Strip Poker

Also by Nancy Bartholomew

Sierra Lavotini Mystery Series
Miracle Strip
Drag Strip
Film Strip

Maggie Reid Mystery Series
Your Cheatin' Heart
Stand by Your Man

Strip Poker

— Nancy Bartholomew —

ST. MARTIN'S MINOTAUR ❧ New York

www.minotaurbooks.com

Library of Congress Cataloging-in-Publication Data

Bartholomew, Nancy.
    Strip poker / Nancy Bartholomew. — 1st ed.
       p. cm.
    ISBN 0-312-26259-0
      1. Lavotini, Sierra (Fictitious character)—Fiction. 2. Women detectives—Florida—Panama City—Fiction. 3. Panama City (Fla.)—Fiction.
4. Stripteasers—fiction. I. Title.

PS3552.A7645 S7 2001
813'.54—dc21

                         2001041899

First Edition: November 2001

10 9 8 7 6 5 4 3 2 1

For my Rangers—You are brave and true

and I love you more than I can ever say.

Acknowledgments

$\mathcal{S}$ierra Lavotini has a mind of her own. She won't do anything I tell her. She's hardheaded. She has high expectations for herself and just about everyone else around her. Hmmm. Wonder where she gets that? I know someone else with high expectations, someone who pushes for the best . . . my editor, Kelley Ragland. Without her, Sierra and I would be lost. We are both very grateful for her guidance.

I would also like to thank Scott Edwards, of the Greensboro Police Department. He is my friend and confidant, but he has also taught me that the greatest weapon is the mind. Without him, Sierra would be stuck in a very small bathroom and I'd be stuck right along with her.

Strip Poker

One

$\mathscr{S}$omewhere around the stage area of your finer gentlemen's clubs like the Tiffany, there is a panic light. When there's a problem in the back of the house it glows red, kind of like Rudolph's nose. It's there, up above the runway, so the bouncers who are watching the front of the house can see it and respond. To my knowledge it had never been used. But on the Saturday before Christmas I saw Bruno, the steroid-impaired bouncer, stare at a spot just above my head. When his jaw dropped like a granite boulder, I knew we had trouble.

He wheeled around and left me at the mercy of a pack of salesmen in for a little pre-Christmas merriment. Lucky for me, the guys didn't see him leave. I was standing at the edge of the runway, wearing my new Santa pasties with the little jingle bells on the tips. I was swaying back and forth, left to right, my hands clasped behind my back, my 38 double D's keeping perfect time as Dolly Parton sang "I'll Be Home with Bells On."

I couldn't figure it at first. Bruno never leaves me. But sometimes my act even gets to the tough guys. They start thinking about their sweethearts or their mothers, or as with this particular production, home and Christmas. But Bruno is not prey to his emotions. He wouldn't turn away to shed a tear. No, he's all business. So when I saw him move off down the corridor toward the office, motioning to Eugene to follow, I knew something was wrong, and

I also figured they were gonna need finesse, a woman's touch, in the form of Sierra Lavotini, headline dancer at the Tiffany Gentleman's Club and troubleshooter par excellence.

I looked over my shoulder at Rusty the stage manager, mouthing to him to hurry it up. His eyes widened, but he nodded. In exotic dancing, true exotic dancing, where you choreograph your routines, "hurry it up" is just not done. It would be like starting *Romeo and Juliet* and then saying, "Let's cut to the chase and get this suicide thing over with." Art is a risky business. You do not rush the creative muse.

Dolly's voice suddenly squeaked an octave higher as the deejay cranked the speed on the tape and I began to half tap-dance my way across the stage. The men loved it. They thought I was purposefully trying to jingle out a tune with my bells. When I hit the switch on my battery-powered G-string, a little sign began flashing over the red-sequined front. NAUGHTY OR NICE? it read.

I turned around and wiggled, stooped in front of the cluster of men, and let them stuff bills into my red and green jingle-bell garter.

"Have you boys been good?" I asked as they pushed and pawed their way toward the runway, all of them eager to ply me with money. It's big money, too, not the little bills the strippers get.

"Sierra," moaned Max, a regular, "when you gonna sit on ol' Santa's lap here and tell me what you want for Christmas?"

I muttered, "When hell freezes over," and smiled. He took that to mean soon, very soon.

Rusty hit the gas on the smoke machine a little too heavy. A huge cloud rolled out across the stage, enveloping us and choking the businessmen in front. When they were done hacking and coughing, I had vanished, rushing into my purple silk kimono and hurrying to see what the trouble was with Vincent Gambuzzo. After all, it wasn't like he had the brains and the manner to work his way out of a tricky situation. He was only the boss and owner of the Tiffany by default—the fault of his father, a used-car dealer who knew Vincent didn't have the brains to sell cars to rednecks on a sucker lot, so he figured to give him an easier job and bought him a nightclub.

I flew down the back corridor, avoiding the public and ignoring the girls who called to me from the dressing room, wanting me to stop in and catch up on the latest catfight. The trouble with being the head woman in a club is you get double the responsibility and nada for extra pay. It was my responsibility to keep the girls in line, but it was also my job to keep Vincent from so totally fucking us up that there was no job. So I ignored the current little brushfire and scurried on, headed for what could easily become a major two-alarmer, given Vincent's gift for trouble.

The back room at the Tiffany Gentleman's Club is cramped and crowded with all the junk nobody wants. It is a catchall room, one step away from the trash Dumpster and the alleged fire exit that everyone uses, regardless of the big signs over the door that read FIRE EXIT ONLY and ALARM WILL SOUND IF DOOR IS OPENED. But the alarm hasn't worked in years, and we all know it, so on the days when we come to pick up our paychecks or need to reach Vincent without walking through the house, we use the back door.

Vincent started a big-stakes poker game in the back room about three months ago, for the purposes of meeting his IRS payments in a semi-timely fashion. I think he saw something poetic in paying off the feds with illegal money. I saw it as just plain stupid and tried to tell him so, but you don't tell Vincent nothing.

When I tried to talk some sense into him, he just sat there in his black wraparound Ray-Bans, choking his three-hundred-pound frame into a too-tight black silk suit with a matching black silk shirt and tie, and giving me the evil jaw twitch. He does this when he's displeased, and Vincent's usually displeased around me.

"Sierra, you're acting like an old lady, worrying about nothin'. Ain't nothin' gonna happen. You know what I think?" he said, leaning back in his swivel chair and trying to lace his pudgy fingers behind his head. "I think it's that cop you've been dating. He's got you all paranoid." Vincent gave up trying to act cool and leaned forward, his elbows resting on the desk. "Next thing you know, you'll be driving the speed limit."

"Bite me, Gambuzzo," I said. "And don't come crying to me when you get popped and your fancy lawyer can't go your bail."

"Do the crime, do the time, Sierra."

Vincent didn't even know what he was saying. It just sounded good and he liked the way it rolled off his tongue. Vincent hadn't known a hard day in his life, thanks to his daddy.

I crept up to the back room, heard the sound of angry voices, and put my hand out to push open the door gently. Cigarette smoke billowed out, choking me, and I heard Vincent say, "Listen, wiseass, play the hand and let's get going. We're both losing, so I don't see why you're looking to bust my balls."

"You're full of shit, Gambuzzo. You're losing to make the house look good," a whiny, high-pitched voice answered.

I slipped inside the room and stepped up behind Bruno. Around a battered oak and metal table sat an assortment of gentlemen, and I use the word loosely. A few of them I recognized, but three I hadn't ever seen before. I knew Mike Riggs, a local charter-boat captain. He was leather-skinned, with bleached-by-the-sun blond shaggy hair that made him look like a sheepdog, complete with dark button eyes that now and then peeked out at the action. His Greek fishing cap sat pushed back on his head and his muscled forearms held his cards close to his barrel chest.

Next to him was Izzy Rodriguez, owner of the Busted Beaver, one of the scummier clubs along the strip down near the beach. Izzy was half Jewish, half Puerto Rican. He was a little man, balding with wiry black hair that he arranged in a careful comb-over, which instead of hiding his scalp only seemed to frame it, making it more obvious. This was completely overshadowed by a long, bulbous nose that seemed to take up most of his face, pushing his eyes into a beady squint. Izzy had a bad reputation with his girls, and the rumor was he was running dope out the back door and prostituted his dancers if they owed him money. I couldn't figure Gambuzzo for letting him into the game. Paying off the IRS was one thing, but using dirty money from somebody who hurt others; that just didn't sit right with me. It crossed the line.

I didn't recognize the man sitting next to Izzy. He looked to be in his mid to late fifties, average size, average build, a fringe of black and gray hair rimming a bald spot, and a cigar hanging, unlit, from his mouth. He wore a shiny red satin baseball jacket that had the word KOKOMO lettered across the back. Above the pocket on the left side it said JOE in loopy white script. I figured him for an amateur.

Sitting next to Joe, on the hard wooden armrest of his chair with one arm stretching across his shoulders, was a ball of fluff that looked somewhat like the Barbie doll I saw on sale last week at the local Target. Beach Bimbo Barbie, I think it was. Beach Bimbo was dressed in candy-fluff-pink spandex, with chunky white sandals, long pinkish blond hair, and pouty, puffed lips that looked to rival Mick Jagger's.

I was surprised Vincent let an observer sit so close to the table, but then I took a second glance. Beach Bimbo Barbie was draped at such an angle as to provide Vincent with a bird's-eye view of her silicone-implanted breasts and a little angel tattoo that danced right above her left breast. She knew what she was doing, and the little challenging glance she shot me let me know she knew I knew it and didn't care. Where Joe from Kokomo was a rank amateur, Beach Bimbo Barbie was a pro. I figured her for a bill a night at least. Poor Joe.

Sitting next to Joe and Barbie was a thin, good-looking man who had no idea how to dress. I thought he was maybe color-blind, with his brown leather jacket and his navy-blue pants. His polo shirt was chartreuse and his shoes were black and cheap, like bad knockoffs of high-top sneakers. I thought he must live alone, or with other men who didn't know women. He was staring at the guy across from him, the guy with the mouth who was fixing to get himself uninvited from the game. He looked anxious, as if he expected trouble.

The whiner picked this moment to jump to his feet, his hand

moving to his waistband, pulling a small gray gun from behind his back. The Beach Bimbo shrieked and Bruno's gun seemed to emerge from nowhere, thick, black, and ugly.

The whiner was a thin, short man with a brassy blond buzz-cut and a weather-roughened face. A cigarette hung from the corner of his mouth. He was wearing black, bug-eyed dark glasses, and I figured if he tried to shoot Vincent, he'd miss on account of he couldn't possibly see. The hand that held the gun was thickly callused, and his fingers were yellowed with nicotine stains.

"You rigged the game," the whiner said.

The bad dresser tried to calm him. "Denny, hold up, man. Mr. Gambuzzo didn't rig nothin'. How could he? He lost his own freakin' club."

I couldn't help myself. "You lost the Tiffany?" I shrieked.

Bruno had frozen at the words, the hand holding his gun dropping to his side.

Vincent, still facing Denny, slipped his hand into his jacket pocket. He pushed his coat forward ever so slightly until it became obvious to everyone that he was holding a gun, too.

"Shut up, Sierra," he growled. "This don't concern you."

Bruno's eyes met mine for a brief, shocked instant.

"Vincent, what are you saying? What do you mean it doesn't concern me? Of course it—"

He interrupted me. "It's a setback, Sierra. I can fix it."

"Fix it? You're gonna fix it? How much're you into him for, Vincent?"

"Shut up!" Denny yelled. His voice was pitched to carry the length of a football field. "I don't do arguments. I'm telling you I want my money back, with interest. You rigged the game!"

No one spoke. No one even moved. There was something wrong with Denny. His arms and legs seemed to jerk involuntarily back and forth. It was weird, the way they moved. And from where I stood, six feet away, I could hear the breath rasping in and out of his chest in rapid, shallow pants. He was sweating but the room wasn't even warm. If anything, it was cold.

"Denny, calm down," his friend said.

Denny looked across the table, trying to focus maybe, and finding it difficult.

"I said shut up!" He raised the gun, pointing it at the center of Vincent Gambuzzo's chest. "Tell your fat bouncer to put the gun away or I pop your chest open and work my way up."

They stood facing each other, two men in bug-eyed dark glasses, guns in hand and not two rational brain cells between them.

"Guys," I started, but never finished. At that moment the back door exploded into a thousand splinters and an army invaded the room. In the chaos of the next few moments, the world we had all known was transformed.

Four huge men filled the shattered doorway, black snub-nosed semiautomatic guns in hand. They wore black combat gear, black helmets with dark-tinted face plates, heavy Kevlar vests, thick black boots, and gunbelts that hung heavily around their waists.

"Down! Down! Down!" they screamed, pushing their way into the room. "Get down!" But their words were lost. The room had erupted into movement. Bruno flew forward, kicking the table over with one huge shove. Beach Bimbo Barbie ran out the door past me, screaming. Denny and his friend moved to the left, the poker game quickly forgotten as survival became the first order of business. Vincent pulled his gun out of his jacket pocket and the next few seconds became a blur of movement.

Kokomo Joe, the amateur, moved toward me, a gun flashing out from a holster underneath his arm. As he reached me, his free hand shot out and punched me dead center in the chest.

"Get out!" he yelled. "Out!" I felt the air whoosh out of my lungs and I was aware of sailing back into the hallway as a small explosion and flash lit the room in front of me.

At that point, I heard gunfire. I couldn't breathe, the wind knocked from my lungs as I lay sprawled out on the cold tile floor of the hallway. I had to help, but I could barely move.

People were running behind me. I heard footsteps and voices and tried to pull myself up as they ran toward me. In the room in front of me, Bruno was working overtime. Using the table and a couple of stuffed sheep from my old Bo Peep routine for a shield, he popped up and down, firing in an attempt to hold the armed intruders at bay.

Vincent and the others contributed to the fray, but Bruno was the best shot. I couldn't make out what was going on inside the room. There was too much smoke and I sat angled to the door. It would've been suicidal to try to get any closer. Instead, I backed up, struggled to stand, and ran down the hallway toward the others.

Eugene, Bruno's doorman, stood in the dimly lit corridor, a black semiautomatic in hand, his mahogany face dark with anger and frustration.

"What the fuck's goin' on?" he asked me. "There's no fuckin' way to get to them."

"I think we're being held up," I answered. "They came in through the exit door."

That was all Eugene needed to hear. He whirled around and headed back toward the house. I knew he'd try the back doorway and I knew they'd kill him.

"Eugene, they got protection. There's four of them." Eugene didn't seem to hear me. He never stopped moving. Rusty ran past him, toward me, his freckled, white face even paler with fear.

"Sierra, I called the cops. They'll be here in a few minutes."

It seemed that the shooting had gone on forever.

Two

The good thing about a smaller town is that the cops don't have to travel far in an emergency. They were there, sirens screaming, within moments. The Panama City Beach Police are tough, mean characters, used to bikers and minor hoods and drunken college students looking to raise hell on spring break. But they weren't a match for the cyclone that was hitting the Tiffany Gentleman's Club.

They fought, guns drawn, shotguns hastily brought out of squad car trunks, with reinforcements called for and all the might the force could muster, but the invaders got away. I heard them blasting their way out the back, their attention turned from the club to making an escape. Eugene rematerialized by my side, then ran past me, headed for the back room, his gun drawn and held high in the air. It was like watching a bad action flick. It didn't seem real until I heard someone moaning and recognized the voice.

That got me to move. I ran down the hallway toward Eugene, stopping just behind him as he cleared the doorway, darting into the room, gun held out in front of him, both hands gripping the butt, finger on the trigger. He came face-to-face with a terrified young cop who screamed, "Drop the gun! Drop it now!"

Eugene, not a fool, dropped the gun. "I'm house security, ass-hole. The bad guys went that-a-way!"

The cop didn't waver, didn't look over his shoulder, didn't

flinch. He waited for the others to verify this before lowering his gun. Eugene, freed to move, reached Bruno as I did. Bruno lay in a pool of blood, still conscious, his eyes focusing on me, a tear rolling down the side of his head, unchecked.

"Hey, babe," I murmured, kneeling by his side, looking for the source of the wound and finding it. Blood was gushing from the right side of his chest. He was pale and beginning to shake.

"Get a fucking ambulance!" Eugene yelled.

"Sierra," Bruno whispered. "Come here."

I leaned closer. "Baby, I'm right here." I stroked the side of his face, my fingers brushing against the sandpaper finish of his beard.

"I can't see you, honey," he whispered. "Sierra, why can't I see you?" He was panicking, his face drawing up into a tight knot.

"Baby," I said, "it's my tits. Nobody can see my face when I'm up this close." I was trying to keep it light, but I was watching Eugene and our eyes met. His hands were pressed firmly against Bruno's chest, but it wasn't helping. The blood seeped through his fingers like red water.

"Hey, hurry those EMTs, will ya?" I yelled.

I was aware of the cops moving around me, but I kept my eyes on Bruno. "Stay with me, baby," I cooed, but it was no use. I was losing him. My throat squeezed shut as I tried to keep a sob from leaping up and out. I had to be calm. I couldn't let Bruno see what I knew: that he was in desperate trouble.

"Hey!" someone yelled. "Got another victim here!" I whipped around to look and saw a cop down on one knee by a body. There was a pause as he leaned forward. "This one don't need no help," he said, the slight quiver in his voice giving him away. "He's gone."

As the words hung in the air, EMTs rushed into the room, past the cop and the body and over to us.

"Move," one said, pushing me aside.

"We'll take it," the other one said to Eugene. But Eugene didn't move until he was pushed aside. Even then he stuck close, his eyes never leaving Bruno's face.

I turned back to the other side of the room. The cop stood up and I could see the victim. Denny the Whiner lay on his back, a bullet dead center through the middle of his forehead.

I looked at Bruno again and saw his eyes fixed on my face. I smiled, the same big smile I gave him every day. The smile that said everything's fine, don't worry, you're bleeding to death, Bruno, but don't worry. I felt like a total idiot, grinning in the face of the Grim Reaper.

The EMTs put an oxygen mask on his face and started hooking up IVs. They were barking terse orders to each other and conferring by cell phone with the hospital. They were rushing, the intensity and strain showing on their faces and in the muscles of their legs and backs as they worked to save my friend.

Cops were streaming into and out of the room. Joe from Kokomo stood talking to one of them, the cigar still dangling, unlit, from his lips. Joe didn't look like such an amateur anymore. The jacket was gone and he stood in his shirtsleeves, the shoulder holster fitted tight against his torso. Joe from Kokomo was a cop, and our collective asses were fried if he was working Vice.

I looked around for Vincent and saw him across the room, eyeing Joe with the same intensity I'd been giving him. The lights were slowly coming on for Vincent, and I could see get-me-a-lawyer written all over his face.

I was so busy looking that I missed seeing Detective John Nailor's entrance, but I felt it. That man couldn't be in a room five minutes without me feeling the heat radiating from him, entering my body, and pulling me toward him like an invisible magnet. So I looked away from Vincent and did a visual scan around the room until I homed in on him. He was bending over the body of Denny the Whiner, but when he felt me watching him, he looked up.

There were a thousand questions in his eyes. The kind between two lovers when one is in trouble, the are-you-all-rights, the I-want-to-hold-you-but-I-can'ts that come with the territory of him doing his job and me doing mine. You put a cop and an exotic dancer together and there's a set of professional issues that immediately cloud the reality of the relationship. This bloodbath made it no different, and I didn't want it to. John's a pro and he needed to be about doing his job, not taking care of me. That would come later, and we both knew it. Right now I wanted him to catch the scum that hurt Bruno. He couldn't fix it. Nobody could do that. But he could catch the sorry bastards who hurt my friend.

Three

                         *B*runo's eyes were closed and his skin was an unnatural shade of gray when the EMTs loaded him up into the ambulance. I tried to speak to him, but if he heard me, he made no move to acknowledge it. How could he have heard me? There were tubes and wires hooked up all over him. The EMTs talked a mile a minute, now and then calling out his name as if he were only sleeping. I felt John's hand on my shoulder as the ambulance pulled out of the parking lot, and realized that I was attempting to follow them on foot wearing only a silk kimono.

"Hey, let's go inside," he said, like maybe it was an ordinary night and we were taking in the stars.

I shook off his hand and looked at him. "I need to get to the hospital."

John nodded but stretched out his hand again, this time touching my arm. "You need some clothes. It's cold out here."

I was shivering, but I hadn't felt the cold. "I've got to go."

"Sierra, Bruno's in really good hands. They won't let you be with him yet. You've got time, honey. Put on some clothes, all right? I'll take you there later."

I knew what that meant. Nailor was blowing me off, slowly. By the time I dressed, he'd be otherwise occupied with the investigation. He wouldn't be able to drive me anywhere for hours. Besides, I didn't need him. I was capable of driving to the hospital all by myself. What was with him, anyway? What was with the caretaking routine? And why was I letting it bother me? Maybe he was just worried about me. This whole relationship thing was starting to bug me. A month ago it had been different. We were still new to it all, nosing around each other, flirting and tempting. Then the whole mess hit the fan, and before I knew it, we were a couple. I hadn't been a part of a "we" for so long, I'd forgotten how it felt. And this felt like a real relationship, not one where I did ninety percent and the guy gave maybe minus ten. With Nailor, he was either in it or out of it. I didn't know what to do with that. It was freaking me out.

I looked back at him again and saw concern mingled with cop-on-duty. Maybe he meant what he said, or maybe he knew he should say it because of our relationship. He looked at me now, like maybe I was acting funny.

"What?" I asked. "I'm fine and I'm gonna drive to the hospital with Vincent. We need to get over there."

But Vincent wasn't going anywhere with me. Joe from Kokomo, along with another detective type, was in his face asking questions. Vincent's jaw twitched and his face was turned purple with the effort not to go ballistic. Around him, cops took pictures and gathered up spent shell casings.

"Okay," Nailor said to me, his voice stiffening, "this is how it's gonna run. Vincent Gambuzzo has some explaining to do. We need a statement from you and everyone else here. I can get with you later, but Gambuzzo's gonna be tied up for the evening."

"I can take her, Detective."

The two of us whipped around. Rusty stood there, his red hair standing straight out from his head where he'd run his fingers through it over and over.

"Eugene just took off," he said to me. "Them cops told him to stick around, but I don't think he even heard them, honest I don't." Rusty looked ten years old trying to act grown up.

Nailor nodded. "It's all right," he said. "I'll stop by the hospital later and talk with him. I appreciate your seeing to it that Sierra gets over there. I'm going to be awhile here." His eyes were on me now. "Do you think you can try to go back over what happened, try to get a description of the gunmen?"

"There isn't much to describe. They all wore body armor and helmets or something over their heads."

He nodded patiently. "That's what pops into your head first," he said. "While you're at the hospital waiting, close your eyes and think back over it. What did they wear? What did the guns look like? What were their voices like? How tall were they? Anything at all that might help us find these guys, all right?"

Then he leaned over and touched my arm. It wasn't at all what he wanted to do, I could see that, but it was the only thing he could do given our public circumstances.

"You think, too," he told Rusty. "You never know what small detail will turn the trick."

Nope, you never knew.

I looked around at the crime-scene team. They were gathered by Denny's body, taking pictures like a pack of tourists. The medical examiner arrived, walked straight up to the body, bent over slightly from the waist, and sighed. He was an older man, maybe seventy, with thick white hair and clear blue eyes that seemed watery when you looked into his glasses. He paused, straightened back up, and looked around the room.

"I thought you said there were two," he boomed.

Nailor looked at me, registered the pain in my eyes, and turned to answer him.

"They told you wrong," he answered. "We've got one in critical condition."

I couldn't wait any longer. I walked down the hallway, rounding the corner to the dressing room. If I'd stayed behind to listen to the standard impersonal cop talk that was sure to follow, there would've been two bodies.

I dressed in the empty room. I didn't know where the others had gone, but I was grateful for the silence, the time to pull my act together and be larger than I felt. When I rejoined Rusty, I was the old Sierra, ready to hit the hospital and deal with whatever came our way.

Rusty's good about sensing a mood. He didn't talk. He didn't question my decision to drive us in my IROC Camaro. He went along. That's what Rusty does. It's his job to figure out what you need and see that you get it. That's why the Tiffany's acts go seamlessly on, one right after the other, without a hitch.

When we pulled into the parking lot and I started to get out of the car, Rusty did the unexpected. He grabbed my arm, his eyes huge with sincerity, and started a nonstop stream of words that came quickly as if he were afraid I'd cut him off.

"Sierra, I don't know how you feel about religion and all. Some folks don't appreciate it if you push it on them and all. And I know a lot of dancers ain't exactly, well, religious types and, well . . ." He drew a deep breath. "I want to say a prayer for Bruno before we go in there. You know, like talk to God before we walk in on whatever's happened. You know, like not waiting to find out he's okay or not okay and making our requests after the fact. I'm wanting to pray now, you know, kind of like we're not cheating by knowing the outcome and praying accordingly."

I stared at him, not knowing what to say. Growing up Catholic, you get a warped view of who God is and how it all works. Life gets tied up in eternal sin and damnation, and before you know it, you're walking down the sidewalk afraid to step on the cracks on account of you might break your mother's back. Praying was something I did, and did regularly, but not like in-church praying. More like a conversation with Her. I know God's gotta be a woman because the more I think about it, the more I figure only a mother could put up with humanity and still have a shred of hope.

Eventually, I felt my head nod, and I reached over and took Rusty's hand in mine. "That would be nice, babe. Why don't you kick it off and I'll just stick the 'amen' in at the right point. Like, you do the talking and I'll back you up."

Rusty's eyes closed and I shut mine, figuring it wouldn't do to challenge Rusty's ritual sense of propriety at this tender moment.

"Heavenly Father," he began.

"Or Mother," I whispered, unable to stop myself.

"Please be with our dear brother, Bruno. It's up to you to decide how it goes, but however it ends up, don't let him hurt. Hold him close to you. Hold all of us close to you, because, God . . ." Here Rusty's voice cracked and tears began streaming down both of our faces. "We just don't know what we'd do without old Bruno around to kick ass—I mean, to watch over us. I mean, you should've seen him the time . . ." I squeezed Rusty's hand, and he seemed to snap out of the reminiscence and continue. "Well, you saw it. You probably helped him do it, but what I'm saying is, please take care of Bruno. We'll try not to question your decision in the matter, but I just thought we'd let you know how we feel and what we hope. In Jesus' name we pray . . ."

And we both chimed, "Amen."

We blew our noses, dried our eyes, and smiled across the console at each other.

"All right," I said, "let's go see about Bruno."

Four

It would turn out to be maybe the longest night of my life. Bruno was in surgery when we arrived, and he was expected to be on the table until well after sunrise. Rusty and I walked into the waiting room just in time to hear Eugene form his posse.

He was standing in the middle of the dimly lit room, right underneath the soundless TV that no one was watching. It was playing an old rerun of *Lassie*. The room was gray, with uncomfortable blue vinyl chairs and loveseats rimming the walls. A wilting fake silver Christmas tree leaned in a corner, tacky red balls hanging from its tired limbs. The staff of the Tiffany Gentleman's Club, most of them dancers still in costume with thick makeup and false eyelashes, sat in the chairs, their attention riveted on Eugene.

In the middle of this lineup, as obvious as two bumps on a log, sat the only outsiders, an elderly man and woman. They seemed too traumatized to move. The woman, gray-haired and anxious, sat clutching a red purse in her lap, as if fearing assault at any moment. Her husband sat beside her, wearing a ball cap that read U.S.S. FREEDOM. He wore the senior uniform: black socks, white loafers, madras shorts and a golf shirt that clashed. He was leaning forward, listening intently as Eugene spoke, now and then adjusting the volume on his hearing aid.

"Here's the situation," Eugene announced. "People come into

the house and messed with the brother. You don't mess with the brother in the house of Eugene. You don't run and you don't hide from Eu-fucking-gene, see what I'm saying, y'all?"

Nods and "That's rights" came from all around, even from the old man.

"Among all of us, there's information. You don't just bust down the door, cap two folks, and walk out and ain't nobody hears a word about it on the street, see what I mean? Motherfucker's shit is gonna be in the street sometime. Somebody gonna know something, and when they do, it's gonna get back to Eugene. You know why?"

The old guy, failing to sense it was a rhetorical question, played straight into Eugene's hands.

"Why?" His wife's eyes closed and she leaned farther back in her seat, as if willing invisibility.

Eugene didn't miss a beat. "On account of we're gonna put the word out that if anybody, anywhere hears a word and don't tell one of y'all or me, they ass is mine. Got that?"

Everyone agreed, but Eugene wasn't finished.

"Them po-lice can do what they want, but we gonna find them motherfuckers first. And you know what we gonna do?"

There were catcalls and shouts but only one "No, what?" from Mrs. U.S.S. Freedom.

Eugene grinned like a rage-crazed banshee. "We gonna bust a cap up they asses the size of New Jersey, and stretch 'em out on the highway like roadkill!"

The room went wild with approval and Captain U.S.S. Freedom jumped to his feet with a mighty roar. "I got twenty live grenades and a torpedo that ain't seen action since the Big One. Let's kick some damn ass!"

At this point, his wife keeled over into the lap of Tonya the Barbarian, out cold.

Whipped into a frenzy of potential, no longer the victims of unspeakable violence, Eugene's followers yelled while Eugene stood like a colonel, his hands clasped behind his back, surveying his troops.

"First we gotta find the assholes, sir," he said to Captain Freedom, "but then we would be most obliged to relieve you of any extra munitions you could spare."

"Damn straight," Freedom replied. "I set only one condition."

Eugene's eyes narrowed warily. "What?"

"I get to come along on the raid." The old guy's face was suffused with color, and his eyes glittered at some memory of unfinished business and partially reaped glory.

Eugene didn't hesitate. "My brother, give me your number, and we will be in touch. We would be honored to have some military guidance and expertise."

Mrs. U.S.S. Freedom sighed, fluttered her eyes, and seemed to sleep peacefully in the arms of Tonya the Barbarian. Tonya looked down at her lapful and attempted to adjust her leopard-skin toga.

"She's sleeping right on the chicken bone I use to hold my G-string," she explained to me. "Ever get a bone stuck in your hip? It ain't comfortable."

Captain Freedom reached over and tugged his wife upright, shifting his position until she slept peacefully on his shoulder.

"Women!" he muttered.

No news emerged about Bruno as the night wore on. We all sat in relative silence, waiting and praying. Eugene now and then paced to the door of the surgical suites and looked through the tiny windowpane. Each time he'd turn away and my heart would break at the agonized expression on his face. He blamed himself for not reaching Bruno in time; I could see it all over him.

Around five A.M., Nailor arrived, tired and grim.

I went to him, questions crowding out anxiety for a moment. "Did you get them?" I asked.

He shook his head. "No. We gathered up every shell casing. Dusted all the surfaces. Interviewed anyone who was even in the neighborhood. It's as if they were beamed down from nowhere, Sierra. It was well-planned and almost flawlessly executed. The only reason they didn't make it was that Bruno just happened to be in the back room with his gun drawn when they came. I think they figured to take the game quickly and disappear. They counted on the bouncers being in the front of the house, where they usually are."

"I guess they didn't count on an undercover cop working the game, either, huh?" I asked.

Nailor shrugged. "Vincent's finally done it to himself this time," he said.

"You didn't arrest him!"

"Didn't have to, Joe Nolowicki'd already done the deed." Nailor looked at me and sighed. "Come on, Sierra, what d'ya think was gonna happen? Not a thing I could do about it, and I would've popped him, too. Illegal gambling and drugs. What choice did he have?"

"Drugs? What do you mean drugs?"

Nailor took out his notepad, read something, and stuck it back inside his jacket. "Cocaine, Sierra. It was right there in the drawer of Vincent's desk."

"Vincent hates drugs!"

"So he only breaks some of the laws in an attempt to make money, not all of them?" He shook his head. "Sierra, we found drugs and evidence of gambling. What else could Nolowicki do? Let him go because the money was for the IRS and Vincent meant well?"

No love lost between Nailor and Gambuzzo, that was always obvious. What else could I expect?

"I guess not," I said. "Did he call Ernie?"

Nailor shrugged. "He was making a lot of noise about a lawyer, so I'm sure he did. But some charter-boat captain named Mike Riggs is holding the paper on the club and says he owns it now, so Vincent won't be using the club as collateral."

Tonya the Barbarian, ever vigilant for the slightest morsel of gossip, jumped up at the mention of Mike Riggs and the club.

"What?" she yelled. She whirled around and faced the other dancers. "Gambuzzo's done lost the club in a game! Some fisherman owns us!"

That was all it took. The dancers and Eugene all started firing questions at once, yelling to make themselves heard, and creating enough of a disturbance that two nurses came running, towing along a security guard.

Nailor finally put a stop to it. In his most commanding voice he boomed, "All right, that's enough! Sit down. Shut up, or I'll start taking you in for disturbing the peace."

I think Nailor thought they listened because he was a cop, but if the truth be told, half of the women listened just because he was a breathtaking specimen of human manhood. The other half shut up because they saw me hold up my hand like we do during rehearsal, motioning them to silence.

"Let me talk a minute," I said to Nailor. "Let me explain it to them. They'll listen to you after they listen to me."

And it would've gone down that way had not a blood-spattered surgeon picked that moment to appear in the doorway. He was young and tired. A kid playing dress-up to my mind, but something in his eyes aged him. He was searching the room, trying to figure out who was in charge.

"Doc," I said, stepping forward, "how's Bruno?"

The doctor looked at me and seemed uncertain. "Um, are you a member of Mr. Bronkowski's family?" he asked. His voice cracked a little, but that was probably because he was staring at my chest and not my face.

"They aren't," I said, "but I am. Up here. It's all right; you can make eye contact. I'm Bruno's, uh, sister."

To his credit, he smiled, a sweet boy smile that lit up his blue eyes for a second.

"I'm Kelly Thrasher," he said. "I did the surgery." He didn't make us wait. "Mr. Bronkowski's not out of the woods. He's lost a lot of blood and he's been through a very stressful surgery, but if we can keep him alive for twenty-four hours, we should be fine."

There was a collective sigh of relief and then Eugene lunged for the doctor, sweeping him up off his feet in a massive bear hug.

23

"Thank you, thank you, thank you!" he cried, tears streaming down his face.

Dr. Thrasher's face was bright red, but he seemed none the worse for wear as Eugene returned him to the ground.

"Now," Eugene said to the doctor, "I am Mr. Bronkowski's security. I'll be right outside his door twenty-four seven, so you don't gotta worry about any assholes trying to disturb your patient. 'Cause I'll tell you right now, the motherfucker that tries—"

Dr. Thrasher cut him off. "We have security, Mr.—?"

"Uzi," Eugene said. "Eugene 'Fully Automatic' Uzi, at your service."

Thrasher smiled slightly and tried to hide it. "Mr. Uzi, your friend's in ICU. We can't have anyone in there except his immediate family, and then only for five minutes an hour. Nothing must disturb Mr. Bronkowski."

Eugene looked ready to pop, so I intervened. "Dr. Thrasher, Mr. Uzi here is Bruno's brother." I stared right into his face, daring him to tell me that it was impossible. But Thrasher was a wise man. He nodded, his eyes twinkled, and he went with it.

"All right. Mr. Uzi, five minutes an hour, no talking, no gunplay." Here Thrasher looked stern and years ahead of himself. "You may, um, surveil the ICU from the vantage point of this chair." He dragged a blue waiting room chair out into the hallway and positioned it halfway between the ICU doors and the waiting room.

Eugene looked at the chair and then at the doctor. He mulled it over for a few seconds, trying to figure if he should push the odds and go for a larger stake. But Thrasher's clear blue eyes never left Eugene's face, and in the end Eugene nodded his acceptance.

"One last thing," Thrasher added. "My security is top dog. In other words, it's their house and you're the guest. Play by their rules. If there's trouble, call them."

"But they're fucking rent-a-cops," Eugene blurted.

Dr. Thrasher, apparently suicidal, took a step closer to Eugene. "Yeah, but they're my fucking rent-a-cops, understand?"

"My brother will, of course, abide by the house rules," I said, glaring at Eugene. "Fully Automatic" my ass.

The doctor, satisfied for now that his orders would be followed, turned and walked back through the swinging doors and into the ICU. Eugene sighed, his shoulders slumping. He reached out and grabbed my arm, pulling me into him, hanging on for dear life.

"He's gonna make it, isn't he?" he whispered in my ear. "I mean, that's what the doctor meant, isn't it?"

"Yeah, honey, he's gonna make it. God ain't ready for Bruno yet. She couldn't handle it!" And I laughed softly into his iron chest.

Nailor, not one to let me stay in the arms of another for long, broke in.

"Eugene," he said, "I'm going to need some help here. You think you could answer a few questions?"

Eugene, sensitive to my relationship, looked up at Nailor and nodded. I knew what he was thinking. He was figuring that the cops couldn't help, but what the hell, keep Sierra's boy happy.

"Thanks, 'Fully Automatic,'" I whispered.

I broke away from Eugene and turned back to Nailor. "Do you need to talk to any of the rest of us?" I asked.

"Just briefly. They can go home after that." I nodded and turned away. We were working, like a team maybe.

"Hey, listen up," I said to the others. "We can't all stay here. Here's what I'm suggesting: Tonya, why don't you cover Bruno's apartment. I think you have a key?" I knew she did. Tonya thought her stuff was smooth, but nobody missed the fact that upon several occasions when Tonya's man had pulled time, she'd spent her free time with Bruno.

Tonya looked disconcerted, but nodded. "I got one. I house-sit now and then."

A, Bruno does not ever leave Panama City proper. And, B, it wasn't Bruno's house she was sitting on, but I let it go.

"Why don't you get over there and check on his cat? You know of any next-of-kin types we ought to get ahold of?"

Tonya looked a little pouty. "We didn't exactly talk about his mama or nothin' when I went over there," she said.

"Well, honey, see what you can find out, all right?" Where handling Tonya was concerned, patience was a virtue. I looked at the others. The U.S.S. Freedoms had fallen asleep on each other's shoulders, but the dancers were all watching me.

"Listen, guys," I said. "We've got to pull together. Vincent lost the house to Mike Riggs, a charter-boat captain. I'm sure it's only temporary, but it don't help that we got robbed and have that to deal with, too. So bear with it. Try and help out Detective Nailor here. Show up for work like it's a regular day. And if you got any no-necked boyfriends that wanna man the door for a few weeks, let me know and we'll hook it up."

"Who's gonna pay us?" one of the strippers asked. "I cain't work if I don't get no check."

Wasn't that just like a stripper? Couldn't see beyond the tip of her nipples.

"You'll get paid, I'm sure," I said, but I wasn't that sure. "What's important is that we're a family and this is a crisis. We gotta stick together." The stripper rolled her eyes and smirked at one of her friends. For a brief moment I considered kicking her ass, but just as quickly discarded the idea in favor of a longer-term payback.

"When the police have what they need, go home and get some sleep. Bruno won't be seeing anyone for a while. If his family comes to town, we're gonna need some hospitality, and I know the Tiffany can produce hospitality for visiting relatives, am I right?"

A chorus of agreement followed. I was thinking hospitality in the form of housekeeping and casseroles. God knew what they were thinking.

"All right, then, I'm going. I'll see you guys at the club tomorrow night. Same time, same—" I stopped. The Tiffany Gentleman's Club was not the same place. Tonight's events had turned the club in a different direction, and despite the way I talked, I didn't have any guarantee that things would be all right. Things at the Tiffany Gentleman's Club might never be all right again.

Five

$\mathcal{R}$usty and I walked out into the crisp, cold air of a December morning in Panama City. Merry fucking Christmas, I thought. As we drove away toward my trailer park, I took in the streetlights all draped in fake green garland and wondered if Bruno was going to be around to see Christmas this year.

Rusty must've been having the same thoughts because when the radio started playing "Grandma Got Run Over by a Reindeer," he quickly switched it off and left us sitting in silence. When I pulled into the Lively Oaks Trailer Park and turned onto my street, I reached over and rested my hand on his knee.

"Rusty, it really is going to be all right."

Rusty said nothing until we'd pulled up into my driveway. Then he turned and looked me straight in the eye. "Sierra, I'm not a kid. You don't have to give me the Big Mama talk you give the bimbos we work with."

I pulled my hand back, stung. "Rusty, I wasn't trying to . . ."

"Yes, you were." He sighed. "Everybody does it to me. I know, I know, red hair and freckles. I look like a kid, but, Sierra, I'm twenty-four. I run the show at work. There're twelve crises a night, and that's on a good one. I'm not a flippin' baby!"

"Yeah, well, I was just trying to be a friend. You don't need to blow up on me just because you're freaking out. I'm sorry, but I'm a little freaked myself, so wise up!"

We both looked at each other, mad as hell and scared, too. Then Rusty looked away for a second. "You're right. I'm scared shitless. How's Vincent gonna get the club back? What if that fishing-boat captain fires me?"

"He fires you, Rusty, and the whole lot of us will walk out with you. All right?"

Rusty grinned. "Hell, just you walk out and the place'll fold."

I opened the car door and got out, then leaned back down and looked through the open door at him sitting there. "Hey, it's a talent," I said. "Either you got it or you don't. Now, you wanna come in and flop on my couch or what?"

Rusty shook his head no and got out of the car.

"I'll just go stay with my sister and them," he said. "She's got the beat-to-shit Silverstream two streets over."

I stood watching him walk away, then started up the steps to my trailer. I shouldn't have bothered. The moment my foot hit the bottom step, two things happened simultaneously: Fluffy, my hairless chihuahua, came flying out through her little doggie door, and Raydean, my psychotic, elderly neighbor, stepped out onto her porch stoop across the street.

"Even a turtle gets the early bird now and then," she said cryptically. She was leaning on her porch railing, pink curlers in her frizzy gray hair, a worn pink chenille robe wrapped none too tightly around her ample middle, and a Hawaiian shirt thrown over her shoulders like a shawl.

Fluffy pranced at my feet demanding breakfast, and Raydean began her slow journey toward my yard, a baby monitor clutched in her left hand and a coffee cup in the other. Well, no guessing as to how she knew I was home.

"Bruno all right?" she asked.

"How'd you know?"

Raydean touched her left temple with a gnarled finger. "Kidneys," she said. "That and the news. You didn't come home on time, neither. Don't take a Flemish to know where you were. So's he all right or what?"

Raydean's eyes darted back and forth, taking in every little detail of her surroundings, scanning the yard for signs of alien life and invasion. Raydean was certifiably insane, and that was on her good days. The rest of the time her psychiatrist called her "floridly psychotic." I somehow always pictured that to mean she was a mass of blooming, tie-dyed hallucinations that swirled about her in cheerful colors, like nodding flowers. Florid seemed so appropriate for Raydean. She bloomed nuts whenever her medication wore off, which was about once a month now that they wised up and put her on something long-acting and injectible. This meant she only fired off her shotgun once in a while at the invisible aliens she called the Flemish.

"Bruno's gonna be fine," I said.

"Oughter be," she muttered. "Too damn dumb to die."

"Raydean!"

She cut her eyes up at me and smiled. "Come on, honey, you've said the same thing any number of times. You don't gotta be nice on account of a near-death experience. I calls 'em like I sees 'em. Besides, you scare folks if you start talking nice about them. They'll think you really think they're dying, and they might just do it to oblige your expectations!"

I shook my head. She was impossible and very probably right.

"Guess that po-lice of yours is on the job, huh?" She turned her head to the side and spit into the little bit of grass I had growing in the front yard. Raydean did not suffer the police gladly.

"Raydean, I'm fixing to go get some sleep, and you ought not to be out in this cold without a coat."

Raydean's eyes narrowed. "Optimal conditions for Flemish." She held up the baby monitor. "Want me to keep extra surveillance on things until you wake up?"

There was only one right answer. "I'd appreciate it."

"Roger," she said, turning away. "I got your back." She looked down at Fluffy. "Come on, you little yard ape, breakfast is on me." Fluffy didn't give me a backward glance. She trotted off at Raydean's side, practically prancing in her attempt to avoid chilling her tiny feet any more than necessary.

"What's that, honey?" Raydean said, leaning to hear something she imagined Fluffy to say. "What's the special?" She straightened back up. "Sausage and gravy. Modified shit on a shingle." And with that, they were gone, vanishing inside Raydean's trailer to spend a morning filled with talk shows and *The Price Is Right.*

I barely made it into the trailer and down the hallway before I was stripping off my clothes and heading for the big bed that took up most of my small bedroom. I paused in the bathroom, stared at my huge Jacuzzi tub, and decided to forgo that in favor of a fast shower. In fifteen minutes I was under my purple satin sheets and sound asleep.

The phone woke me up, ringing insistently. I grabbed it before it could totally shatter my dreams and held the receiver to my ear.

"Got your po-lice at ten o'clock, fixin' to enter the premises without a warrant. You need backup, or you got this one covered?" It was Raydean, on the job.

I sighed and snuggled down deeper under my comforter. "I got this covered," I murmured, and replaced the receiver. Then I waited, listening as the key slowly turned in the lock and the door softly shut behind him. I heard him take off his shoes, leaving them by the kitchen door, then walk softly down the hallway to my bedroom.

I feigned sleep, peeking as he started to undress. First he took off his tie and loosened his collar. Next went the shirt, and I couldn't help but squirm as he turned around and began to un-buckle his belt. Nailor naked was becoming one of my favorite sights.

He was taking his time, arranging his shirt neatly over the back of the one chair in the room, carefully folding his pants and draping them over the seat. I snuck a quick look at the clock; it was almost eight A.M. I'd been asleep for about an hour and a half. Nailor had to be exhausted, but when he turned around and dropped his box-ers, I knew he was also an eternal optimist. I like that in a man.

He crossed the room and slipped under the covers beside me.
"Done watching?" he whispered as he pulled me to him.

"How did you know?"

"Sierra, your act is so lame."

"Nailor," I said, turning over to face him, "bite me."

Nailor laughed, kissing me and beginning a slow nibble on the side of my neck. "Gladly."

His lips moved down my neck, touching my shoulder, his tongue leaving a fiery trail as he slowly worked his way to my breasts. What had begun playfully was now becoming a serious intention on his part. I responded by moving my hands down his sides, running them across his back and down, closer to what had become a very large sign of his level of desire.

"Oh, Sierra," he said, sighing, "you are so beautiful, sweetie."

That's when it happened. It was as if a switch clicked inside my head, and what had been a ten on the Richter scale of desire dimmed to an eight. It wasn't anything Nailor was doing. It was me working a number on myself. Nailor was continuing on his path, doing what normally sent me over the edge, and I was responding, but as if I were some distance away.

Sweetie? Nailor had called me *sweetie.* Suddenly I was a basketcase. I couldn't relax. I was going through the motions, all the while arguing with myself. *God, that feels good,* my body would say. And my head would answer back. *Sweetie. What is this sweetie stuff? You can't do this. This is going to be a disaster. You can't go letting yourself fall for him like this. You know what happens. Every single time. You give yourself away, and look, your heart gets broken.*

And then the other half of my head started answering. *What's wrong with you? He's a good guy!*

Yeah, right. He seems like a good guy. Maybe that's an act. And maybe that's a little too boring. I like bikers. I like bad boys.

My head shook its head. *You poor stupid idiot!*

My body broke it. *Hey, will you guys knock it off! Do you feel what he's doing here?*

And then I moaned as Nailor's tongue slid across my belly and his fingers moved to part my legs ever so slowly.

For once my body and my head were in agreement. We felt *that*. But only to a point. I opened my eyes and looked down at his shoulders. Strong, tanned shoulders that rippled as he moved. John Nailor had the sexiest shoulders, I thought. I reached out and stopped him, pulling him up to me.

"Now," I whispered. "I need you inside me, right now."

Nailor frowned. "No, you don't," he said, and made an attempt to move back.

"Yes, really, I do." And then I moved to make his retreat impossible. He sighed as I touched him, guiding him inside me. He gave up to what felt totally right and moaned as we began to move ever so slowly.

"Oh God, Sierra," he said into my shoulder. "This feels so good."

But my head wasn't listening. Something was really wrong here. I was sabotaging the one true happiness I'd had in years. Truth be told, it was maybe the only true romantic happiness I'd ever felt. What in the hell was wrong with me?

Right before we fell asleep, he pulled me against his chest and lay there holding me. His fingers gently stroked my hair.

"Sierra," he whispered, "where did you go?"

I struggled up onto my elbows and stared at him. "What do you mean?" I asked.

He brushed a tendril of hair away from my face and stared at me. "You know exactly what I mean, babe. You can't con a con. What's wrong?"

I shook my head, my heartbeat quickening a little. "I guess it's just Bruno and everything. I can't let loose. I mean, that's understandable, isn't it? After all, it's not every night a girl gets shot at, her friend critically wounded, and her boss loses the freaking club."

Nailor nodded, as if he still didn't buy it. "It's a lot, I know, but, babe, when we connect, the rest of the world always goes away. I'm thinking I'm gonna have to keep an eye on you."

I smiled and kissed him. "A little sleep and I'll be fine."

John smiled back and then looked serious again. "Don't worry, sweetie," he said. "Bruno'll be fine. I bet he's out of the hospital in time for Christmas."

That's when the second ton of concrete hit me, weighing me down until there was no pretending. Christmas. What was I going to do about Christmas? I always went home, but how could I do that with my friends in trouble and the club at risk?

"I was gonna go home for Christmas," I muttered. "There's no way I can do that now."

Nailor was getting sleepy on me. He pulled me closer to him and stroked my hair again. "Don't worry, honey," he said, his voice a thready whisper. "We'll make this a great Christmas, best you ever had."

With that, John Nailor drifted off to sleep, leaving me lying there listening to the only sound in the room, the strong and steady beating of his heart.

Six

I should never have given into technology, but it was on sale, so like a backwoods tourist on my first trip to Atlantic City, I sold out to temptation and became the owner of a cell phone. Like a further fool, I gave people the number, so they called me. I could've turned the thing off, shoved it under my car seat for emergencies, but no, I couldn't do that. "What ifs" surrounded me. What if someone needed to reach me? What if there was an emergency? What if, what if, what if?

So when it started chirping as I drove across the Hathaway Bridge, I reached reflexively, rooting to the bottom of my purse, half dumping everything out in my attempt to catch it before it went to voice mail and I had to start punching numbers.

"Hey!" I yelled into it, grasping the steering wheel with one hand and attempting to hear the incoming call over the surge of air that blew through the T-tops in the Camaro.

"Sierra." Vincent's voice boomed out into my ear, forcing me to hold the phone out and wince. "Where the fuck are you?"

"Vincent, it's five-thirty. Where else would I be? I'm on my way to work."

Vincent continued almost as if he hadn't heard me. "Listen, we got a setback here."

A setback? He was calling what we had a setback? I was thinking of it as a red-hot emergency, or a thermonuclear meltdown, but not a setback. Setbacks are for hangnails or bad hair days.

"But Ernie's on his way, so don't worry about it."

I was coasting down off the bridge, heading for the beach, my foot hitting the accelerator a little harder as I listened.

"Vincent, shoot it straight. What are you talking about? Have you been arrested? I thought Ernie was taking care of that last night."

"Yeah, he did. This is kind of a little different." Vincent sounded like a teenager explaining why he was late for curfew and it was driving me nuts.

"Vincent, how about you quit the dance and talk."

"I'm under arrest for murder, Sierra."

That was shooting straight. I gripped the phone for a minute, unable to speak. "Okay, what are you talking about?"

"He didn't tell you? That prick you call a boyfriend didn't fucking tell you?" Vincent's voice rose in a crest of anxiety. "Somehow those assholes say I shot that dick Denny. Apparently the ballistics came back on the bullet in his tiny brain, and they say it matches up to my gun! They say the gun has my prints and no one else's. They say I got gunpowder residue on my hands. Now, what the fuck is that?"

For once I didn't know what to say. I just sat there at a red light, clutching a little black phone to my ear and looking stupid.

"Sierra, hello! You still there?"

"Yeah," I said softly, "I'm here. Vincent, I don't understand."

"You don't understand? What's to understand? It don't make no sense. I didn't shoot nobody. I shot at somebody, but they was robbing the place. I didn't have time to shoot no pissant Denny."

"It's a mistake," I said.

"Damn right it's a mistake, and you gotta take care of it."

"Me?" I turned out onto the beach road and got a glimpse of dazzling blue water and sugar-white sand. December on the Panhandle of northwest Florida. It couldn't get any better . . . or worse.

"Yeah," Vincent continued. "You gotta help me. You think

some two-bit lawyer in a Hawaiian shirt who plays the ukulele is gonna be able to get me outta this? I don't think so."

"Look, Vincent, there's a mistake here, all right? I'm sure—"

"Sierra, this ain't Candyland. Something's going on here and I need you. Besides, I ain't got the jack to pull in no high-powered team of private eyes and lawyers. I'm in a temporary financial situation. Maybe it's time to call your uncle."

"Uncle?" I was stalling for time. I knew who Vincent meant.

"Sierra," Vincent sighed. "Don't you think with your *connections* you could, you know, *do* something?"

Okay, so Vincent Gambuzzo was laboring under the assumption that I was hooked up to the "Big Moose" Lavotini syndicate out of Cape May, New Jersey. So maybe I let him think this on account of it bought me some clout when I needed it, but the reality of the situation was that I didn't know "Big Moose." I mean, he had heard of me, but we had not been formally introduced. I used his name once too often, and word had finally reached him up in New Jersey. So far, he hadn't issued a cease-and-desist order in the form of a visit from one of his henchmen, but I wasn't going to press the issue by using his name in vain.

The familiar white stucco of the Tiffany Gentleman's Club loomed up ahead of me, only there was a problem. The huge neon sign had been covered over by a large square of plastic that said: BIG MIKE'S HOUSE OF BOOTY. I gasped and Vincent was on me.

"What? What? You hit something? I told you about driving and talking. It's illegal, Sierra."

Then don't fucking call me. "No, Vincent, I just almost missed my turn, that's all. Now listen, you gotta calm down. I'll talk to Nailor. I'll find out what's going on. This is temporary. You won't be in there for long."

"I will be if they deny bail," he said. "Hell, if they set bail at much over twenty dollars, I'll be in here for years."

I didn't respond, I was so distracted by the sign in front of me. Big Mike's House of Booty! The silhouette of a naked woman, her breasts pointy and her hips thrusting outward, let it be known in no uncertain terms that Big Mike's was gonna be nothing like the Tiffany Gentleman's Club. I shuddered and pulled into the parking lot. I was going to have to talk to Big Mike, try to make him understand a little about the exotic dancing business.

"How's Bruno?" Vincent asked.

"I called the hospital right before I left," I said. "He's conscious, but they're keeping him doped up on account of the pain."

Vincent sighed. "Damn, I really made a mess of things."

I looked back up at the new sign and cringed. A mess was an understatement. "Listen, I'm here. I've gotta go inside. Vincent, try not to do a number on yourself. I'll call Nailor. Something's wrong here, but we'll get it straightened out."

Gambuzzo had radar. "What's Mike done to the club?" he demanded.

"Nothing, jeez, I just got here. I'm not even inside!"

"Sierra, don't run no shit with me. I can feel it. What's he done?"

I sighed. "The sign says 'Big Mike's House of Booty.' "

"I'll kill him! I'll freakin' kill him!"

In light of Vincent's current situation, I thought making terroristic threats from the pay phone at the county jail a little inadvisable.

"Vincent, just let me handle it. Big Mike's a little excited, that's all." I reached for my gear bag and climbed out of the car, the cell phone still glued to my ear. On the other end I could hear Gambuzzo hyperventilating.

"Gotta run, big man," I said. "This is gonna be fine. Don't worry."

Vincent was still huffing and puffing when I hung up, but there was nothing I could do about that. The Tiffany was vibrating with the sound of loud tasteless rock music, the kind with no discernible beat that appealed to a class of clientele that the Tiffany did not desire. Poor Mike, he needed some expert guidance, and I was just the girl to lead him down the right path.

Vincent was going to have to do his part. He was going to have to find the money to pay off Mike before our reputation was completely ruined.

Things were no better inside the club. For one thing, Rusty wasn't working the stage. I couldn't find him at first, and then I saw him, working the lights.

"What are you doing?" I called up to him. Rusty gave me a pained look, hit a switch, and looked back at me.

"Waiting for you, basically," he said. "Then I'm blowing this pop stand."

I looked around. In the spot where Rusty should've been, I saw Big Mike. He was wearing the headset Rusty used to direct the show, its microphone pulled up close to his fat lips. He looked like a kid in a candy store. When he saw me he motioned me over, a big smile on his face like he was inviting me to his birthday party.

"Hey, come on over here, gal!"

I approached with caution, strolling across the concrete floor like it was nothing but an ordinary day at the park for me.

"Shouldn't Rusty be doing that?" I asked. "I mean, don't you have other more important things to tend to?"

Big Mike had changed from the night before. His wiry hair was slicked down with pomade; he was wearing a button-down shirt that couldn't quite cover his huge beer gut without showing a little skin, and he'd shaved, in an attempt to look respectable, I supposed.

"See, that's just the problem with this joint," he boomed. "Gambuzzo didn't take a personal hand in the management of the place. I'm here to make sure it runs right." I followed his glance out onto the stage and was instantly horrified. Big Mike had five girls out on the catwalk and stage area. Five strippers, not to be confused with your artisans like myself, all dancing with no apparent theme or choreography. They were just flashing meat, and lots of it, in an attempt to blatantly solicit money. No class. No seduction, just sex for hire on a platter. It was disgusting.

I looked back over my shoulder and saw the dancers queued up in the doorway of the locker room, waiting to see what I was going to do. I turned back to Mike, who seemed to be also waiting for a response from me.

"Mike, in all due respect, this is not the Tiffany way. We are not about screwing a pole for money. We are not low-class hookers. We are women of desire. Our clientele expects that. That's what they want."

Mike frowned and pointed to the edge of the runway. "Then you'd better tell them that, 'cause they sure seem to want it bad enough!"

A cluster of twenty-year-old airmen stood barking like dogs, gripping their crotches and indicating that they did indeed want something. Of course, it's hard to grab your pants and insert money into a girl's garter at the same time, so the strippers' garters were nearly empty. I decided to try another tack.

"Mike, you know this is only temporary, right? I mean, Vincent'll get the money and pay you off, he could even do it today, so let's not—"

Mike spun around and stared at me. His eyes weren't sleepy sheepdog eyes anymore; they glittered with something I hadn't seen in him before: greedy determination.

"Sierra, this club's mine now. I don't care if he offers me twice what I took it for, I ain't selling." He barked out a thick laugh. "You think I'm not gonna jump on this golden opportunity like white on rice? Hell, you think I like taking drunken executives out twenty miles and baiting their hooks and waiting on them like they was royalty? Reel their fish in, bring 'em cold beer, hell, I do everything but hold their dicks while they pee. I ain't about to give this up for that!" Big Mike laughed. "Honey, you can tell ol' Vince I know where there's a used charter boat he can buy for cheap! That is, if he ever gets his ass out of jail!" And Mike was off, laughing at his newfound change of status, pleased as punch with himself.

I stood there and watched him, my attention flickering between him and the strippers on the stage. I couldn't do this. I wouldn't do this. I was aware of Rusty's eyes boring a hole in my back, and the girls waiting for me to do something. But I couldn't move. I was frozen.

Mike finally stopped laughing and looked back over at me. "What you doing standing there, Sierra? Ain't you supposed to be working? Hurry up and change. I want you and the next four girls in the alphabet out there in five minutes. Scoot!"

I just stood there.

"Hey," he said, not noticing that I hadn't made a move, "and don't put on one of them gussy things you always wear. Put on a thong-back and pasties. We don't need to stall off giving these men what they want. Window dressing is not allowed in Big Mike's House of Booty."

That did it. The slow burn ignited into an inferno.

"Yo!" I said.

Behind me I heard Tonya's voice. "Here she goes!"

Big Mike turned around. "What?" It was a big dumb "Whut?" The kind of "Whut" that made me want to sucker punch him for being stupid, but I didn't. Somehow I didn't.

"Okay, let me lay it out for you, Hot Stuff. This isn't your club, not for long anyway. And we aren't your dancers. We will not prance out on stage like flat-backing hookers. We will not lower our standards. We will not compromise our integrity."

Behind me a few girls started calling out "Yeah" and "That's right, honey!"

Big Mike smiled like maybe I was a difficult kid. "Sierra, I didn't ask you about your values. I told you. Now, honey, I understand that in Vince's house you were the alpha dog, but, baby, here you're just a bitch like all the rest. So go squeeze your ass into a thong and trot it on out here, girl, or you won't be making a trailer payment this month."

I'm sorry. I slapped him then, and it felt good, right up until he pulled his fist back to return fire. That's when Eugene appeared out of nowhere, a black tower of rage and aggression.

"Motherfucker!" he yelled, grabbing Mike's fist and holding it like a child would a lollipop. "You messing with my sister?"

Two men materialized out of the darkness of the backstage, gripping guns and looking very much like they might use them as easily as they had probably used grappling hooks the day before to bring a sailfish aboard Big Mike's boat.

Big Mike slowly pulled his fist from Eugene's grasp, straightened his collar, and glared at all of us.

"Those of you who want a job will play by my rules. My rules are simple: Get naked and get your ass onstage. Now!"

There was a general movement by the locker room door. Five girls, the lowest of the strippers, materialized dressed in next to nothing. Fifteen girls filed past them and walked over to the back door, gear bags in hand and determined looks on their faces.

I looked at Rusty and Eugene, then over at the girls by the back door. Inside I felt like I was going to bust out crying, but outwardly I knew I looked cool as a cucumber.

"All right, guys," I said. My voice was barely louder than my heartbeat. "Let's blow this pop stand!"

I turned around and saw an unexpected face in the shadows. Izzy Rodriguez stood just inside the back entrance, watching the scene unfold. I didn't know why he was there, but I could guess. He was just like any other predator, looking to take advantage of a bad situation. Whatever his business, it had nothing to do with us.

I took a deep breath and started walking, my back to Big Mike. I was walking out of the club that had been my home for almost three years. I was leaving it in the hands of a man whose sole bent seemed to be the destruction of all the Tiffany stood for. I was leaving a sinking ship, and yet I felt I had no other choice. Only now I had the working lives of at least fifteen other people in my hands.

Seven

$\mathscr{B}$y the time we reached the parking lot, the wait staff and the bartenders had joined us. Everyone looked grim, their faces shadowed by the overhead lights, drawing the lines of worry into sharp relief. We looked like characters in a black-and-white melodrama.

I was not going to make the mistake I'd made with Rusty again, so I decided against a pep talk. Instead I leaned on my Camaro and waited to see what was going to jump off.

"My husband's gonna kill me," one girl said, her voice small with worry.

"Hell, mine's gonna throw a party!" another said, her voice thick with sarcasm.

Tonya stepped forward, a chicken bone holding her hair up in a little ponytail that sprouted from the top of her head like a golden fountain. "I think y'all are looking at this wrong. It's a temporary vacation. You know any one of us can get on at any of the clubs around here, and not just the bad clubs like the Beaver. I mean the good ones. Dancers stick together, good times or bad."

Tonya looked at me, waiting for me to pitch in. I pushed up off the hood and looked at my coworkers. For a moment I could see them as they really were, just frightened little kids.

"Tonya's right," I said. "Times have been tough before. The

other clubs have a shortage of talent. I'm sure we can work out a visiting-artist gig."

Bubbles, a short little thing with huge boobs and big blue eyes, gasped and looked at me. "Sierra, what about Marla? She's been in Mississippi with her mama all week, but she's coming back tomorrow. Who's gonna tell her about Vincent?"

This got everybody's attention, and not just because Marla was my rival and the woman voted most likely to get under my skin in the shortest amount of time. Marla and Vincent had recently developed their professional relationship into a serious romance, so serious, in fact, that I had a vague uneasiness about my toehold as top dancer. Maybe Vincent would be so blinded by love he'd overlook the true talent at the Tiffany and give his squeeze top billing.

"Bubbles, don't sweat it. I'll go over there and tell her."

"She is gonna freak," Tonya said.

Freaking was going to be the least of what Marla would do. Turning Marla loose in a crisis involving her beloved would be like turning King Kong loose in a cable car. We were looking at pure disaster, unless it was handled right. I figured to have enough past baggage and debts owed to get us through this, but you never knew with Marla. Her fifty-two-inch tits could be all the brains Marla had going for her. She might not be able to see that cooler heads needed to prevail. Whatever. I figured to worry about all that when I saw her.

"All right," I said, facing the others. "Let's get out of here. Call my house tomorrow and I'll give you an update. If anybody gets ahold of a club that wants some of us, call around and let the others know."

"Hey," a male voice said. I turned and knew without looking that Izzy Rodriguez had overheard me.

"Seems like you girls might be kind of stuck," he said, strolling over to join us. He was chewing on the end of an unlit cigar, his teeth yellowed by age and poor hygiene. "I mean, I couldn't help but see what went down in there, and I must say that was a bold move." He looked over at me. "And perhaps a foolish one." He let the words hang in the air for a second, long enough for the seeds of doubt to take hold in any mind that wasn't firm in her conviction.

"But don't y'all worry. I could use y'all." There was a flush of relief on the faces of the youngest talent. But the older ones, the ones who knew Izzy and his reputation, they stayed right where they were, their faces unmoved.

" 'Course now, I couldn't pay you like Gambuzzo did, but hell, it's something."

I stepped away from him, positioning myself between Izzy and the girls. "That's nice, Mr. Rodriguez," I purred. "We'll be in touch." Like when it snows in July, I thought.

Izzy ignored me. "Auditions at ten A.M. tomorrow," he said, starting to walk away to the white stretch limo that waited in a darkened corner of the parking lot. "Don't y'all be late!"

I waited until the driver opened Izzy's door and then shut it behind him before I spoke.

"Don't do it," I said. "Rumor is, Rodriguez is running dope out the back door and prostitutes his girls. Don't get mixed up in that."

I had high hopes that they'd listen, but I knew we'd lose a few. The younger ones with kids to support or a worthless boyfriend who wanted money at any price, they'd be the ones to go. They'd be the ones I couldn't reach.

I thought about the easy ones the whole way back to the trailer park; the vulnerable ones were always the first to fall prey to the trap. Exotic dancing is not for lightweights looking to collect fast money, but those are the ones who wander into the life and end up victims. Sierra Lavotini was nobody's victim, and if I had my way in this war with Mike Riggs and the rest of the world who had lined up against Vincent Gambuzzo, I wouldn't make victims out of my staff either. 'Cause see, they were my girls and I was responsible for them. I'd led them out of their jobs, and I'd cover them until we were back in again.

Fluffy was sitting on the kitchen stoop when I arrived home. She was shivering in the early-evening air, but obviously was not quite cold enough to move inside. She was smiling. Life at Ray-dean's must've been good.

"You look like the cat that ate the canary," I said.

Fluffy grunted and let out a long, slow dog belch.

"Back at you," I said, and walked into the trailer. The light was on over the stove, and the kitchen was bathed in a warm yellow glow that for a second reminded me of Ma's kitchen, and then just as quickly depressed me. No Christmas with the family this year. I looked over at the refrigerator. My airline ticket was stuck to the door, held by a magnet made to look like Santa Claus. Ho, ho, ho.

Fluffy rubbed her face against my ankle, as if she knew.

"Ain't nothin' for it," I muttered, and picked up the phone. Why put off the inevitable? Might as well call them and let the blues begin. I looked at the ticket again. I was due to leave in thirty-six hours. There was no way to wrap this one up and make the world okay in less than two days, one day really if you counted this day as half shot and the departure day as nonexistent because it was a morning flight. Nope, there was nothing to do but call.

I sat counting the rings. My brother Joey caught it on the third one.

"Lavotini," he barked.

"Lavotini," I answered.

"Sierra?"

"You know another Lavotini female that ain't over sixty?" I said.

Joey laughed. "Yeah, as a matter of fact. The former Mrs. Francis Lavotini, or your cousin Donna, or any one of a half-dozen other women in this family aside from you. Figures you're only seeing yourself, you little princess."

"Hey, whoa! I am not a freakin' princess."

"Couldn't tell it by me."

The whole time I was bantering with Joey I was also listening, straining to hear who was around in the background, hoping for a taste of home that comes of hearing Ma bustling around the kitchen or Pa yelling out something. It was after dinnertime, but oftentimes my brothers ate with Ma and Pa, then sat around talking fire department business until after nine or ten. I just wanted a little piece of that now, but all I heard was silence.

"So, Joey, listen. Is Ma around? I gotta tell her something no good and I'd rather get it over with."

Joey's voice shifted an octave deeper. Joey's creeping up on thirty but sometimes I forget. I keep him frozen in time somewhere around fifteen. Maybe it's on account of he's so laid-back and low-key that you forget he's growing up in front of you. Maybe on account of he's the closest brother to me and I don't feel any older than a kid myself. Who knows?

"Sierra, Ma, she don't need no more bad news right now. So if this is something big, tell me."

Joey's voice was somber and it scared me. "What do you mean, Joey? What's going on?"

Joey's voice dropped still lower and he was half whispering, as if he didn't want to be overheard.

"Just tell me what's up. I can't really talk too good, you see what I'm saying?"

No, I did not see what he was saying, but I knew it was frightening me and that he was very, very serious, so I did as he asked.

"I can't come home for Christmas," I said.

Joey made a noise like a loud buzzer. "Wrong answer. Try again."

I was pacing around the kitchen, the long phone cord moving with me, Fluffy right at my side.

"Joey, I'm sorry. You know I want to be there. I just can't come. There's trouble at the club. If I don't do something, a lot of people could lose their jobs or worse. We got big trouble here, hon."

"Sierra," Joey whispered, "we got bigger trouble here. Trust me on this."

"Is it Pa? Is something wrong on the job?"

Joey snorted. "What, him? There ain't nothing wrong on the job, Sierra. That's piddlety shit compared to what's up. But I tell you one thing, if he don't start acting right about this, I'm gonna whip his tired ass!"

"Joey!"

"I'm serious, Sierra. We need you up here and I don't mean *want* you, we freakin' need you."

My heart was starting to pound. "Joey, quit fooling around. What's wrong?"

But Joey wasn't budging. "All's I'm gonna tell you is this, Sierra: Ma and Pa need you. They were waiting to tell you until you got up here, and you have to come."

Joey was a firefighter, just like two of my other three brothers. He didn't exaggerate. If he said something was wrong, it was. If he didn't want to say it over the phone, then it ranked up there as a national emergency. My family was like that. When trouble hit, they closed ranks. Look how many times they'd come to me. No, the Lavotinis were tough. They didn't go outside the family in an emergency. They didn't talk about it to outsiders. They just took care of the problem, no matter how big or small.

"Sierra," Joey whispered. "I don't want to tell you and have you all upset and by yourself. I'm just telling you it's bad and you need to come home."

"Joey, all right. You want me to come sooner? Try and fly out tomorrow?"

Joey thought for a moment. "No, don't do that. I don't want them knowing I spilled it. Don't talk to nobody. I don't want it getting back to them, all right? It'll wait until you get here, but not any longer." There was silence for a second, then he spoke again, but this time I heard the tears in his voice.

"Sierra, pray, all right?"

If I could've come through the phone, I would've.

"Hold on, honey," I whispered. "I'm on my way."

Eight

I hung up and the phone rang again. Joey, I thought, thinking twice and deciding to tell me after all.

"Okay, what's wrong?" I said. There was the briefest hint of a pause, then I heard Eugene's voice, frantic, the sounds of the hospital in the background.

"They called a code on Bruno," he said.

"When?"

"Now! Sierra, he's dying. They're all in there. They're shouting and they got all these machines." Eugene's voice broke off. In the background I heard faint voices and beeping.

"I'm on my way," I said, and hung up. Bruno wasn't going to die. He couldn't die.

I ran out the door, hopping into the Camaro and squealing rubber down the asphalt. I was five minutes from the hospital. Five minutes feels like an eternity when you're hoping someone won't die on you. I drove blindly, my mind reviewing old movie clips of Bruno pulling some drunk tire salesman off me, or touching my shoulder like he knew how I felt when my friend Ruby Diamond died. Bruno was stupid—Raydean had that much right—but he was my kind of stupid. He was loving stupid. His errors were due to trying too hard, not wanting to be less than he was. Okay, so he wanted to be a pro wrestler. Okay, so he believed the WCW matches were real. But that was Bruno for you, always wanting to believe in heroes.

I was full-out crying by the time I pulled into the medical center parking lot. It didn't help to see Eugene outside, crying as hard as me and smoking a cigarette.

I ran up to him, almost afraid to look him in the eye, not wanting to hear it. "What happened?" I asked.

"He died on his way back into surgery, Sierra," Eugene said. "They were right by the elevator, running, when his heart stopped again." Eugene shivered and took a long drag on his smoke. "They brought the fucking paddles right out there in the middle of the hallway. Some nurse was on his chest, beatin' the shit out of him, and then they zapped my boy right there."

Eugene was seeing it, his eyes staring out into the lot. "Motherfucker wouldn't start up. They pushed some needle right into his fuckin' heart, and I'm screaming, 'Wake up, asshole!' But Bruno wouldn't do it."

Eugene looked over at me then and smiled softly. "Motherfucker took four zaps to start his heart up again. Do you believe that? Four times." Eugene shook his head. "They zap me once, I'm gonna wake up! He was dead, Sierra. They were looking at their watches like they be thinkin' my brother was fuckin' wasted! Son of a bitch showed them. His ass is on the table again with that little boy cuttin' on him. And I done told him, too. I said, 'Don't mess up with the brother.'"

"Oh, I'm sure that put the doc right at ease. Threaten his ass and see if his hands shake while he's cutting!"

Eugene looked back at the parking lot. "I was just trying to make sure this didn't go down like some managed-care HMO bullshit."

"Managed care? What are you talking about?"

Eugene smiled. "Baby, before I was a bouncer, I ran the claims review department for an HMO. Them people'll waste your ass to save a buck. I got burnt out on the con job, you know what I'm saying?"

I looked at Eugene, really looked this time. The Tiffany Gentleman's Club never asked too many questions when they hired staff. After all, Gambuzzo just wanted to know his bouncers could clean house. It didn't occur to him to find out what other skills his security team harbored. Eugene was a brain, a brain on hiatus from the corporate world of health care. Go figure.

"Well, your intentions were clean, my friend," I said, "but your methodology was lacking."

Eugene pitched his cigarette into the parking lot and turned to open the door. "We'd better get back up there," he said.

I started in after him, then caught the reflection in the glass door. Eugene wasn't rushing back to wait in the ICU waiting room; he was avoiding the owner of the silver Miata that was pulling up to the front door.

"Sierra!" Marla's shrill voice cried. "Just a damn minute!"

Eugene was gone. I turned around and stepped over to the curb where Marla sat in her little toy convertible. Her long black hair was held back by a silver lamé scarf that matched the car's paint job. Her perfectly manicured fire-engine-red nails drummed the steering wheel, and her false eyelashes were in no way passing for natural. She looked like a dime-store mannequin in a B-grade fifties movie.

" 'Bout time you got back," I said. I didn't mean it, but it was something neutral to say, something to hold off showing all my cards until I figured how much she knew about the situation. With Marla you gotta not overwhelm her with facts. Her tiny brain can't hold but so much at a time. Beyond her limit, Marla is all emotion — negative, wailing, uncontrollable emotion.

Marla eyed me like I was maybe a day short of fresh, and started in. "What are you doing about Vincent? Have you talked to that . . ." Here she paused to find a word that wouldn't lead to her immediate demise. "Man," she finally said. "Is he going to take care of things? Why can't Vincent come home right now?"

I stood there staring at her, waiting for the well of questions to run dry. "Marla," I said finally, "Bruno just almost died. He could be dead now for all I know. Let me deal with this first. I'll get back to you."

Marla's face changed, softening. "I thought he was better," she said.

"Setback."

Marla switched off the ignition and stepped out of the car. "Okay, let's go inside."

"Marla, you can't leave your car here. This is the entrance to the hospital."

Marla straightened up to her full five-foot-eight-inch height and looked through the glass front door at the security guard, an elderly man with a hearing aid. She adjusted her red tube top, licked her lips, and stared right at the old man, as if she were only studying her reflection. Then, with a fake start, she pretended to notice him, tossing her hair back like Veronica Lake in the good old days. She smiled, bit her lower lip softly, and stuck out her B-52 bombers. The security guard was putty in her hands.

"Let's roll," she said. She sauntered past the security desk, tossing her keys in the old man's lap. "I'll be back, sweetie," she purred, "but if you don't mind, I think the left rear tire's a little low."

The guard couldn't even answer; Marla made sure of that. She leaned down and slid her arm across his shoulder, her tits practically down his throat, and kissed him on the cheek. "You are so cute!" she cooed.

I was sick.

The elevator doors chose that moment to open and we vanished before the guard could recover. Marla's face changed back to its normal snarl and she was on me again.

"If your boyfriend can't clean this mess up, maybe you oughta call that Uncle Moose of yours. It's a downright shame you cause all this trouble and then can't clean it up!"

"Cause trouble? I don't see how you can think I had a thing to do with Vincent getting his ass in a sling."

Marla sniffed. "Between your cop and your relatives, I can't see how this isn't your fault," she said. "Vinny don't go looking for trouble like you do."

"No, Marla," I said, "Vincent doesn't have to go looking for trouble. He's a magnet for misfortune."

Marla raised her eyebrows like I was suddenly using big words deliberately in an attempt to confuse her.

"You know, Vincent's got enemies," she said. "Jail is not a good place for him. He has needs, strong needs. I just can't see him lasting long in prison."

I was not gonna go there with her. I did not want to know about Vincent's "needs." What he needed was to be off a murder rap.

"Marla, what we need here is to find the guys that robbed the place. We need to figure out how someone else got ahold of Vincent's gun and shot Denny. Or we need to prove that the ballistics test is wrong. But one thing we don't need is to hear about Vincent's sex drive."

Marla sniffed. "Well, I should hope not," she said. "Me and Vincent are quite happy in our relationship. Besides, you are definitely not his type!"

I sighed and stepped out of the elevator. What we had here, as usual, was Marla trying to communicate with higher life forms and failing. Maybe Raydean was right about the aliens taking over the world. Maybe Marla had lost her mind to the Flemish.

Eugene was standing by the door to the surgical suite, his face practically pasted up against the glass window. Beyond him I saw nothing but the empty hallway leading to the operating rooms.

"Why don't you come talk to me," I said to him. "Why don't we see if we can come up with something on those guys?"

Eugene reluctantly left his post and wandered up. "All right," he said, but his eyes were still glued to the closed doors. I was on the verge of telling him that it would be all right, that Bruno was one tough cookie, when the surgical suite door flew open and a young nurse in green surgical scrubs scurried out, the front of her uniform bloodstained, and her mask pulled just below her chin.

"Eugene?" she called.

Eugene walked up to her, his eyes searching her face for a sign.

The nurse smiled slightly, but seemed a little intimidated by Eugene's bulk. "Dr. Thrasher wanted me to bring you a message." Eugene nodded. "He said to tell you he's got your back." Here she seemed a little uncertain of herself, but Eugene smiled. "And the doctor also said Bruno is gonna be fine, they're just repairing a tear in his artery. Dr. Thrasher said for you to take a load off and go eat something. He'll be out in about an hour and a half. Bruno is gonna be fine," she said again. She sounded just like a little parrot of Dr. Thrasher.

"Tell the doc I said I owe him another one," Eugene said.

The nurse nodded and walked back toward the suite. She was petite, with a perky little butt that Eugene seemed to find fascinating.

"You gonna offer her a job or go get something to eat?" I asked. Eugene, a new man again, turned to me and smiled.

"You just jealous 'cause she's tiny and got a bigger butt than you do," he said.

I didn't dignify this with an answer. "Well, are you going to go eat something or not?"

Eugene shook his head. "I'm not leaving."

"How about we go get you something and bring it back?"

Eugene started to shake his head no, but reconsidered. I was willing to bet he hadn't eaten since this whole mess had begun.

"Well, maybe a little something," he said. "Like maybe some meatloaf, if they've got it, and a cheeseburger, all the way, mashed potatoes and fries, a salad, two cartons of milk, and get me some chocolate cake if they've got any. If they don't, just bring a couple of whatever desserts they got. And if there's no potatoes, try for spaghetti. I gotta carbo-load."

Marla, sensing I was going to leave her alone with Eugene, sprang toward the elevator and started popping the button. We rode down to the ground floor in silence, made our way to the antiseptic cafeteria, and proceeded to load a tray up with every bland dish Eugene's starving stomach could demand. Marla followed along behind me, sighing and now and then tossing a food item onto the tray. I was not going to ask her what was on her mind, because it was clear that was what she wanted me to do. I figured let Gambuzzo pry stuff out of her. Marla was not my problem. But that made me think about Vincent. Vincent was my problem.

I looked over at Marla and decided not to tell her I was leaving town for a few days. I didn't want to be the one to break it to her that Vincent was going to spend his Christmas behind bars. Instead, I started lining up my options, figuring what I could do in the next twenty-four hours to find out what had gone down in Vincent's office that could've resulted in him being buttoned for a murder.

The cafeteria closed down after we left. Marla carried one tray and I carried the other and we still struggled to get all that food up to the third-floor waiting room. She didn't talk, just sighed now and then and looked up toward the ceiling, as if that was gonna help her plight.

"Supper's on," I called out as I stepped off the elevator. Eugene turned, revealing visitors. John Nailor stood there, Joe Nolowicki by his side, a notepad in hand and a serious look on his face. Clearly I was interrupting something.

"Detective," I said, nodding at Nailor and sliding the tray onto a table that occupied one corner of the room.

"Ms. Lavotini," he said, his deep voice sliding over my name like a caress. I shivered.

"Did I leave anything out?" Nolowicki asked Eugene. For a moment the three men turned away from us as Eugene thought it over.

"No, I think that's about right," he answered. "I couldn't really see from that angle, but I did get a real good look at the shooters. With all the confusion, it would've been easy for Mr. Gambuzzo to drop his gun. One of them could've picked it up."

Nolowicki wasn't going with Eugene's speculation. His eyebrows shot up and he stared right at Eugene. He looked out of place without a cigar. "Anyone could've picked that gun up, but only Gambuzzo's prints were on it," Nolowicki said.

Eugene was right back on it. "Maybe they wore gloves, or wiped it. You didn't get a full print off the trigger, did you? And you couldn't get one off the butt, not with that plastic handle."

Nolowicki shrugged. "Well, only one person threatened the victim with that gun, and that was Gambuzzo, so I'm sticking by it."

Nailor stepped around Eugene. For some reason he was letting Nolowicki ask all the questions, and he wasn't intervening. What was this all about? Surely he didn't think Vincent shot anybody?

"What're you doing here?" he asked me. "I thought you were working tonight."

He walked toward me, closing the distance in a few steps but taking his time, knowing, I'm sure, that I watched him. That was the thing about Nailor. He didn't showboat because he didn't have to. He moved in a slow, deliberate way that made him incredibly attractive. It was his self-assurance. I like a man who knows where he's going and doesn't have to worry about how he gets there.

By the time he reached me, my doubts had vanished. Everything else on my radar screen had faded into the background. It was the smell of him, the spicy leathery scent, that made me want to pull him closer. It was the way he looked at me and smiled that slow, sexy grin that reminded me of his lips on mine.

"I went to work," I said, "and then I got to thinking it was maybe time for a career change." My eyes never left his. We were communicating on another level about all the things that were best left unsaid until later.

"Career change, huh? Well, I've heard those things happen. Would this career change involve the rumor I heard about the Tiffany's new name?"

"It would indeed," I said, almost whispering as I moved even closer to him.

Nailor nodded toward the elevator. I looked back at Eugene and Nolowicki. Nolowicki was listening and nodding, but he still appeared to be unchanged by whatever it was Eugene was telling him. Marla was keeping a low profile over by the windows, but I knew she was soaking it in. Every little word was going somewhere inside that devious mind of hers, and I knew she'd use the information at some point.

The elevator doors opened and Nailor pushed me inside and hit the red stop button. The door closed behind us, and in an instant he had pulled me to him. I felt him inhale, then kiss the top of my head.

"I missed you," he said.

"I missed you, too," I answered. "But what are you doing here with Nolowicki? I thought you were the primary?"

"Your place later?" he whispered in my ear, ignoring the questions.

I nodded, my throat suddenly tightening. God, how I wanted this man. I wanted to lie in his arms, lay my head on his strong chest, and forget all about everything but him. I flashed to an image of him, naked, hovering above me, and then just as quickly shook it off. I couldn't. Not now. I had to take care of Vincent.

"Sure, my place," I said. "I want to know everything that's going on."

His hands slid up and over my breasts, touching my nipples and feeling them harden beneath his fingertips.

"Really?" he whispered. "All right, I'll tell you everything that's going on, step by step." He was trying to get by me, trying to ignore the questions and go where he wanted us to go.

I pushed away from him, turned and hit the red button. This was pointless.

The elevator door opened again and I stepped out. "Talking," I said. "Talking is very important. I need to know what else you've found out."

Nailor sighed and in his eyes I saw something change. He knew it wasn't going to work. He knew what I was feeling. That was the trouble with Nailor; he almost always knew what I was feeling.

"I'll meet you back at the trailer," I said, and almost ran away from him, back to the sanctuary of Eugene and the waiting room. Nailor followed, his footsteps echoing behind me. Life had prepared me for lots of things, but Nailor wasn't one of them.

Marla had apparently had all she could take of Nolowicki talking about her beloved Vincent. In the brief time we'd been gone, Marla had edged closer and closer to Nolowicki and Eugene. By the time I crossed the lobby and re-entered the waiting room, Marla was a nuclear warhead and the hapless detective was the target.

I almost felt sorry for him. There he stood, the top of his bald head gleaming in the weird glow of the fluorescent lighting, his red jacket pale compared to the angry flush in Marla's cheeks, listening and pinned almost to the wall by Marla's huge tits.

"My Vinny is a prince," Marla was saying. As she spoke she kept moving closer, inching her way right up into Nolowicki's face. "You go around telling people that he uses drugs, that he has them in his desk! That's horse poop and you know it! I think you all are trying to frame my man!" She whirled around and looked at Nailor, her eyes huge black wells of pain and distress.

"Why don't you look for the real killer?" she continued. "Why don't you pick on that bimbo that was there, huh? Maybe she shot the little guy and left her dope behind. Ever think of that?"

Nolowicki, to his credit, decided to play peacemaker. "No, Miss er . . . what was the name?"

"Marla the Bomber," she said. "And that's all you need to know because I wasn't even there that night!"

Joe Nolowicki looked over at Nailor, gave him a cop look I'd seen a million times, a hey-watch-this sort of nonwink.

"Well, Marla, now maybe you can help us out. Maybe you can tell us all about the Vincent Gambuzzo you know. Maybe show us around his place and explain a few things about the real man."

Marla was going to go for it. I could see her turning it over in her head. She cocked her head and examined Nolowicki. "Maybe I just could," she said, and a small, sly smile broke out across her face. "But not at Vinny's place . . ."

That's right, I breathed silently, don't let him in without a warrant.

"No," Marla continued, "we'll be much more comfortable at my place!"

Joe Nolowicki smiled, but it was just as phony as Marla's. "Now, that would be right nice," he drawled. He looked over at Nailor. "Can I catch up with you later?" he asked.

Nailor frowned, obviously not liking it. Nailor was straight up, clean. He didn't work a con or lead a witness. It wasn't his style, but on the other hand, what could he do? Nolowicki was another investigator working a different angle. So he nodded and the deal was sealed.

Eugene was back by the surgical suite doors, hoping to get a glimpse of Bruno or to catch Dr. Thrasher on his way out of surgery. He looked like a big black Labrador retriever.

I slipped up behind him and laid a hand on his shoulder. "I'm gonna go," I said. "I'm gonna see if I can't catch a little shut-eye and then get up with Gambuzzo. You call if there's any change, all right?"

Eugene nodded, not looking away for more than a moment. "I'm cool," he said.

Nailor walked up to us. "Eugene, I've just got one or two more questions for you, and then I'll leave you alone, okay?"

I took that as a cue. I slipped away, leaving each detective to his subject, and rode the elevator down to the ground floor. When I walked through the front door, I came face-to-face with the elderly security guard. He was standing by Marla's car, a dewy-eyed, wistful expression on his face.

"Ain't she something?" he murmured as I walked past. Somehow I just knew he didn't mean the convertible.

I hopped in my car and tore off out of the lot, wanting to put some distance between myself, John Nailor, and the events of the past twenty-four hours. I reached over and cranked up an old Allman Brothers tape. "Ramblin' Man" broke the silence of the late-night air. I cranked up the heat full-blast so it could compensate for the open T-tops and settled back, trying to fight my mood. Whatever in the world was happening? In less than twenty-four hours my boss had lost the club and gotten himself arrested for murder; one of my best buddies was in intensive care, clinging to life; I find out that my parents were in some kind of desperate trouble; and in the midst of all that, I was suddenly made aware that I'm in a real, honest-to-God relationship.

I looked in the rearview mirror, sensing his presence again before seeing him. There he was in his new unmarked Crown Vic, gaining on me. By the time I entered the Lively Oaks Trailer Park he was just off my bumper. The two of us were up the steps and inside the door, barely managing to avoid crushing Fluffy as Nailor backed me up against the kitchen wall and started unbuttoning my blouse.

I fumbled with the buttons on his shirt, finally pulling it open and away from his body. I wasn't aware of any Greek chorus of doubt in my head this time. The only thing I wanted was him. I took his hand and pulled him toward the bedroom, stumbling in the darkness, knowing nothing but the way I suddenly ached for him.

He tried to slow me down, pushed my hands away as I grabbed for him, and forced me to wait while he ever so slowly undressed me. He sat on the edge of the bed and pulled me close, his lips trailing their way from my breasts to my belly.

"Nailor, come on," I said. "Don't make me wait this time."

I pulled his clothes off and pushed him back onto the bed, but he wouldn't let me rush him.

"We have all night," he whispered as his lips brushed my ear. "So I'm taking all night. Get used to it, Sierra. I'm not like the other men you've known. With me it's all about you. I'm going to spoil you, Sierra."

I felt myself go weak. My stomach flipped over and the desire that had threatened to engulf me fanned to a five-alarm fire. I didn't think about anything but him and the two of us making love.

My body belonged to the process and nothing I could do would stop it.

He pulled me to him, his fingers spreading my legs, moving inside me, his tongue following his fingers until I moaned and began to move with him. I lost track of time. My ears started to ring. I pulled him closer, up and into me, joining with him and crying out as he filled me.

We moved together, my hands sliding down his back, pulling him deeper inside, until I felt him cresting and taking me with him. We came, shattering against each other, pulling each other closer and deeper, lost in the sensations that moved us. And then it happened.

"I love you, Sierra," he whispered.

My eyes flew open and I stared at him. He was looking right at me, and if I judged right, he was as surprised by his words as I was. He closed his eyes and lowered his head to my shoulder, feathering my skin with a soft kiss. I couldn't see him, couldn't tell how he was reacting, but I knew what those words had done to me.

"You want something to drink?" I said, moving away from him and rolling to the side of the bed.

"Sure. How about water?"

I looked over at him. He was lying back, his arm behind his head, studying me with that cool detective stare of his.

"I was thinking more along the lines of some of Pa's Chianti," I said.

"Scared you that bad, did I?" he murmured.

I jumped out of bed then, pulling on my purple chenille robe and stepping over the pile of clothes on the floor.

"Don't be ridiculous," I said, moving for the door. I started down the hallway at light speed, almost running in my need to escape.

"You're the one running away," he called.

"No, I'm just the one who's thirsty. I mean, you wore me out!" Then I was out of his range, safe in my kitchen, pouring Chianti into tumblers while my hand shook like a leaf. Nailor loved me?

He couldn't mean that. After all, the words were said in the heat of passion. How could he love me? He didn't know the half of me. And I didn't know the half of him.

I leaned up against the kitchen sink and took a big swig of wine, forgetting for the moment that Nailor's glass was sitting beside mine. I needed time and space to think.

"Sierra, you coming?" His voice seemed to echo down the narrow hallway.

I turned away, looking outside through the darkened kitchen window. A face, ugly in the dim light, darkened by a full beard, stared back.

I gasped, opening my mouth to scream and hearing no sound escape.

The figure held his finger up to his lips, a sinister smile creeping across his face. Like a flash of lightning, the apparition vanished, leaving only darkness.

Nine

I screamed, and this time the sound came out loud and clear. The terrible face filled the window again, surprise written all over the man's features, surprise mingled with frustration. He rolled his eyes, shook his head impatiently, and vanished.

Nailor came on the run, fumbling to fasten his pants while trying to hold his departmental-issue gun in his right hand.

"Jesus, Sierra, what's wrong!"

I pointed to the window, trying to calm myself. "There's a man out there!" Fluffy was going crazy, barking and tearing off for the doggie door. I tried to block her way, but she squeaked by me and was gone with Nailor right behind her, his gun held high in the air. I ran behind them, the cordless phone in my hand, dialing 911 as I tried to keep Nailor and Fluffy in sight.

Fluffy was barking in the distance and Nailor was running hard after her. I heard him yell, "Stop! Police!" But whoever it was kept on running. A minute later I heard the sound of a motorcycle roaring off into the distant night and knew they'd lost him.

The 911 dispatcher only needed to hear Nailor's name before he responded by dispatching half of little Panama City's police force. The two cars arrived, sirens screaming and lights blazing, only to run into a half-naked detective and a tiny chihuahua.

Nailor, winded, glared up at me from the bottom of the steps. "What'd you call them for?" he muttered.

"That's what you do when you have a prowler, Nailor, you call the police."

Nailor looked disgusted. "Honey, I am the police."

Raydean emerged from her trailer, Marlena the Shotgun by her side, and a wary look on her face.

"Well, I know you're the police," I said, "but you might've needed backup. I was trying to help you out, Nailor. You don't need to go off on me!"

Raydean spat over the railing of her tiny stoop and surveyed the scene. "I got your backup right here," she said, racking the slide of her gun. "You want me to dispatch them impostors?" She was looking at the patrol cars, her left eyebrow a skeptical inch above the other one.

"No, honey, not them," I said. "They're the good guys. There was a man looking in my window, that's all."

Nailor, not finished with me, muttered, "Yeah, like I need backup for a Peeping Tom." He walked over to the closest cop and began talking in a low, quiet voice. Whatever he said prompted a few snickers and an impatient bark from Fluffy. The younger cop was looking from Nailor to me and smiling like he'd figured out some big secret. Oh well, that was just all part of the general hoopla that came with me and Nailor getting hooked up, however informally. Now we'd be the continued talk of the department and probably most of Panama City.

The two cops got back into their cars and drove off around the trailer park, searchlights bouncing off the darkened trailers. Few residents had bothered to get up and investigate the blue lights and sirens. It just wasn't that unusual for the Lively Oaks Trailer Park to see police activity.

Raydean, reassured by the departure of the two officers, decided to go back to bed, but not before she issued a few choice words to Nailor and me.

"You two have got to get your ducks in a row," she said. "Just because you shoot off a few fireworks in your bedroom, it don't mean the rest of us has got to get involved. Now I need my beauty sleep, so let's keep it down, y'hear?"

Nailor, used to Raydean, nodded and slowly climbed the steps to the back door. I was tempted to correct her, but didn't. I'd have all morning after Nailor left to set Raydean straight about Nailor and the future of our acquaintanceship.

Once inside, Nailor went straight for the tumbler of Chianti, took a long swallow, and then turned his attention to me.

"All right, what'd he look like?"

I wanted to tell him he looked familiar, like a friend of mine's boyfriend, but that was impossible as the two had vanished into the sunset and a witness protection program long ago. And I caught myself censoring the information on account of not wanting him to think I had men popping in on me at all hours of the night. Instead I told him exactly what I'd seen and gave him the best description possible.

Nailor listened, leaning against the counter and drinking as I talked. He looked completely comfortable standing there. He wore only his trousers, no shoes, and no shirt. His bare feet were tanned and I found myself staring at them, wondering how he'd like me to massage them later. I shook it off and focused back on the conversation.

"Any of your customers ever try to follow you home?" he was asking.

"A time or two," I said. "But Raydean or I always handle it. I think by now the word's gotten out that uninvited guests are unwelcome."

Nailor didn't seem especially reassured. "It's a risky business you're in, Sierra."

I bristled. "You too, my man, but you don't see me trying to warn you off of it."

Nailor smiled, but his face was tight. "I'm observing, Sierra, not warning."

"Whatever."

Nailor picked up Pa's jug of wine and poured more in both our glasses. "Let's go back to bed," he said. He was trying to push it aside and move on, but I wasn't so sure.

"I'm not going to change just because we're involved, Nailor."

He turned around and laughed. "God, I hope not!" The mood was broken. We started out of the kitchen and headed for the bedroom only to have the phone ring. I rolled my eyes at Nailor.

"Guess who?" I asked. "Five bucks says it's Raydean reporting aliens."

Nailor laughed. "No takers there." He moved past me and headed back down the hallway as I grabbed the cordless phone and followed him.

"Hello?"

I could hardly hear the voice above the loud roar of an unbaffled motorcycle.

"You idiot!" he said. "I need to talk to you. What did you go and sic the cop on me for? And what're you doing, shacking up with that creep?"

I knew the voice. It was my friend, Frankie the Biker, back in town and looking for trouble as usual.

Nailor turned around and made a face at me, clearly thinking I had Raydean on the line.

"No, honey," I said, "everything's fine. Nailor's here with me. Don't worry about that prowler."

Frankie caught on. "I've gotta see you and I don't need no cops around. There's a problem and I think you know all about it. Can you lose that asshole by lunchtime?"

"Sure, honey," I said soothingly. "No problem."

Frankie sighed. "Good. I'll call you later. Boy, is Denise gonna be pissed when I tell her you're screwing a dick."

"Well maybe that'll just be our little secret," I said.

Frankie roared. "Like hell! I told her you had the hots for him and she didn't believe me. No way is this gonna be a secret!"

"Yeah, but you do owe me."

There was a pause as Frankie considered how I'd helped him

and Denise out of a huge jam before they rode off and disappeared on me.

"Not that big a favor," he said. "I gotta keep Denise happy, and trust me, this'll make her real happy!"

Nailor was sliding under the covers when I clicked the phone off. I dropped the robe, aware of him watching my every move.

"Weren't we in the middle of something?" he murmured, pulling me close to him.

"Maybe," I said, slipping my hand under the covers and beginning a little exploratory research.

Nailor moaned as I touched him and his eyes slowly closed. "Yeah, that's it. We were in the middle of something."

I moved closer, my fingers finding all the little spots Nailor loved, but inside I was thinking a mile a minute. What was Frankie doing back in town? There could only be one answer. This all had something to do with the robbery at the club.

Nailor's fingers were doing their own dance across my skin and I felt myself respond. A sigh escaped my lips and I moved a little to the left, landing his fingers right where I wanted them. For a second I relaxed, giving in to the feel of him, the sheer enjoyment of his skin against mine.

Maybe Frankie was going to present me with the key to the robbery at the club. Maybe the whole mess with Vincent and the murder charge would all be taken care of by Frankie's information and I could go home for Christmas without a care in the world. Except, that is, for leaving Nailor behind.

I reached for him, pulling him tighter against me. When he sighed I felt guilty. Right now, Nailor was completely happy thinking we were going to spend Christmas together. But come the morning, I was going to pull the plug on his expectations. Surely he'd understand. I looked at him and felt a pang as he smiled down at me. Sure, he'd understand, but he'd still be alone. What if he didn't have anywhere to go?

The thought of Nailor alone on Christmas morning was almost more than I could take. For some reason, that one image tore at me until I was suddenly aware of a tear snaking its way down my cheek. What in the hell was wrong with me?

I brushed the tear away before Nailor saw it and tried to refocus my attention on the current moment's activities. It was all the tension, I supposed. I was getting all mushy over a man who was perfectly capable of handling a simple holiday without me.

"Mmmmm," Nailor moaned softly. "I can't wait to wake up with you on Christmas morning."

Great. Just great. If I didn't go home, something awful might happen, and with a Lavotini, family comes first, no question. But if I left Panama City, not only was I letting the club, the dancers, and Vincent down, I was ruining John Nailor's Christmas morning.

For a moment I entertained the idea of taking Nailor with me, but I couldn't bring an outsider in on a problem so huge Joey wouldn't even discuss it over the phone. No, this wasn't the time to bring home a man, even if that man was John Nailor.

I thought of my brother Joey's last words to me—"pray, Sierra"—and shivered. Something was horribly wrong in Philadelphia and I was going to have to fly up there and face whatever it was alone.

Ten

*I*n my dream I was home for Christmas. Pa had trimmed the tree in bright red glass balls. But when I stepped over to look more closely, all I could see were the distorted reflections of my friends, each one imprisoned in a glass globe, each one crying out, "Help me, Sierra!" I reached out to touch them and my fingers came away covered in blood.

I sat up, gasping. Nailor was gone. In his place there was a note written on his small, lined notepad paper. "I'm working until six. Get dressed up. I'm taking you out."

I moaned and rolled over on my stomach. Hearing me, Fluffy came tiptoeing into the room, jumped up on the bed, and stuck her cold nose in my armpit.

"All right, already, I gotcha. It's time to wake up!"

Fluffy snuggled up closer until I wrapped my arm around her and hugged her tight.

"You know I love you, right?" I said. "You know it's you and me against the world, right?"

Fluffy smiled and licked the side of my arm. I scratched behind her ears and laid there for a second, enjoying the warmth of my bed and the quiet of a trailer park morning. Everyone who was leaving for work had left two hours ago. And those who weren't working still slept. It was unusual for us to be up. On a typical worknight, I wouldn't have collapsed into bed before five A.M.

I looked over at the clock. Ten A.M. The faint smell of brewed coffee reached my nose. How could that be?

"You make the coffee, girl?"

Fluffy only scratched a spot behind her ear and hopped off the bed, waiting for me to follow her. My kitchen had been invaded by one of Raydean's Flemish aliens. The coffeepot was almost full of fresh coffee. The two wineglasses from the night before had been washed and turned neatly upside down on a square of paper towel. And Fluffy's food dish showed the signs of having been filled recently along with fresh water in her bowl. Nailor.

"Okay, girl," I said, pouring a cup. "I should love this, right?" Fluffy nodded. "Well, I do." I looked around at my kitchen and felt warm inside. I felt like I did when I was a kid and Ma had chicken-noodle soup and fresh muffins ready if I walked home from school for lunch on a cold day.

I sat there, drinking my coffee and thinking about Nailor, a stupid grin plastered across my face. This was definitely an uncomfortable feeling for me. New. The last guy I thought I loved was Tony and that ended in total disaster. In fact, if I looked back on it, I couldn't recall a time when thinking I was in love turned out good for me.

I managed to keep thinking about Nailor all through my shower.

Raydean's phone call finally burst the bubble on my little romantic sojourn.

"Good," she said when I answered. "You're getting ready. I'll be by to get you soon as I can. I reckon we take the Plymouth. It makes more of a show at these sorts of occasions."

I sank down on the edge of the bed and cradled the phone against my neck. If I reached across just so, I could get lotion on my legs and accomplish two things at once.

"What occasion, Raydean?"

She snorted. "Why that poor dead boy's funeral, that's what. Says right here in the paper the funeral's at one followed by the family receiving guests back to their house. Don't you read?"

I spread a thick coat of raspberry cream lotion down the front of one leg and started slowly massaging it into my skin. Raydean never missed a good funeral and this one promised to have all the thrills she could handle. After all, here was a whiner cut down in the prime of life, a murder victim no less.

"I can't come," I said. "I've got a business meeting."

"The hell you say!" Raydean countered. "Honey, what kind of detective are you? This is what you do. You go to the funeral and watch for suspects."

I sighed silently. "Raydean, the men who robbed Vincent are hardly liable to show up there. It'll just be a bunch of family and friends."

"And good eatin'," Raydean threw in. "Ain't nothin' like a funeral for good vittles. What time's your meeting?" Raydean managed to make the word "meeting" sound like an encounter in a motel room with a married man.

"Noon."

"Well, all right," she said. "I'll just pick you up and we'll be a little late, that's all. How long's your meeting going to last?"

I poured lotion on the other leg, switching the phone to my other ear. "That won't work, honey. I don't know how long it'll take and I don't know where it is yet."

"Humph!" Raydean clearly didn't like my answer. "Don't sound like too much of a meeting to me. Sounds more like wishful thinking. You didn't get enough of that boy last night, you gotta wait on him to call and hope for a nooner?"

"Raydean! That's not it at all. This is something different. I'm working my own angle on this case." Then I became inspired. "Tell you what, you go to the funeral and make notes." I lowered my voice to sound secretive. "I'll meet with my source then slip over to the family's house for the receiving."

Raydean bit. "Good plan. Now let's have us a code word so I'll know you." I figured up mentally how soon Raydean would be due for medication. She had to be about due.

"What's the word, Raydean?"

"Well hell, honey, thought you'd figure that one all by yourself. Just walk up to me, make eye contact, and say 'hello.' That'll clue me in right there that it's you."

I lay back on the bed and stared up at the ceiling. "Sounds like a plan," I said. Raydean, confident in her condolence casserole's ability to gain her entrance into yet another funeral, hung up with the furtive air of a master spy. I made a mental note to call her friend and my landlady, Pat, so we could drive Raydean into the mental health center for her shot.

The phone rang again just as I finished dressing. I was wearing black, just the thing for meeting with a biker and then paying a condolence call.

"Sierra," Frankie said, "meet me out back of the community college at the picnic tables. Ain't nobody gonna know us there. Fifteen minutes." He hung up before I could say a word.

Maybe Frankie and Denise were in more legal trouble. I didn't really think so. Denise and I had worked together at the Tiffany, and while Denise didn't dance pro, she could've turned at any time. She was a hell of a looker and sweet on Frankie to boot. Denise wouldn't put up with Frankie rejoining the biker life, and Frankie wouldn't jeopardize what he had with Denise. No, I figured Frankie to be carrying a message or getting ready to drop a dime on somebody.

Fluffy was waiting in the Camaro when I opened the door. Her look said "don't even think about not taking me."

"You sure you want to see Frankie?" I asked.

Fluffy let out a low growl.

"Well, just so you're sure. And then there's a funeral after that. You'll be waiting in the car. It'll be boring. I can't even leave the radio on for you. And if it gets cold, all you'll have is your blankie."

Fluffy rolled her eyes and stared out the window, clearly ignoring every warning I was issuing.

"All right, just don't come crying to me when it doesn't turn out the way you want it to."

Fluffy yipped and I cranked the engine. There was no accounting for dogs and crazy people. I was surrounded by unpredictability. I looked over at my dog. She was standing on the passenger-side bucket seat, her toenails gripping the black leather. Fluffy loved adventure, the smell of unknown places, and the challenge of peeing in a new location.

"So what's the music for the occasion, girl?" I asked. I pulled two cassettes from their holder and looked over at her. "Shawn Colvin?" Fluffy seemed to shake her head. "Yeah, you're right, not rowdy enough for this venture." I held out the other cassette, as if she could read it.

"How about this?" I plugged it in before she could issue an opinion. Travis Tritt started singing "I smell T-R-O-U-B-L-E." "Now that's music I can relate to," I said. Fluffy ignored me. She watched as we swooped down into the parking lot of the college, wide and open, facing St. Andrew's Bay.

Frankie sat on top of a picnic table, dressed in his standard black leather jacket, boot-cut jeans, and Harley T-shirt. In the daylight, if you looked past the beard, he was easier to recognize. His hair was much longer than it had been the last time I'd seen him. The lines around his mouth and eyes were a little deeper, but the essence of Frankie was there. He still smoked unfiltered cigarettes. He still smiled with a lopsided grin, but now the smile seemed genuine, not the sinister leer he'd sported before Denise calmed him down.

"You ain't changed a bit," he said as I approached him. "Still got them great tits and those long-assed legs."

"Yeah, well you ain't lost your mouth either," I said. For a second I flashed back to the way we'd met, him on his Harley, his friend kicking poor Fluffy senseless. I'd tried to kick his ass that day, hopped up on adrenaline and unafraid even though he towered over me.

"Where's Denise?" I asked, like this was nothing but a social call, like he was a regular citizen and not with a price put on his head by angry bikers who didn't particularly care for him resigning from his gang.

"She couldn't make it on account of she don't know I'm here yet."

I walked right up to him and stood just beyond his reach, challenging him to invade my personal space, letting him know I was in no way threatened by him.

"Break it down for me, Frankie," I said. "What's this about? You're taking a hell of a risk coming here. The Outlaws might not have a presence here anymore, but one of their friends could spot you. They don't forgive people they think betrayed them."

Smoke got in Frankie's eyes, making him wrinkle up and squint at me. "I've still got some friends here," he said. "But you have a way of pissing people off. I don't know how you do that." He laughed, but there was a harsh ring to it.

"I'm down in Key West, minding my own business, when I get a call from some former, shall we say, acquaintances. You got any ideas about that?" he asked.

I sighed, reached for one of his cigarettes and then thought better. Now was not the time to start smoking.

"Yeah, I think I have an idea. Your friends must've been looking to rob Vincent's game."

Frankie nodded and looked off out at the water. "Word is, a guy got shot."

"Two guys got shot," I said. "And one of them was my friend."

Frankie shrugged. "You get so fucking sentimental," he said. "I don't give a shit about that part. All's I'm saying is, you're running around town saying they plugged a guy and they're saying they didn't and you should let it lie at that."

"They shot Bruno," I argued.

Frankie shrugged again. "That's part of his job, Sierra. He got in the way. But they didn't do the other guy."

"How can you say that?" Frankie was starting to irritate me.

"On account of they were using completely different weapons and one of the guys saw the little runt get plugged."

"Oh, and I am filled with brotherly love and respect for this upstanding citizen who is witness to a cold-blooded murder and has stepped forward to identify the real killer!"

Frankie blew smoke in my direction. "Still a wiseass, huh?" he said.

"Well, come on, Frankie. Think it through. An armed robber says, yeah we robbed the guy but we're not killers? And I'm supposed to believe that? Give me a break!"

"That's the word, bird," he said, climbing down off the table and stretching. "I was just trying to do you a favor. See, the way my friend sees it, the cops don't really care about them. They got Gambuzzo. They got him on a multitude of charges. Who cares if some guys rob an illegal game?" He shook his head and answered his own question. "Don't nobody care . . . until you start saying they done more than attempted robbery and assault. You start making a federal murder case out of it, and the cops'll get more interested. What they're saying is, take their advice, they didn't do it, leave them alone."

"Or what?" I asked.

Frankie smiled, the sinister smile this time. "Now you get it," he said. "Or what, indeed." He walked right up to me, so close I could smell the cigarette on his breath. "Or they'll be dropping by to shut you up." He looked at me, his eyes burning into mine. "Sierra, I owe you, but don't make me fight off these guys. They're assholes. They'll kill our asses. Just listen to what they said and move on. Is that so hard?"

I shook my head. "So who did they say did it?" I asked.

Frankie smiled like maybe I was listening finally. "Some guy."

"Aw, come on, Frankie!"

Frankie raised both hands, palms out. "Shit, I don't know. The guy who called me said all he knows is it wasn't one of them, it was some other guy."

"A big guy? Gambuzzo or what?"

"He didn't say, Sierra. I don't know!"

"Oh that's wonderful!" I said. I started walking toward my car, watching Frankie's reflection bounce off the windshield as I moved. "You tell them they have my undying gratitude. And then you tell them I want to talk to them."

Frankie started after me. "Yeah, right, Sierra. I don't think you get me. You don't *talk* to these guys. They talk. You listen."

I whipped around. "I'm serious, Frankie. Hook me up to talk or I'll tell Nailor to start driving toward Key West."

I had pushed the wrong button and suddenly I knew it. Frankie covered the distance between us in two strides, grabbed me by the back of my hair and pulled my head back against his chest.

"This is the end of what I owe you, honey. Now it's time you started owing me. You compromise me or my fucking family and I'll skin you while you watch. You got that?"

I nodded. "Family?"

"Denise is pregnant," he said. "We don't do stress."

I took a deep breath and relaxed back against him, hoping to take the pressure off my neck. Fluffy came flying out of the car window, barking, charging Frankie, only stopping when I called her name.

"Fluffy, stop, good girl, it's all right. He's not hurting me." But Fluff wasn't sure. She stood watching, her teeth bared, growling. I squirmed and turned my attention back to Frankie. "All right. Okay. I'll leave you two out of it," I said. "But you gotta get the word to these guys that I want to talk."

"Sierra, you're a serious nutcase. These jokers'll kill you."

"Let go of me," I said, wrenching away. "That hurt!"

Frankie didn't seem to mind. He just stood there looking at me like I was seriously demented.

"Deliver the message, Frankie," I said. Behind us I heard Fluffy growl. My backup.

Frankie shrugged. "You know what?" he said. "I'm just going to do it. I'm going to hook it up and I'm going to be there to make sure it comes off okay." I started to speak but he held up his hand. "And you know what? Then we're even. In fact, after that, you owe me." He smirked again. "And it won't be nothin' personal if I decide to collect one day." He started stalking off toward his bike.

"Frankie, set it up for after Christmas," I said. "I'm going to Philly for a few days."

Frankie just shook his head. "I'll see if they can work you in," he said. "Of course, at your convenience!"

I'd pissed him off good, but there was nothing I could do to help that. Vincent Gambuzzo was an innocent man and one of Frankie's ex-friends might be able to help prove that. What was a little riff between friends if it meant saving another friend's life?

Eleven

$\mathscr{D}$enny the Whiner was buried in a small church cemetery on the outskirts of the Panhandle village of Mexico Beach. By the time I scouted out the family home, I'd reached the edge of Port St. Joe and could smell the stink of the paper mill.

His house was a small redbrick rectangle that showed all the signs of hard living and hit-or-miss attention. A concrete seahorse stood guard over the weed-laden front garden bed, its white paint peeled and the tip of its nose chipped by some long-ago accident. The grass in the yard was burnt off by the drought that had plagued most of Florida this fall, and a baby stroller sat sagging on the tiny front porch.

Cars lined the small street, among them Raydean's former police cruiser, and people stood in small huddled groups in the front yard. Somehow I found it difficult to believe that Denny had many friends. I figured most of the people here were curiosity seekers.

It was one of those warm December afternoons that Florida is famous for, mid to upper sixties, bright sunlight, and blue, blue sky. I left Fluffy curled up on the backseat, wrapped in her faded yellow blanket, and headed for the front door. Denny the Whiner had a real last name and I struggled to remember it as I stepped onto the front porch and entered his home. Watley. Dennis Watley, the paper had said, thirty-six, with three young children and a wife, Rebecca.

I spotted them instantly. While hordes of young children ran through and around the legs of the adults, the Watley children sat still as statues on the sofa beside their young, beautiful mother. Luckily, none of the kids bore much of a resemblance to pinch-faced Dennis. They were tall and rail-thin like their mother, with dark hair and eyes and clear, pale skin that seemed almost trans-lucent. The four of them sat as if they were still in shock, watching the goings-on around them with vacant, slightly puzzled expres-sions.

Raydean was in a corner of the room observing the scene on the sofa with a terribly sad look on her face. I walked up to her, breaking her view of the family, and smiled softly.

"Hello," I said, giving emphasis to the word so she'd remember our code signal and maybe jar herself out of whatever state she'd fallen into.

She looked up at me and a slight air of irritation seemed to cross her features. "Sierra, this ain't the place nor the time for playing super spy. Do you not see them poor young'uns? And look at their mama, 'bout to bust a gut with another young'un. God Almighty knows that's a tragic picture."

I turned back and looked again, then faced Raydean. "I know, sweetie," I said. "It must be so hard." But inside a part of me was thinking, "Who wouldn't be relieved to lose Denny 'The Whiner' Watley?"

I spotted Denny's badly dressed friend from the poker game. He was standing in the kitchen doorway, a sad, forlorn expression on his face as he watched the Widow Watley reach down and rub her hand absently over her pregnant belly. A gray-haired woman, looking like an older version of the young widow, stepped up to Denny's friend and handed him a glass of tea, motioning that he should give it to Denny's wife.

I watched him walk up and speak to her. She seemed startled at first, taking the glass of tea and placing it on the coffee table in front of her, but then she looked over at the children and lapsed back into whatever thoughts she'd had before he walked up. Denny's friend stood there, looking helpless for a few moments, then wandered back to his watch post by the kitchen door.

I looked past him and saw Mike Riggs standing in the kitchen, talking to an elderly lady and holding a coffee mug like maybe he wished it was a beer. Even dressed for a funeral, Riggs still looked like Barney Rubble. Every now and then I'd see him glance nervously around the room, like he was maybe hoping to avoid someone, or like he wasn't supposed to be there and was just waiting to get thrown out.

I looked over at Raydean and saw her watching me. I nodded toward Riggs and raised an eyebrow. If Riggs was nervous, Raydean was just the girl to take advantage of the situation.

She smiled slowly, instantly figuring Riggs as a potential alien. She nodded and pushed off from the wall, heading toward the nervous sea captain. Raydean made her move just the way the alligators used to push off from the sunny riverbank in the old Tarzan movies.

The surprise guest of the afternoon was Izzy Rodriguez, the owner of the Busted Beaver. From the way he was watching Mrs. Watley, I figured him to be scouting for new talent. He looked hungry, like he was figuring the best angle to use to score her. It made me sick. I moved away from Raydean and toward Rodriguez with an eye toward letting him know what a sick piece of scuzzbag he was.

He saw me coming and smiled, but it was one of those wary, enemy smiles and we both knew it.

"Thought you didn't crawl out of your coffin 'til after dark, Rodriguez," I said. I was smiling so's the people nearby would figure us for friends.

Rodriguez looked at me, his beady little eyes hard chips of coal. "That's no way to talk to your future employer," he purred. "I'm gonna need a dishwasher and you're gonna need a job. If you're lucky, I might let you lick out the toilets."

Okay, open warfare, me and him, I was good to go. "Turd like you, I didn't think you'd be wanting it clean," I said. "Ain't that like it always is with you, Izzy, dirty?"

I saw his fists clench and knew I was getting to him. I smiled. "Bet you're here to offer the little widow a loan at an interest rate she can't possibly afford. Guess that's how you play it once you bust a cap on her husband."

Izzy didn't flinch. "Nice try, honey," he said. "But amateur hour don't start for another fifteen minutes. Perhaps you oughta go brush up on your detecting techniques and try it again."

Well, I hadn't expected a lay down. "So why're you here then?" I asked.

"Could ask you the same."

"Could, but I got a reason and you don't." Raydean, looking over my way and sensing trouble, broke off her conversation with Mike Riggs and started moving slowly in our direction.

"Maybe," Rodriguez said, "I want to buy a fishing boat. Maybe I feel bad because another club owner shot an innocent man. Maybe I don't want the Watley family to get a bad idea about the entertainment industry in Panama City."

"Bullshit," I said. "You aren't telling me why you're here, but trust me, I'll find out."

Raydean joined us, a scowl deepening as she sized Izzy up and found him lacking. Izzy stared right back at her, his eyes coldly appraising. Big mistake on Izzy's part. Raydean didn't like people who stared.

"Flemish, ain'tchu?" she asked, invading Izzy's personal space by a good six inches.

Izzy, mistaking Raydean for an elderly relative, smiled. "I didn't know Mr. Watley well," he murmured.

"Hell, I reckon you didn't know him a'tall," Raydean answered. "You're not from around here, are you?"

Izzy tried to back up, but bumped into the wall, trapped by Raydean's bulk and her enormous flowered hat.

"I'm from here," he sputtered.

"Yeah, right," Raydean said, reaching not at all subtly into the depths of her flower arrangement, plumbing for a hat pin. "You think I fell off the turnip truck yesterday, don't you, boy?"

She extracted the pin, hiding it in the palm of her hand. "I got me a surefire test for your kind," she said softly.

Izzy, still smiling, leaned back as far as he could, but it wasn't far enough. From the angle of Raydean's approach, I could see a possible 911 call coming. I bumped her, throwing her pitch off just enough to land the four-inch needle in the side of Izzy's left rear anterior. But better that than the dead center target she'd been working on.

Izzy screamed and Raydean jumped backward, a puzzled expression on her face. "Ain't never heard a one of 'em utter a death scream like that," she said. "I was figuring for him to kind of pop and go flying around the room like a leaky balloon."

Izzy pushed past us and barreled out the front door at a dead run. Raydean, for her part, merely tucked the hat pin back in her bonnet and looked after him, shaking her head.

"Grief," she said to the near-silent room. "It's a turrible thing."

The room remained silent for maybe ten seconds before everyone once again resumed their condolence behaviors. The well-wishers, or whatever you call them, seemed to be mainly made up of Rebecca's family and her friends. Denny didn't seem to be very well represented at all.

I snagged a glass of too-sweet punch the color of lime-green Jell-O and struck up a conversation with the plump woman in charge of ladling out cups of the sticky goo.

"Friend of Denny's?" I asked, trying for all the world to pass for a dumb blonde.

The woman sighed, leaned toward me, and looked around to make sure she wasn't heard. She was about as subtle as a balloon in the Macy's Thanksgiving Day Parade.

"Frankly, I think we're well rid of that'un," she said. "Don't get me wrong," she added. "He was a good provider, but he made her life a livin' hell, what with his drinkin' and his druggin'." The woman stared back at the sofa and the four lost souls sitting there. "All Becky ever done was homeschool and love up on her young'uns. But he dogged her, expected her to do all the work, tend the yard and raise the young'uns, while he was out getting shot at a poker game and such as that!"

I shook my head, aware that Raydean had joined us.

"Poor Becky," Raydean said. "I knowed that man was wrong for her."

The punch lady nodded. "You should've seen her in high school—perkiest little thing you ever did see. Could've had her pick of 'em, but no, Denny's what caught her eye. He seemed like such a nice guy back then, but you never can tell about a man, can you?"

"Aha!" Raydean cried. "I knowed it. Self-esteem problems, weren't it?"

The punch lady looked confused and picked anxiously at a spot on the tablecloth. "Well, I don't know them fancy terms, but I can tell you this: She never felt worthy, not with Willie Baldwin for a father. Cut from the same cloth, he and Denny were. I ask you, what was wrong with all them nice boys that wanted her? And look over at him," she said, nodding toward Denny's friend. "Turk's half sick in love with her, but she wouldn't leave Denny. Now you go figure that!"

A gaggle of teenagers flocked around the table making any further investigating impossible. Raydean, sensing the end, looked over at a particularly wild-eyed boy whose black hair had frosted blond tips frizzed out in a quasi-afro.

"How 'bout them Nine Inch Nails?" she asked.

"Smooth," the boy answered.

Raydean cocked her head and popped a pimento-cheese finger sandwich into her mouth. "The force be with you," she whispered, and turned away.

We left without ever speaking to Rebecca Watley and the children. Raydean stepped out into the sunshine, stripped off her hat, and shook her head to loosen her tightly wound curls.

"Amen," she said as we stepped off the porch. "Ain't nothin' like a funeral to set the world to rights." She stopped in her tracks and pointed down the street to the car parked directly behind mine. "Well, lookee here," she drawled. "You gonna make a lapdog out of that one yet!"

John Nailor was leaning against the side of my car, scratching Fluffy behind the ears as she hung half out the side passenger window. When he saw me he frowned, like even though he'd found my dog and my car, he still hadn't expected to see me there.

He was wearing my very favorite navy-blue suit and a white starched shirt. His tie was a deep red. I knew he'd smell good, just the way I knew he was pissed off at me again. Some things you can just come to count on in a man, and John Nailor was no different. He walked toward us, his eyes dark circles of displeasure.

"Hat pin," Raydean whispered to me. "Concealed deadly weapon."

I burst out laughing, which certainly didn't help the situation. "It's the sunlight," I said to her. "It's right in his eyes. That's why he's frowning."

"In your dreams," Raydean shot back.

Nailor stopped three feet away from us and pulled out his notepad. "I've got you on assault," he said to her.

"You got nothin' of the kind, honey," Raydean answered. She spoke to him as if he was a misinformed pupil and she was his slightly irritated teacher. "What you have is a thwarted attack by a homo sapien pervert with alien overtones. Now, I'd report it myself, but since you're offering, make sure they know the quadrant and vector. They always like to know the precise location." Raydean turned away and headed back to her own car.

"Oh," she said, tossing a last word over her shoulder, "if you'd be so kind as to throw in the longitude, latitude, and exact minutes, they'd probably eat you up with a spoon!"

And he let her go. I figured he wasn't going to make a federal case out of Raydean anyway. What, take a sleazy, dope-dealing, stripclub owner's word against that of a known psychotic elderly maniac? No contest. The jury would go with Raydean every time.

But Nailor wasn't thinking about any of that. His attentions were focused on me.

"Can we talk business a second?" he said.

I looked around, like maybe he was talking to someone else. "Sure. What're you doing here?"

Nailor shrugged. "Nolowicki and I wanted to interview some of the witnesses from the other night and I wanted to see who showed up for the funeral."

"Nolowicki's here?" I asked. "I didn't see him."

"Well, I don't think he was looking to announce himself. He's here somewhere."

Nailor led me over to my car, his hand warm against the small of my back. I wanted for some foolish reason to turn so he'd be forced to take me into his arms, but I fought the urge and won. This was business. Of course, nothing turned me on like the prospect of business with John Nailor.

He waited until I leaned against the front fender, side by side with him, before he spoke.

"About Gambuzzo," he said.

"Yeah, what about him?"

There was a long pause. "Vice wasn't the only squad investigating him," he said. "The DEA's got an informant saying that Vincent's dealing rock out of the back of the house."

I pushed off of the car and jumped in front of Nailor. "Well, I don't care who said that, it's not true. I know Gambuzzo. I know the house. He wouldn't do that. He *isn't* doing that."

Nailor was watching me, a slight smile crossing his face. "I know," he said simply.

"Then why'd you tell me that?"

Nailor was watching me that way he did when his cop brain was thinking one thing and his man brain was thinking another. He was amused and serious all at once.

"Just wanted to see what you'd say," he said. Then he straightcned up and looked me right in the eye. "Sierra, maybe you're accustomed to being the only one doing the thinking in a given situation, but I'm not stupid. In fact, on this one, I'd say I'm a step ahead of you."

That griped me. Who was he to tell me I didn't know what was going on?

"Sierra, Vincent didn't kill Denny Watley. That's my gut feeling. Now, Nolowicki thinks different, but he doesn't know Gambuzzo. This is just too clean. And frankly, I know Vincent's a candy ass. As much as he'd like the world to think different, he's just the son of a used-car dealer trying to make out like he's tough."

I didn't say a word. What could I say?

"But my gut instinct isn't going to spring Gambuzzo. We've gotta find out who did kill Watley and we've gotta find out without stepping on Detective Nolowicki's toes and before Carla and her DEA task force come running down here looking to settle a score with you and packs Vincent off on a twenty-to-life vacation in the federal pen."

Two things hit me simultaneously: Nailor said *we* had to find out who killed Denny the Whiner. And Nailor was giving me the heads-up that his ex-wife, the DEA agent, was back in town and loaded for bear, which, by the way, suited me just fine.

"What do you mean 'we' have to find out who killed Denny Watley?" I asked. For now, I was going to ignore the Carla Terrance situation.

Nailor smiled. "Sierra, I got two ways I can go with you. I can try to work around you, or I can try to work with you. I'm thinking it's time to try working together on this. After all, you've got some contacts who won't normally talk to me, and I've got some information you could use to make those contacts talk to you." He shrugged, his eyes doing a long careful inventory of my body, then coming back up to look at me. "So, you wanna try it?"

My stomach flipped over as a horde of butterflies started doing figure eights around my insides. Yeah, I wanted to try it, whatever "it" was.

"I'll take it into consideration," I said.

"So we'll discuss it at dinner?"

I licked my lips and he noticed, smiling slowly and enjoying my discomfort.

"Yeah, dinner ought to do it." *And by the way, I'm going home for Christmas.* Nailor was already standing by the door of his black Crown Victoria, his fingers curled around the door handle.

"I'll pick you up at six," he said, his eyes issuing a challenge.

I gave it right back to him. "See that you do."

After Nailor pulled away from the curb, I turned, spotting the Widow Watley crossing the backyard toward a large freestanding garage. Now was as good a time as any to express my condolences. Maybe she knew her husband's enemies. Maybe she needed a soft, womanly shoulder to cry on. I slipped across the yard behind her, trying to think of my opening line, trying to picture myself less like a dancer and more like a mother, or a best girlfriend. But I needn't have bothered. Just as I reached for the door handle, I heard her voice and knew that a sister wasn't what the Widow Watley was looking for.

"What are we going to do?" she was saying, her voice soft and muffled. She started to cry.

"Hey, don't do that, baby."

Wasn't that just like a man? Don't let a woman have a good cry, oh no. God forbid we should have feelings.

I couldn't see the man, but I could guess who it was. I stooped down and gently pushed the door open a few inches more.

"Everybody's going to find out," Becky Watley said.

"Hush, baby. It's going to be all right."

"No," she wailed, "it won't!"

And that's when I made my move. I darted up a few inches and looked inside. Becky Watley's back was to me and she was wrapped in the arms of Turk, the bad dresser. Their attention was entirely focused on each other, so I pushed the door a little wider, slipping into the almost darkened garage and ducking behind two large trash cans.

"Becky," Turk said, "it was going to happen sooner or later. I just didn't think it would happen like this."

What? I asked him, silently. *What?*

Becky Watley drew back from his shoulder. "You weren't supposed to let anything happen. Not yet. Not until . . ."

Her next words were lost to me. When I moved deeper into the shadows, hoping to get a better view of the couple, I stumbled, stretching my hands out to keep from falling forward onto a sack that lay just in my path. I bit my lips together, hoping not to make a sound as I fell. I hit as quietly as I could, considering that I had just landed on something warm and wet and most definitely human.

Twelve

My mouth opened, the scream bubbled up in my throat, but then stopped. I pushed up off the body and bit down on my lower lip as hard as I could. I looked back at the couple standing mere feet away from me and tried very slowly to breathe. The body in front of me was only sleeping. Yeah, I told myself, that's it. He's just drunk and passed out. Don't be an idiot, Sierra. No way is this person dead.

I reached out and touched the body. It was warm. I breathed a sigh of relief. The guy wasn't dead. He was drunk. The guy was small, dressed in faded jeans and a black leather vest. Next to him was a black leather cap, the kind Frankie and almost every other biker I knew wore. I leaned closer, examining the man. He looked wizened, with wrinkles that hung off his skinny neck like chicken leather, and harsh, wind-roughened lines around his eyes. He smelled of alcohol and vomit. I backed off, trying not to breathe through my mouth.

"Honey, you can't do this to yourself," Turk was saying. "You've gotta think about the baby now, our baby. Try not to be upset."

Becky Watley was still crying. "I know," she said, "but what if they find out? What if the girls find out? I can't let that happen. This has to be kept quiet."

I leaned over the body, straining to hear every word.

"They won't," Turk said. "I'll take care of it. I won't mess it up this time."

I looked down at the body. There was something not quite right about it. And then I realized the guy's eyes were open, fixed and blue, staring straight up at the ceiling. Drunk men don't pass out with their eyes open, I told myself. But dead guys, now, they do that all the time.

I began whispering to myself, trying not to scream, not to panic. I reached out again and touched the man's chest, willing it to rise and fall, hoping to feel his heart beating against my palm. Nothing.

I was screaming silently, no longer focused on the widow and her lover. I made myself examine the man. His neck seemed a little crooked, like maybe he'd passed out sideways. Only he wasn't passed out. Nope, this guy was class-A dead, and his neck was broken. And his killer was probably standing ten feet away from me, holding the mother of his unborn child.

"Stay calm, honey," I whispered to myself, backing up in a crouch, creeping out of the garage. "It's going to be okay. We'll just walk back to the car, get the cell phone, and call the police."

I backed the rest of the way out of the door, still almost on all fours, right into a pair of legs wearing trousers and shiny black leather shoes.

"Miss Lavotini, isn't it?" Detective Nolowicki asked, and I screamed. This time it came out nice and loud.

Nolowicki jumped, then reached out to grab my arm. "What in the world is wrong with you, lady?" His tone was flat and thick, like maybe he was from Chicago or somewhere in the Midwest. He was looking at me as if maybe I was wound too tight and he should anticipate fireworks.

"It's . . . there's . . . okay," I said, trying to draw air into my lungs. I closed my eyes for a second, made myself take a deep breath, and then tried to say something the man could understand.

"There's a dead guy in there," I said. "He's lying behind the trash cans."

Nolowicki looked at me, his eyes not registering. He didn't

seem concerned, or panicked, or like he was intending on taking any action. Instead he was looking at me like maybe he needed to get me a nice cool glass of punch, like maybe I had the vapors.

"I'm telling you," I said, this time trying to put the command back in my tone, "there is a man inside, a biker-looking, older guy, and he's dead. And there are two other people in there. And the body's still warm, so I think it just happened."

Nolowicki was watching me, still not appearing to believe me, only now he was starting to frown.

"Meathead," I said, "the guy in there might've killed the other guy! Will you do something already?"

And that's when Nolowicki moved. His right hand reached inside his suit jacket, pulling out the gun that sat strapped to his left side.

"All right," he said, his voice calm but still strong like Nailor's. "Wait right here. Don't move from this spot, okay?"

Now we were getting somewhere. "Okay. I'll be right here." Of course, Detective Nolowicki didn't take that as me saying I'd be there to back him up, that I'd help out if he needed it, but I felt better.

Nolowicki pushed the door wide open and vanished inside the building, his gun held high and by his side, just like a movie. He was gone for about a minute before reappearing in the doorway.

"There's a dead guy, all right, just where you said. But there isn't anyone else in here. Maybe you were hearing things." He didn't wait for me to answer. He flipped open his cellphone and called the police.

I heard the words "possible homicide" and knew Nolowicki didn't get it, not yet. There was no possible to it.

"Hey," I said, as he flipped the phone shut. "I not only heard voices, I saw the two people talking and I know who they are."

Nolowicki stared at me. "Well, why didn't you say so!" he barked. "We could've stopped them! Who was it?"

"I did say so! It was the widow and her boyfriend, some guy named Turk."

I was thinking that if Nailor had been there, he would've listened to me, gotten it the first time, and been lightyears ahead of the stupid vice cop. It didn't help matters that I went ahead and told Nolowicki my thoughts. When I reached for my own cell and called Nailor, it further cemented our bad relationship.

"Don't go anywhere," Nolowicki said as I started walking away from him toward my car. "I'm not done asking you questions."

I whipped around and looked at him like he was Fluffy's leftovers. "You may not be done, but I am. I'll do my talking to a real homicide investigator, not some quasi-vice-narcotics dipshit who thinks my boss is running rock and that I'm hearing voices!"

I kept right on walking until I reached my car, knowing he wouldn't follow me when he had two other more likely suspects to round up.

In no time at all, police cars from the tiny town of Port St. Joe were screaming toward the Widow Watley's, and Detective Joe Nolowicki had the entire community in an uproar. Of course, that sort of thing is to be expected when you come running into a house with your gun drawn and held high in the air, screaming for the poor grieving widow not to move and scaring her poor grieving children half to death. You expect a mob reaction when you start off an investigation like that, especially when most of your mourners are fishermen used to handling bullies and big fish in small ponds.

I stood outside, listening to the hostile voices, watching the chaos erupt, and waiting for the cooler head of one professional homicide detective to arrive. I figure that was the only way I noticed Izzy Rodriguez slinking off the property, ignoring the police order that no one was to leave. After all, when had Izzy Rodriguez ever listened to the law?

Thirteen

$\mathcal{B}$y the time John Nailor arrived, called back in not only by me, but by the Port St. Joe police department, the crime scene was shot straight to hell. No one listened to poor Nolowicki. They all ran straight out to the garage to look at the dead guy, and then collectively agreed that they'd never seen him before in their lives. To further gum up the works, no one would admit to seeing the Widow Watley leave the house, swearing she'd been right on the couch all afternoon, in plain sight of everybody.

As for Turk, why, nobody'd seen him at all. In fact, very few people even remembered what he looked like. As far as they were concerned, Nolowicki was an octopus and they were all clams, sealed up tight and not willing to crack so much as an air bubble's worth of information to the police.

Nailor looked fit to be tied after about thirty minutes of wrangling with the locals, and Nolowicki was nowhere to be seen. I figured they'd sent him off to avoid an all-out riot. Or maybe he was following up on another of his half-baked ideas.

I slipped back inside the house and watched the police work. All they were getting was name, rank, and serial number from the mourners. The widow had gotten so worked up she'd had to go lie down upon her doctor's orders. Masterful, I thought, given all I'd heard in the garage.

I moved my base of operations out into the kitchen, figuring it would be the hub of anything I needed to know. The kitchen is always the headquarters for the women, and the women are always the ones that know. So I picked up a dishtowel, slipped up to the sink, and proceeded to blend in with the others, drying and passing the plates on to the next lady in line.

"Cain't imagine them bothering her the way they did! As if she knew a thing," one sniffed.

"And looking for Turk like he's a criminal!"

I dried a saucer and handed it to the elderly lady beside me. "I can't believe it," I sniffed. Big mistake. The others looked at me, suddenly noticing that I wasn't one of them, and proceeded to dry their plates in silence.

Great, I thought, some detecting you're doing. I dried for a few more minutes, then moved toward the back porch, intending to drape my towel over the railing to dry. But as I stepped out onto the back stoop, I half tripped over a small form. The eldest Watley daughter sat on the top step, her head resting on the arms that wrapped her knees to her chest, quietly sobbing her little heart out. At her side sat Fluffy, all concern and wet-tongued kisses.

"Oh," I said, ignoring the tears, "you found Fluffy. I am so glad!"

The girl's head shot up and she turned, trying to wipe away the tears so I wouldn't see.

"I hope she wasn't any trouble," I said, plopping right down beside her and offering her my hand. "I'm Sierra Lavotini. This is my little girl, Fluffy."

Fluffy yipped softly and the little girl struggled to smile and take my hand. She couldn't have been more than twelve.

"Sarah," she whispered, hiccupping with the effort not to cry. "Sarah Watley."

"Oh," I said. "I'm so sorry about your dad."

Sarah's eyes filled again. "Thanks." She looked away, staring at a spot on the wall, thinking, I guess, that we'd leave. But she didn't know Fluffy.

Fluffy nudged her way under the little girl's arm, forcing her way up into her lap and licking her right on the tip of her nose. Sarah smiled again, but tears spilled over the reddened rims of her eyes and streamed down her cheeks.

"I know you miss him," I began softly.

Sarah shot a quick, angry glance at me. "No," she said, "no you don't know, 'cause I don't miss him! He was mean to us, and worse to Mama! I'm glad he's dead! Glad! You hear me?" Her voice rose with each sentence, bordering on hysteria.

"Really?" I said. "Then why are you crying?"

Sarah really thought I was stupid now, but she was putting up with me because Fluffy was being her most charming and adorable self, licking the little girl and sighing with pleasure whenever Sarah stroked her head.

"I'm crying because the police found a dead guy and for some reason they think my mama and Turk know something they're not saying! What do you think I am, stupid?"

"Nope," I said. "Not you. Aren't you the oldest?"

Sarah flashed me another look. "Yep. So what?"

I stretched my legs out over the steps in front of us and rubbed my kneecaps. "Nothing. It's just a known fact that the oldest is usually lightyears ahead of her siblings in maturity. You can fool a younger kid pretty easy, but not the oldest. They catch on quick."

Sarah nodded ever so slightly and focused her attention on Fluffy.

"So if you say they didn't have nothing to do with it, why, I'd take your word."

"Well, they should, but they don't. Stupid cops!"

"Yeah, cops don't always know what's what." I took a quick look over at the girl and saw the frown lines ease up. "Why, I could take one look at your mama and Turk and see that he was taking the best care he could of her. Now, how could he kill a guy when he's looking after her?"

Sarah nodded her agreement so I went right on. "He loves her. I know we women can see that as plain as the nose on your face. And somebody oughta help figure out who did dump that dead guy here and get on with it. After all, your mama can't take much more stress."

I talked fast, but like I was absolutely certain of what I said and like it was perfectly okay to acknowledge what everyone took for fact.

"I know," Sarah said. "I know all about it."

"Good," I said, and reached inside my purse for a piece of paper and a pen. "Then here's what we'll do: I'll write down my name and phone number on this piece of paper and you keep it and show it to your mama later, after all this dies down. Tell her I'd like to help her any way I can. You just tell her I know all about how it is to be in a mess. Tell her I know all about her friendship with Turk and I'd like to help, okay?"

Sarah stared into my eyes, checking me out every way a kid can check out an adult, and apparently finding me harmless.

"Okay," she said at last. "Are you part of the police or a detective?"

I smiled. "No. I'm just good at figuring out the puzzles and helping when it looks like nobody else will."

My heart was thumping, just hoping she'd go for it and get the message straight to her mom. "*I know about your friendship with Turk.*" I figured those words alone would be enough to get Becky Watley on the phone, even if it was only out of fear and curiosity. And if the truth be known, I did feel a little bad about causing her more stress. But I also figured it like this: Becky Watley had already picked one loser, maybe Turk was another one, and maybe Vincent Gambuzzo wasn't going to have to take the fall for a man who wanted to steal another man's wife.

I stood up, brushed imaginary dirt from the back of my dress, and let Sarah carefully hand Fluffy to me.

"You call me anytime you need me, Sarah, okay? You or your mom or whoever you think needs me, okay?"

Sarah nodded again, slipped the paper with my phone number into her pocket and sat staring at me as I walked around the side of the house to my car. I walked, careful to keep a lookout for

Nolowicki, ignoring the fact that he told me to stay put. After all, I had my own personal "in" with the police department, and if that detective wanted to question me until all hours of the night, I was ready, willing, and very, very able.

I reached the Camaro without being noticed. Then I drove off, careful not to chirp tires or rev the engine too loud on account of my Catholic upbringing demanding respect for the newly departed, not that they could hear me.

Fourteen

I was back home and asleep within thirty minutes. It was as if someone had slipped a Micky into my lime punch. I slept for almost two hours before the alarm went off at six. Although I seriously doubted that Nailor would be able to keep his date with me, it didn't hurt to be prepared just in case. So I struggled to wake up enough to slide down into my Jacuzzi and the frothy, lavender-scented bubble bath that would leave me soft and smooth, just like Nailor liked. Fluffy tiptoed up beside me and whined. I looked over at her, pretending I didn't understand.

"What do you want, girl? You trying to tell me you made coffee?"

Fluffy was having none of it. She stamped her little front paw, then jumped up onto the wide rim of the Jacuzzi. I relented and reached up above my head for the blue Styrofoam kickboard and placed it gently into the tub, holding it steady with both hands as Fluffy daintily stepped onto it and settled down for a relaxing float.

"Better?" I asked.

She moaned, like I was an idiot.

"You're the one floating on a kickboard," I said. "You know many dogs who do that?"

Fluffy wisely ignored me.

"Say, maybe you could call Nailor later and break it to him we won't be here for Christmas."

Fluffy opened one eye and stared at me. She wasn't happy. Fluffy hated her dog carrier, and she hated airplane rides even more. Fluffy was not cut out for the cold winter weather of Philadelphia either.

"You know what I think?" I asked her. "I think this is a hell of a time to be leaving town. I mean, the stuff with Vincent and Bruno is one thing, but we've got trouble on top of trouble."

Fluffy's ears pricked up, she was listening to every word.

"Well, it should be obvious what our other problem is. I mean, Carla Terrance has picked a hell of a time to come nosing back around Panama City." Fluffy sighed. I didn't have to tell her about the bad blood between me and John's ex.

"I mean, think of it like this: the two of them, alone on Christmas Eve, just two cops working a job, hungry, tired, lonely. Fluff, my girl, that's a recipe for disaster."

I sank a little deeper into the tub, trying to convince myself that if Nailor went back to his ex I wouldn't care.

"Maybe they're made for each other," I whispered. "Maybe it's better just the two of us."

Fluffy belched, the mark of total doggie disapproval.

"Well, you're the one who loves him, not me." Fluffy stood up on the board and stared at me. "Okay, so maybe I like how he looks at me sometimes, like he's got a secret and a promise all rolled into one." Fluff was listening. "Or the way he keeps me on my toes. I like that I can't just walk all over him."

Fluffy whined and yipped once.

"I know, girl. There's something about the way he touches me, too." I closed my eyes and sighed. "It's too bad I can't take him home for Christmas. I just can't stand the idea of him being all alone . . . or worse yet, with her."

Fluffy yipped again, her tail wagging a million miles an hour. "I know, girl," I said, my eyes closing again but my imagination showing me a million mental images of Nailor. "You think it's great when he scratches *your* itch. Honey, that ain't nothing compared to the way he scratches mine!"

"Is that so?" Nailor said, stepping from the doorway into my line of vision. I jumped, tipping the kickboard over and dumping Fluffy right into the lukewarm bathwater.

Nailor reached down and scooped poor, indignant Fluffy out of the water and wrapped her in a towel.

"How long have you been standing there?"

"How long have you been itchin'?" he drawled. He stepped closer to the tub, grabbing a towel as he approached and holding it out to me.

"Come here," he whispered.

"Make me," I said, the challenge laid out before us.

"I reckon I don't have to," he said. "I reckon you'll be coming all on your own."

And he was right. He sat on the edge of the tub, leaned over, and kissed me, his tongue slipping slowly inside my mouth, his lips hungry and insistent. His hand reached behind my head, supporting me as his lips kindled a flame that spread throughout my body.

He stopped abruptly and leaned back watching me. I looked into his eyes and I was hooked. It was the way he'd stood there with his red tie loosened just enough to make me want to take it off . . . the way he guaranteed satisfaction just by the self-assured manner he had of waiting for me to realize I needed to feel him against my skin. Any woman who walked away from that was a total fool, and Sierra Lavotini was certainly no fool.

I stood up slowly, running my hands down my sides, smiling and sluicing off bubbles. So he wanted to show me a thing or two, huh? Well, we'd just see about that.

He waited until he had me where he wanted me, naked and in bed, sweaty and satisfied, before he started talking. He ran one fingertip down my side, trailing it around my nipple and delighting in watching it harden in response to his touch. He spoke so softly I almost missed the words.

"Sierra, you don't have to worry about me. I had a life before you and I won't fall apart if you go."

"What are you talking about?" I asked, and I almost couldn't meet his gaze.

"What you said earlier, before you knew I was there. That you aren't going to be here for Christmas."

I looked up at him then. "John, something's wrong up there," I said. "I've gotta go home. I'd take you, but . . ."

Nailor placed two fingers over my lips and silenced me. "Sierra, I don't own you. You've got to go home. It's no big deal."

"Yes it is," I said.

His finger trailed across my stomach creating a swirl of tingling skin. "No, honey, it's not." He leaned back and looked at me. "I'm guessing you have some thinking to do. I've been feeling you pull away." I moved to protest, then thought better of it. Instead I felt tears welling up behind my eyes.

"You're afraid you're going to fall in love with me, really fall in love, and that scares you. You think if you love me, I'll die like Tony, or leave you like all the others."

"No, I'm not afraid of that!" I said, but there was no use in trying to fool him. He knew.

Nailor pulled me to him and held me close. "Yes, honey, you are. You're scared shitless and we both know it." He paused for a moment, then went on. "Maybe it would be a good idea for us both to take a little time to sort this through."

I pushed away and stared at him. "What do you mean? Are you having second thoughts about us?"

Nailor's eyes softened, but I couldn't tell what he was really thinking. "I just think we need some time. You aren't the only one who's been hurt before. I could use a little while to sort things out, be clear about where we're heading. I don't want to be going down one path thinking one thing and have you be thinking something else, that's all."

This was not at all what I had intended. What was going on?

I closed my eyes and willed it all to vanish, but this wasn't a bad dream.

"Okay," I said. "We'll take some time."

Nailor was moving to the edge of the bed, reaching for his clothes, no longer vulnerable and available.

"I'll take you to the airport," he said. "When do you leave?"

"In the morning."

That shocked him. He stopped for a second, momentarily angry. "Sierra, when were you going to tell me?"

"Tonight. At dinner." I looked at him and saw that I'd hurt him. "I kept trying to tell you," I said, "but I guess I just wanted it to all work out somehow."

He was reaching for his shoes, slipping his feet into them, taking his time and considering what he would say next. I had the horrible feeling I knew what would come next. He was going to walk out the door and never come back.

"Tell you what," he said. "I don't really feel like going out. I reckon you've got packing to do and I'm pretty tired. How about giving me a rain check?"

His eyes were so open and sad, but he smiled like it was no big deal at all, and for a moment I knew exactly how he felt. We were feeling the very same thing and couldn't, wouldn't own up to it.

I smiled right back. "Sure. I know you're tired. We'll do it when I get back."

"What time's your flight?" he asked. His hands were stuck deep into his pockets and he had the look of a man who was already halfway out the door.

"Eight," I said. "I should be at the airport by seven-fifteen."

He nodded. "I'll be here to get you about a quarter till. That work?"

I straightened up and looked into his eyes. I wanted to say a hundred other things, but all I did was say, "Thank you, that'll be fine."

He took three short steps to my side, pecked me on the cheek, and was gone, the sound of the door closing behind him the last thing I heard before I sank back onto the bed and gave myself over to self-pity. How was it possible for things to get so messed up in such a short amount of time?

I sat there for I don't know how long, thinking about Nailor and me and the whole mess I'd made of every relationship I'd ever known. When I heard the car drive up outside, and Fluffy yip once and then go silent, I hopped up, hoping he'd changed his mind. But it wasn't Nailor. It was Becky Watley, looking pale under the light of my back stoop, pale and very, very pregnant.

I opened the door and wondered for a second if she'd be able to fit through. I think she knew because she smiled a little and ran her hand over her enormous belly.

"Don't worry," she said. "Baby's not due for a week and I'm always late anyhow." Then the smile vanished. "I need to talk to you. My daughter said you said something about Turk and maybe you could help me find him."

That was all she had. Her voice trembled and broke as she said his name, the tears following and the composure fleeing.

"Hey," I said, reaching out and pulling her into the kitchen, "now don't do that." I was thinking the upset could bring on labor and Sierra don't do home deliveries. "Come on inside. Sit down on the sofa. Shhh, just get a grip and tell me all about it."

Becky Watley shivered and let me lead her to the green futon in the living room. When she noticed the open bay window she seemed to panic.

"Don't you have curtains?" she asked.

"Sure, sure, don't wet your pants. It'll just take a second." I bustled about closing things and rearranging the thick curtains so that not so much as a sliver of streetlight shone through.

"All right," I said, settling down next to her. "What's the deal? What's going on that's got you so freaked out?"

Becky folded her arms over her stomach and looked at me. Now that the outside no longer scared her, she was going to check me out. I looked right back at her, trying to look as nonthreatening as possible. I mean, I didn't exactly figure the Widow Watley to have a lot of options, what with her husband dead and her boyfriend on the lam for maybe murder.

"Okay," she said. "I don't know what else to do and I need help, so here goes." She took a deep breath and let fly, every bit of it escaping like hot air from a spent balloon.

"I heard you know about me and Turk. I don't know how you found out, but it isn't what you're probably thinking." I didn't want to interrupt her, didn't want her to know that I was as empty as a vacuum when it came to having all the answers.

"Turk loves me, and I love him, but we didn't kill my husband. We couldn't, even if we'd wanted to. Denny was doing too good a job of that all on his own."

Becky looked at me, like maybe I would contest her statements, but when I didn't she continued. "He had a brain tumor. It was small, but the doctors told him it was going to grow and one day kill him." Becky sighed and looked down at her stomach. "They said that though they couldn't operate, he might live for years, but Denny didn't care. He just drank that much more, and used all of his paycheck on crystal meth. It was like he figured no tumor was going to kill him if he could do it himself."

She sat up a little straighter, tossing her stick-straight black hair over her bony shoulders, trying to look tough.

"You think it was wrong, watching out for him, making sure he didn't kill himself with the drugs. You think it was cold of me to wait for the tumor to take him, but I've got girls to raise. Turk don't make enough to take on four children and a wife, and he shouldn't have to."

I started to say something, but there was no point; Becky Watley was past the point of caring.

"Denny would've wanted it this way," she said. "The Denny I married would've done the same thing. He wasn't always mean. That thing in his brain did that. It turned him, made him into the cruel man everybody around here knew. But when we were first married, there wasn't a better man. But that man left Denny's body a long time ago and, well, sometimes you just need someone to lean on. I didn't mean for it to get like this."

A tear leaked down one cheek, but Becky seemed not to notice. I stretched out a hand and patted her knee.

"Listen," I said, "who am I to judge? I don't know the players here. I'm just trying to help out a friend."

Becky Watley didn't trust easily. "What friend? Are you working with the cops?"

"No. I work with the man the police say shot your husband. I don't think my boss killed Denny. I just want to find the guy who did it so they can let an innocent guy go."

"Well, it wasn't Turk!"

"Hey, I'm not saying it was. I'm not thinking that at all," I lied. "I'd just like the chance to talk to him."

Becky shook her head slowly back and forth. "So would I," she said, "but he's gone."

"What do you mean?"

She shrugged like it puzzled her but was maybe inevitable, like she was used to bad luck and trouble.

"I know he saw something he shouldn't have seen," she whispered, "and now he's scared. He said it's not safe to be around me, but he won't tell me why and he won't come back until he knows it's safe."

Now, what did that mean?

Fifteen

Nailor looked as bad as I felt the next morning. He arrived right on the dot of 6:45, looking like he hadn't slept either. He picked up my suitcase, threw it on the backseat and turned to open the passenger side door, all without saying a word. When he finally did speak, his voice was hoarse and raspy with fatigue.

"This all?" he asked, picking up my carry-on bag with one hand and Fluffy's dog carrier with the other.

I was wearing black. A black Harley jacket, courtesy of a former "friend," black straight-legged pants, a black turtleneck, black high-heeled low-cut boots, and black sunglasses that hid my lack of sleep and the fact that I'd spent half the night crying.

"That's it," I said, forcing my voice to attempt cheery but sounding more like a cracked-voice adolescent boy.

The curtains moved in Raydean's window and then I heard the sound of one lock after another turning as she opened her front door and stood somehow looking like a kindergartner being left behind on the first day of school. In her arms was a large round bundle wrapped in aluminum foil.

I looked at her and Nailor and realized that in the swirl of the last few days, I hadn't even managed to go Christmas shopping, let alone wrap anything up or bake anything to leave with them.

"Sugar," Raydean said, "this here's for your mama 'n' them."

She rushed right on. "I'm figuring we'll have us a little Christmas of our own when you get back, do our present exchanging then. Won't we, Lieutenant?" she called, favoring Nailor with an expectant expression on her face.

"Sure," he said, smiling at her like he meant it. "That's a good idea. You cooking or you want me to bring the doughnuts?"

Raydean pretended to consider the question. "Why young'un," she said, "you cain't never take too many precautions. Let's us do both. That way, if the scan don't run clean on the doughnuts, we'll have us a backup food source."

Nailor nodded like he understood the threat of alien contamination and slid behind the wheel of the Crown Victoria. I walked across the street, up Raydean's walkway, carefully avoiding the booby-trapped third square of concrete, and up onto her stoop. She handed me the foil-wrapped cake and would've run back in the house had I not taken her into my arms and hugged her so hard she was nearly swept off her feet.

"I'll be back the day after Christmas," I said. "I'm flying out in the late afternoon, so it'll be after suppertime when I get in."

Raydean nodded. "Me and Pat're gonna set up the tree today," she said. "Pat's fixing to take me to the mental health clinic for my shot. Said she wants to avoid the Christmas rush." Raydean snorted. "Like the mental health's gonna have a run on families looking to buy gift certificates!"

Nailor backed the car out of the driveway and sat idling in the street, a sign that time was a'wasting to his way of thinking.

"I love you, Raydean," I said. Fluffy, standing by my side, whined and yipped once. To Raydean this meant Fluffy echoed my sentiment.

"I love y'all too," she said. "But bring me back a cheese steak, all right? And not one of them touristy things they make down on South Street. I want some meat on mine!"

I laughed and started back down the steps to the car where Nailor sat waiting patiently.

"Cheese steaks, hoagies, and soft pretzels," I called back over my shoulder. "We'll have a feast. December twenty-sixth. Eight P.M."

Raydean hooted. "Let them Flemish be advised: Foreign food don't get no better than Philadelphia!"

I slid in beside Nailor, and Fluffy hopped in beside me, trembling. Whether it was from the cool morning air or the anticipation of an airplane flight, I couldn't tell, but I found my own hands shaking as we rolled off down the street. Nailor drove with the calm assurance of a man who spends hours behind the wheel.

"We got an ID on the victim," he said, purely professional, easier than talking about what was sitting right in front of us.

"Who was he?"

"Local biker. Everybody called him Tinky, but his name was Edward Little. Small-time dope dealer. A few arrests, nothing big, really. That's all we have so far."

I stared out the window, looking at the gaudy Christmas decorations that covered little Floridian bungalows.

"Was he a friend of Denny's?"

"Not that we know of. Nolowicki said maybe he was Denny's dealer, and that seems as good a theory as any, but then we don't know why he'd come to his funeral."

I nodded and turned away, staring out the car window, unable to focus on the details of Nailor's investigation or anything other than the fact that things between us just weren't right. I thought about telling him about Becky Watley and Turk but decided against it. After all, I didn't know enough to give him more than a "he said–she said." I didn't have anything firsthand.

The sky was a brilliant blue, just right for flying, and it was unseasonably warm. Nailor approached the airport, and for an instant, I could see the water of the bay, sparkling in the sunlight. The terminal stood out like a tropical reminder of everything I was leaving: green tin roof, Art Deco architecture, clean and bright. Florida was nothing like Philly. It was breathing and three-dimensional.

Nailor pulled up to the curb, right by the curbside check-in, and hopped out of the car. It was then I realized he had no intention of coming inside. He wasn't going to draw out a long good-bye, or stand by the terminal gate waving as I walked away from him. Nailor was doing it clean.

He handed my bags over to the skycap, waited while I coaxed Fluffy into her crate, and then turned to me, smiling as if I were merely stepping into the grocery store for a gallon of milk.

"Have a good Christmas," he said. "Take care of that family of yours."

It might've flown. We might've pulled it off, cool and casual, had a stupid tear not escaped, spilling over onto my cheek.

"Hey, what's this?" he whispered, reaching up to wipe the tear away.

"The sun's really bothering my eyes," I said. And then spoiled it all by stepping into his arms.

"Yeah," he said. "This Florida sunlight really takes it out of you." He kissed the top of my head and held me for a moment, until the skycap interrupted us and it became evident that I was going to have to turn my attention to leaving.

I felt Nailor slip something into my pocket, a small box with a bow on the top. And there I was with nothing for him.

"Don't do that," I said. "Wait until I get back. We'll have our own Christmas."

Nailor broke the embrace and stepped back so he could see me. "I want you to have something for Christmas morning," he said. "We'll do the rest when you get back."

Fluffy whined and I wanted to. Instead, I smiled. "I'll be back in three days," I said. "I'll bring you a big surprise."

He reached out and cupped my chin in his fingers. "Just bring me you, safe and sound, all right?" And then he kissed me.

I spent the entire time waiting for the flight huddled in a stall of the ladies' room, crying into a soggy tissue. Somehow I missed the call that came on my cell phone, missed it until I reached to turn the phone off before boarding the plane.

I pressed in the buttons, looking to see who'd called, hoping it was Nailor, but the caller ID only said RESTRICTED NUMBER. I punched in the code to hear my messages, hoping like hell to hear his voice, wishing with all my heart that Nailor could say something magical to make it all better. But it wasn't him, and what the recorded message said wasn't at all magical.

"I need to talk to you," said a deep male voice I didn't recognize, muffled and indistinct. "You're breaking some very important rules, Sierra. Maybe you don't know what happens when you break the rules."

I stood still for a moment, willing my heartbeat to slow down, forcing myself to turn off the phone and put it away, aware that the flight attendant was growing more and more impatient with my delay.

I looked outside again and made myself stand just a little bit straighter, just in case somebody was watching, or thinking maybe I was afraid. Good, I thought, someone is pissed off. Then maybe I'm close.

I looked around the empty waiting room. Maybe I was close, but maybe the killer was too.

Sixteen

As I stepped onto the plane I figured the temperature would probably reach eighty degrees that day in Panama City. It didn't feel like Christmas, despite the wreaths attached to the light posts and the Christmas carols on the radio. It never felt like Christmas in Panama City, not to an ex-Yankee. For me, it isn't Christmas until I step off the plane in Philadelphia on Christmas Eve, and Ma starts to cry.

Pa tries to act like he doesn't know us, on account of we're both crying like babies and clinging to each other. Pa resents public displays of affection. For him, affection is saying, "I'll go get the car so's your Ma don't hurt her corns walkin'."

He drives the car up to the baggage claim and parks, big as the moon, right in front of the cop who's blowing his whistle and threatening to ticket any imbecile dumb enough to leave his car unattended.

"Hey," Pa yells, whipping his fire chief's badge out and flashing it like he's maybe the freaking mayor, "have a little respect, here. I got business inside."

The cop quits blowing, but he doesn't look sorry. They never do. It would be like a dog backing down off another dog in his own territory. So he just stares at Pa, who stares right back, and then Pa walks inside to grab my bag outta Ma's hand.

"What, what? You gotta throw your back out on Christmas Eve?

Give me that!" That's how Pa tells Ma he loves her. Ma was trying to prove she loved me by grabbing the bag off the carousel before I could see what she was doing.

Pa whips the power-steering wheel half to death as he pulls away from the curb and heads home. He doesn't like venturing far from his little corner of Philly. He says you never know what kind of insane lunatic will take a potshot at you downtown. I say, "Yo, Pa, didn't Vinny Donatelli wack Big Red Runzi not three hundred feet from your own Sons of Italy Social Club?"

"That was different, Sierra," he grumps. "That was business."

Oh yeah, totally different, I think.

Pa makes it home in record time, under twenty minutes. We drive out of the airport, shooting up onto Penrose Avenue over the top of the stinkin' Schuylkill River, past the refineries with the orange flames that shoot up into the starlit Philadelphia night. Past the auto salvage at the foot of Passayunk, where the old guy sells soft pretzels in the daytime. Right past the Montrose Diner, where Pa takes me for a slice of pie and coffee on our way back to the airport. Moyamensing Street takes us under the Schuylkill express-way. Then Pa pulls out onto 20th Street and I'm in my old neighborhood. It's freaking beautiful. I start watching for Mifflin Street, my heart pounding like the Mummers String Band warming up for the parade. When I see the spire of St. Edmunds, just ahead there on 23rd, I cross myself and hold my breath. Pa is about to undertake his life-threatening parallel parking job.

"Piece of junk car!" he swears. But I don't care, because I'm home.

I jump out of the car behind Ma, who was angling to leave as soon as Pa started swearing. I can't beat her to the door and it wouldn't matter if I did. There are six locks to be undone, three more than last year, and I long ago quit trying to keep up with the keys.

"Sierra, wait," she shrieks, laughing as I try to bust in ahead of her. "Let me cover your eyes. I got a surprise in there."

"Aw, Ma! Give me a break here! I'm freezing and I gotta go!" But Ma isn't listening. She is trying to wrap her work-gnarled fingers around my face, standing on tiptoe, even with me half-squatting to help. I know what's coming. It is the same every year, and every year we must repeat the ritual.

I hear the door swinging open, and Perry Como on the ancient stereo. It smells like spaghetti inside, warm and moist with steam. Garlic bread. Baking. Home. I hear people, too. People trying to be quiet, muffled snickers and movement. Behind me Pa puffs up the steps with my bag.

"What you got in this thing, Sierra, bricks?" he yells, 'cause Pa always yells, he never speaks. I think that's from being a Chief, yelling at fire scenes. "Ma, move it! Her bag weighs a ton. You want me to get hemorrhoids here?"

"Surprise!" the voices shout out, and Ma propels me forward into the living room, letting her hands fall away from my eyes.

There they all stand, big hulking men, my brothers, laughing and running up to me. Grabbing me in their arms and twirling me from one to the other. Francis, David, Alfonse, and Joey, all there, smiling like big goofs, beers in their hands.

Behind them the table is set with Ma's best china and a white lace tablecloth. The dining room is so small that with us Lavotinis all grown there is barely space to squeeze into our chairs. Francis, the oldest, lights the candles and pours the Chianti. Ma bustles around in the kitchen, shooing us all away when we try to help. Later, after mass and after Ma is tipsy with the one glass of wine Pa will convince her to drink, they will dance. My brothers and I will pretend not to notice at first, but then, as always, we will be drawn to the door of the kitchen.

There, in the dimly lit room, they come together, whirling around on the old linoleum to music we have heard since childhood. There he holds her and she gently lays her head on his shoulder. They have done this every Christmas Eve for as long as we can remember. Even in the years when five children lived at home and times were tough. Even when they couldn't imagine where the money would come from to pay for those presents under the tree. Still they danced.

We hold our breath, watching, not wanting to disturb the strange-to-us moment when our parents become adults in love, and we, the children, outsiders. But they see us, they always do finally see us. Ma blushes and Pa gets all flustered.

"What's the matter with youse?" he yells, and we all giggle. "Can't a man dance with his own wife, in his own house?"

"Yeah, Pa, sure," we all answer, because now he is smiling at her again. Suddenly, his arms and hers are open, and the children are enfolded, even now as adults. It is a ritual. A reminder that in my world there are certain things I can count on, certain truths that will always hold, no matter how far away I am, or how hot the Florida sun is on my homesick body.

But this year it was all different. I was coming home a day earlier than usual, and I was leaving right after Christmas, instead of my usual New Year's Day departure. This year something was terribly wrong, and I knew how bad it was the second I stepped off the plane and found Francis waiting for me instead of Ma and Pa.

Francis looked grim, despite his attempt to smile and hug me. His face looked gray and there were thick circles under his eyes. He was trying to be the oldest brother and act tough, but I could read him and I knew he was aching inside. He was scaring me with his silence. I waited, forcing myself not to ask, until he'd led me away from the gate, drawing me into an empty waiting area.

"Where's Ma?" I asked him.

"She's in the hospital, Sierra," he said. "She made us swear not to tell you until you got here and I could take you to her." He paused, sucked in his breath, and let out the big secret. "Sierra, Ma's got breast cancer."

I don't remember leaving the airport. I know Francis picked up my luggage. I know we somehow found his car and drove away, but looking back on it, I find nothing in the memory files, just the feeling of blind, white-light, panic. Ma needed me and I wasn't there, and couldn't get there fast enough.

Francis was in his stiff-upper-lip, emotions-in-check, standard-operating mode. He presented me with the facts just as they had occurred, nothing omitted.

"Ma had a checkup or something," he said. "That's when they found it. Apparently, Ma knew it was there, but she kept telling herself it was something else."

"*It*" was cancer, I wanted to scream at him, but I didn't. Instead I let him go on and on, flooding me with every fact he'd been hanging on to, knowing he had to do it his way or lose it completely.

"They went in yesterday and did a complete mastectomy," he said. "It was in over half her lymph nodes," he said. "That ain't good, but they're gonna do chemo and the doc's the best in the business. Joey's girlfriend works in his department at Penn. Ma's gonna be all right. She's in a lot of pain right now, but that's to be expected."

Francis was working his way to Thomas Jefferson Hospital, talking and dodging traffic, his eyes focused on the road ahead, all emotion carefully sheltered by his dark aviator glasses.

Expected? The pain was to be expected? Well, I hadn't expected it. "Why the hell didn't somebody tell me?" I yelled. "You sons of bitches!"

I reached over and punched his arm so hard the car swerved.

"Damn it, Sierra! Stop it! Ma wouldn't let us tell you!"

"So fucking what?" I yelled. "Don't you know when to think for yourselves?"

Francis stopped at a red light and looked over at me. "Our hands were a little full up here, Sierra. Ma was in trouble and Pa's acting like a total asshole. He's completely losing it, Sierra, so pardon me if we couldn't quite get around to you."

It was the Lavotini way, scream, yell, beat on things, and then get rational. We weren't at the rational point yet.

"What do you mean Pa's acting like an asshole?"

Francis turned his attention back to driving. "He won't go to the hospital. He's sitting down in the basement, drinking. I never seen him like this. I tried to get him to go to her and he took a swing at me, Sierra. He's a fucking loser."

"Ma's up in the hospital going through this alone?"

I was shrieking. I was wild inside. It scared Fluffy, because a high-pitched yowl escaped from the backseat, where she sat cowering in her crate.

"Fluffy, babe, it's all right," I said, trying to calm down and failing miserably. "Francis, who's with Ma?"

"We all are, Sierra. Didn't nobody leave her."

"And what about Pa?"

We pulled into the parking deck of the hospital and Francis rolled down the window and reached out to take a ticket.

"Didn't nobody leave him either," he said. "We're taking turns. We got family coming over out the ying-yang, and Ma's church ladies are practically haunting the place. You can't move for the people wanting to do good."

"Then what's with Pa?" But I knew. Pa loved Ma so bad he couldn't deal with the threat to her. It was Pa's job to make sure nothing ever happened to Ma or his family, but this time he couldn't take care of Ma's problem. He couldn't fix Ma and he couldn't handle that.

"Pa is being an idiot," Francis pronounced calmly. He pulled into a parking slot, shut off the engine, and got out of the car. I followed him, tossing Fluffy a doggie treat and a promise.

"I'll be right back, Fluff," I said, but my voice broke as I tried to speak and the words came out in a whisper of tears.

We rode the elevator to Ma's room in silence. The whole time I was preparing myself. In all of our lives, nothing had ever gone wrong with Ma. It seemed to me she had never so much as had a cold. And the only injury I could remember was from the time she and Raydean played commando while Ma was visiting my place and feeling particularly powerful. What was Ma feeling now?

Francis stopped outside a wide door and looked at me, mouthing the word "Ready?" I nodded and he pushed open the door.

The room was the same color all hospital rooms are in my head, a pale shade of tan. They can dress them up any way they want to, throw a picture on a wall, pitch in a burgundy recliner, but still it's not the room you remember, it's the people in it. I stepped inside and the only thing I could focus on was my brothers and Ma.

Joey, Al, and David were all sitting in chairs pulled up to the bed, looking subdued and strangely frightened. They glanced up at me, all at once, and their eyes were sunken and dark with fatigue. Ma lay on the bed, pale and silent, her face contorted with unexpressed suffering.

I stepped up to the bed, silently slipping past my brothers to take her hand in mine.

"You hurtin', Ma?" I whispered.

Her eyes slowly opened and she focused on me, tears spilling over her lashes and running down her ashen cheeks.

"Oh, Sierra, honey," she said, her voice cracking with thirst and pain, "it hurts bad." She took a shaky breath, then whispered, "I'm sorry, honey. I wanted to be feeling better when you got here."

This was not Ma. I turned to my brothers and noticed how lost they seemed to be. They had the same look in their eyes that I'd seen in Dennis Watley's little kids.

"Okay, Ma," I said, trying to sound like I was gonna lick the world. "Let me talk with your nurse and get you fixed up."

Joey spoke up. "She wouldn't take nothin'."

I looked back at Ma. "Why not?"

Ma's eyes fluttered. "I was waiting. I didn't want to be asleep when you and your father got here."

"Ma, when Pa gets here and sees you looking so bad, he's gonna freak. Now let's get you some medicine and a different nightgown, and you'll be looking good when he comes." She started to protest, but I leaned down and stroked the hair away from her forehead. "Ma, he'll wait if you're sleeping."

The tears started flowing again. "He ain't coming, Sierra. He don't want to see me like this. He don't want to look at me no more."

Al jumped up out of his chair and went to stand by the window, his back to us, but anger written all over the way he held himself, his fists at his sides.

"Ma, it ain't that, trust me. Pa's never been good in hospitals. He can't take not being able to help, and seeing you in pain makes him feel even worse. Let's get you taken care of, and then I'll go find Pa." And when I did, I was figuring to give him a good piece of my mind.

Seventeen

When we got back to the car, things were not as they should've been. For one thing, Fluffy was a basketcase. When Francis unlocked the door, Fluffy snapped and barked like we were both strangers. Then when she heard my voice, she began whimpering.

I figured she'd had enough emotional trauma for one day. While Francis went through the motions of getting us out of the parking deck and on our way home, I shifted my attentions to the poor dog. I turned around in my seat and reached back to undo the crate door. That's when I found the slip of paper with my name on it sticking out from the bottom of the cage.

I looked back at Francis, tempted to say something to him. He was talking to the garage attendant, paying his tab and collecting his receipt. I unfolded the paper slowly, trying to figure out when someone could've slipped a note under Fluffy's crate. After all, the car had been locked. There was no sign that the locks had been tampered with, only Fluffy's hysteria.

"*We will talk . . . soon,*" the note read.

I looked at Fluffy. She was trembling. I opened the door to her cage, pulled her out and brought her up into the front seat.

"Hey, Fluff," Francis said.

"It's all right, baby," I crooned. Fluffy snuggled deeper into my arms, still shaking. I started to tell Francis about the note and then stopped. He and my other brothers had been through hell. Whoever was looking for me could wait. I had an assortment of past boyfriends and associates, any one of them very capable of breaking into a car and leaving a note. Maybe this was their idea of courting. I reviewed the list of men not currently serving time and realized that even among those losers it was a thin idea to think they'd be searching for me in this manner. Nope, this was trouble. I just wasn't sure what kind of trouble.

I glanced over at Francis. I had four strong brothers. No way was this bozo note-writer going to get through them to hurt me. Anyway, if he'd wanted to hurt me, he would've hurt Fluffy. Besides, how was I to know when the note arrived in Fluffy's crate? Someone could've slipped it into the cage while we were at the airport in Florida. Nah, this wasn't an immediate threat and Francis didn't need any more stress. I tucked the note into the pocket of my pants and tried to put it out of my mind, but a little thrill of fear shot through my chest and settled in to kindle a low flame of anxiety that wouldn't go away. Somebody was looking for me.

Francis turned onto our street and began jockeying for position among the cars lining the curb. He slid into a spot between an ancient Cadillac and a beat-to-death Beamer.

He shut off the engine and looked at me. "Sierra, when I told you I ain't never seen Pa like this, I meant it. He's drunk. I've never seen the man loaded. He can hold his Chianti, but he ain't drinking Chianti. He's drinking liquor."

I shrugged. "Francis, we've all got our ways. Nothing ever happened to Ma before. He's taking it hard."

Francis shook his head like the Chief should always be on duty, always in control, just like Francis. Only Francis wasn't any better than Pa at handling what was going on. He walked around like a powder keg, and sooner or later he was going to lose it every bit as bad as Pa. But Francis and I had covered this ground and it wasn't going to get any better by me beating it into him. So I opened the door and started to step out of the car.

"I'm just trying to tell you, Sierra," he said.

I looked back at him, cradling Fluffy and glaring at him. "I know what you're trying to do, Francis. But what I'm trying to tell you is this: I understand Pa. I'm not saying I can do more or less than anybody else. I'm just saying maybe I can help him."

Francis snorted. "Pa don't need help. He needs to sober up and be a man."

Before I could stop it, the words flew out of my mouth. "Oh, like when you and the ex split up? He should be a man like that?"

Francis just stared at me, not believing what I was saying, not believing he heard me, the look of disbelief etched clearly across his face.

"Francis," I said, "I'm sorry. That was unfair and untrue."

He wouldn't even meet my eye. He got out of the car, locking it slowly and carefully behind him, then brushed past me as he walked up the stairs to the row house. I followed, trying to find the words to undo the terrible wrong I'd done him. Losing his wife had been the worst thing that had ever happened to him. Losing her to his best friend had been almost more than he could bear. Now I had to bring it up, play off his weakness by returning to revisit it with scorn.

Aunt Dolores undid the locks and pulled the heavy front door open before I had a chance to say anything more to Francis. Pa's sister stood there pulling on her thick black wool overcoat and frowning out at us, disapproval written all over her pudgy face.

"He ain't come up," she said to Francis. Then, "Hello, Sierra," to me, and a cursory glance that seemed to say: "I knew it. You look just like a stripper."

Dolores made no bones about how she felt, ever. She was thick-set, with bleached blond hair that always showed coarse black roots, and the thin line of a mustache that never seemed to vanish with bleach. Dolores was sensible in a way that made the rest of the world look foolish, no matter how responsible they were. A devout Catholic, she never missed mass. She never ate meat on Friday, despite any papal dispensation. Dolores confessed to Father Max for hours, it seemed. I always figured her confessions were about nothing, or else she wouldn't have complained all the time that he fell asleep on her. Father Max has yet to fall asleep during one of my confessions.

I walked by her as she made her way out of the house, past the little huddle of church ladies who bustled about in Ma's kitchen, and down the steps to the basement. Fluffy, sensing a battle, jumped out of my arms and scampered back up the steps. Even the church ladies seemed safer, I figured.

Pa was sitting on the worn gray sofa that Ma had long ago dismissed from aboveground duty. He was wearing a sleeveless white T-shirt, his thick arm muscles ropy with age. He held a bottle of whisky in one hand and a faded photograph of Ma in the other. He was crying, tears running down his cheeks and into the gray stubble of a three-day growth of beard. His hair was rumpled and pressed to the side of his head from where he'd slept on one arm of the couch. He was a mess, just as Francis had said.

I stepped down off the last stair and walked over to him, sitting down beside him and slipping my arm around his shoulders.

"Oh, Pa," I whispered. "She's gonna be all right."

I wasn't even sure he'd heard me. He sat without moving for so long I became frightened and thought maybe he'd completely lost it. When he did speak, his voice was almost a whisper.

"They cut her, Sierra," he said. "And still it's eating her. And it's gonna keep on eatin' her until she dies, just like it did her mother, and her mother before her."

This was something I didn't know. "Grandma died of cancer?" Pa nodded. "And her mother too?"

Pa looked over at me briefly, like it was nothing at all unusual for me to be sitting on his workshop sofa, even though he knew I hadn't been home in a year.

"Sierra, your mother's been afraid of this all her life, and now look what's happened." A tear escaped and ran down his cheek. "And I can't do a goddamn thing about it!" His voice rose and he brought the bottle to his lips, as if drowning out the words.

"Pa," I said, pulling the bottle down and gently taking it from him. "Ma is fine. She just needs you."

Pa wouldn't look at me. "She ain't fine. She's got it in her body. They talk like they're gonna save her, but what kind of talk is that? Experimental drugs, my ass!" He paused and I sat waiting. He twisted at an invisible thread on the sofa. He stared at Ma's picture, and finally he said it. "I don't know if I can handle it, Sierra. If I walk in that room and she looks at me, she'll know."

"Know what, Pa?"

He sighed. "Sierra, I don't love your Ma for how she looks on the outside. She's the most beautiful woman in the world, but what if I can't make her see that?"

"Well, Pa, you can't make her see that by sitting here drinking, that's for damn sure."

He moved a little on the sofa, restless. "What am I gonna say to her? She's gonna look at me and know what I'm thinking. What if she says, 'Am I gonna die?' What do I say? How do I look at her and say no?"

Fluffy picked this moment to walk down the steps and come up to the couch. She hopped up beside Pa and crawled into his lap.

"Pa, she ain't looking for you to lie to her. She's looking to know you still love her. She's looking to hear you're still there, that no matter what, you're the guy. You're the man that has loved her forever and will go on loving her long after both of you are dead and buried. That's all there is to it." I took his hand and squeezed it until he looked up at me. "Pa, it's okay to be afraid. It's okay to be petrified, but you gotta be that with Ma, not without her."

Pa's gaze drifted to the steps like he was hoping maybe someone would walk downstairs and explain the entire situation to him in a way that made everything better. "Pa, listen to me. Tomorrow's Christmas Eve. Ma's coming home tomorrow. We've got work to do. You've gotta pull it together and give Ma a Christmas. You can't let her come home and see we ain't making it." I patted his knee. "You know what I think, Pa?"

"What do you think, Sierra?"

"I'm thinking Francis and Joey should go get the tree and set it up. Then after you and I go to the hospital, you can get the decorations down from the attic and I'll go to the store and get the groceries."

I sandwiched in the part about Pa going to see Ma like it was a given, but I was holding my breath. I heard Pa suck in a breath too, then hold it, considering.

"Okay," he said. "We go, but you leave me there. I want youse kids to go do all that Christmas shit. I'm staying with Evie."

I felt the tears of relief clogging my throat and forced them back. "Okay, if that's what you want, that's what we'll do."

Pa stood and headed toward the stairs. "I gotta go get cleaned up," he said. "Give me a half hour. Oh and, Sierra?"

"Yeah, Pa?"

"Welcome home, sweetie."

Eighteen

When the phone rang, I was in Ma's kitchen, where she should have been on Christmas Eve, whipping up the filling for our traditional angel cake. I cradled the receiver against my neck and answered, the whole while focused on whipping the cream.

"Sierra?" the voice said.

It took me a moment to realize that I hadn't given anyone but John Nailor my number. It took another second to figure out who was calling.

"Frankie? How'd you get my number?"

"It's in the book, Sierra, along with a number of your finer relatives. It didn't take a miracle. Now listen up. I got you hooked up to talk to this guy Dimitri the day after you get back. You're meeting us at the Oyster Bar on Beck at eleven. You got that?"

"No problem."

"Good, then I got something else to tell you. Izzy Rodriguez is looking to link up with your new boss. Word is he's there every night and making himself useful by telling your fishing-boat captain what's what with running a club."

That didn't make sense. Why would a snake like Izzy suddenly turn humanitarian and help out a potential new rival?

"I don't work there anymore," I said.

"No shit," Frankie laughed. "The House of Booty's got a new

headliner. Some blonde that looks like a Barbie doll and slithers like a snake. Girl might give you a run for your money. Bitch can dance."

I was having a bad feeling. "Would this powder puff be sporting a tattoo above her left boob?" I asked.

"Yeah, just like her name, Angel."

I slapped the wire whisk against the side of the crockery bowl. "You got any more Christmas Eve cheer for me, Frankie?"

He chuckled. "Yeah," he said, "your boyfriend's thinking with his little head. He let Gambuzzo out for Christmas dinner. I don't know how you did it, but Gambuzzo's sitting over at his girlfriend's house, surrounded by unmarked police, enjoying a little holiday cheer."

Someone in the background called out, and Frankie's attention was diverted. When he spoke again, his entire voice had changed. He sounded rushed and anxious.

"I gotta go."

"Frankie, wait. I need to ask you something."

"Gotta go, Sierra," he said, and snapped his cell phone shut.

I stood there in Ma's sunny kitchen, listening to Perry Como sing about chestnuts roasting on an open fire and worrying about a biker, a cop, and a used-car salesman's son. In the living room, Al and Joey struggled to put the tree in its stand, swearing when it didn't stand up straight and blaming each other for the problems of the world and other assorted issues. This was not Christmas as I had ever known it.

I stepped to the edge of the dining room door and peered into the living room.

"Youse guys," I said to my brothers. "It's almost lunchtime. Pa and Francis will be home with Ma anytime now. How about you knock it off with the language and start cooperating?"

The front door opened at that moment and Francis stepped inside, his face taut and gray with tension. Behind him I could hear Pa, his voice as soft as a whisper, coaxing.

"Baby, let me carry you," he was saying.

And we all heard Ma's breathless answer. "No. What do you want Mrs. Dominichi to think, eh? I can do it."

But she couldn't. They paused for minutes on each step and not one of us moved. Francis wouldn't look backward. He couldn't and Ma wouldn't have wanted him to. This homecoming had to be done her way. Ma was trying to act as if everything was normal and we were to go along with it or die trying. I knew what she was doing. She was sealing off the hurt and the vulnerability, and we were to do it too. That's the Lavotini way. You take it on the chin. You shake it off. And you don't mention it again. It's the code.

When Ma finally stepped through the door, she looked around at us all, taking in the undecorated tree, sniffing the smells from her kitchen, and noticing the stricken looks we all were trying desperately to replace with frozen, wooden smiles.

"Al," Ma cried, "what's the matter with you? What are you doing letting your poor brother do all the work by himself? Look at that tree. Is that what you call a tree? It's crooked."

Al stepped forward to take Ma's arm, guiding her toward the steps up to her bedroom.

"No, you don't!" she said, swiping at his head with her good arm.

Pa intervened. "Let us help you up the stairs, Evie," he coaxed.

Ma turned on him. "What? I'm not going to bed. I'm going to sit right down here on this sofa and make sure these knuckleheads get it done right."

"Sierra!"

I jumped. Ma was in commando mode and there was no fighting it.

"Yeah, Ma?"

"You get the eel for the sauce?"

"Yeah, Ma. Sure."

Ma nodded. "All right, then. Is it on?"

I was aware of answering her, but I was also aware that in our tiny row house, time was standing still. We were all frozen with the desire to do it right, to help Ma pull off the grand charade, but at the same time, our hearts were in our throats and our souls were aching with the desire to make this horrible reality go away. Our Ma was invincible, wasn't she?

"I got minestrone. I got sauce. I got the cassata working."

Ma smiled softly, but she couldn't hide a wince as Pa gently guided her to the sofa and lifted her legs up onto the cushions.

"Sierra, bring me a glass of your Pa's Chianti," she whispered. From one corner of her eye, she tracked Al moving toward the door, trying to escape either from his emotions or his job. It didn't matter to Ma.

"Oh no, you don't, buster," Ma said, her voice still a husky whisper. "You and Joey start with them red balls, and be careful you don't break them. They was handed down from your grandmother to me. One day your children, should the good Lord bless you with a woman patient enough, will have these ornaments. You drop one of them and you're cutting into your legacy."

Pa was standing by Ma's side, almost wringing his hands. Ma looked up at him and frowned. "What are you doing here?" she said.

"Evie, I . . ."

"So you would break with tradition too?" she asked.

Pa didn't know what to say. Every Christmas Eve, Pa went down to the firehouse to cook supper for the single men who volunteered to work while the married men took off to be with their families. Sometimes Ma joined him, but more often than not she stayed home, cooking for the hordes of relatives and friends that would stop by on Christmas Eve and Christmas Day.

"I am fine, sweetie," Ma said. "Now leave me be to get these children on the right road." Ma looked around at all of us and sighed, but it was a pleased sigh. "I guess you people would fall apart without me," she said.

I turned my back and headed for the kitchen, my throat tight and my eyes burning. "Yeah, Ma," I whispered to myself, "we would all be lost without you."

Nineteen

$\mathcal{O}$n Christmas morning I woke up in my old twin bed upstairs in my old bedroom, the room that Ma kept like a shrine to me, unchanged from the day I moved to Upper Darby with my girlfriends. I lay there, staring up at the ceiling, my eyes wandering from there to the cabbage-rose wallpaper and the gold-and-white mirror that hung over my dressing table. I strained to hear any sounds from the street, but I heard nothing.

I rolled over and reached to pull the curtain away from my window. A thin coverlet of snow blanketed Mrs. Mattagoni's slate rooftop. I rolled back, leaving the curtain open so I could watch the light breath of snow continuing to fall. My hand brushed the bedside table, knocking into the tiny package John Nailor had given me.

I picked it up and pushed up onto one elbow. I could open it now, here, up in my room alone. I could open it in private and not have to answer my brothers' questions or see the hope in Ma's eyes. Still, I made it last, picking at the tape that sealed the ends of the tiny box. What had he done? And where was he right at this moment?

The paper and bow fell away, gold and white giving way to a small gray jeweler's box. Too large to be a ring, too small to be a bracelet.

I pried the lid up, feeling the hinge give and snap as it popped open. Inside was a smooth silver locket on a thin silver chain.

I picked it up and slid my thumbnail between the edges and gently slid it open. John had taken a picture of Fluffy and slipped it into the left side. On the right side he had carefully written the words I LOVE YOU, SIERRA.

I sat there in bed, holding the locket, for one moment letting myself feel it. I loved him too. Deep down inside of me, I suddenly knew it. While I was wrapped up in my fears and doubts, I knew, undeniably, that I loved him.

I reached over, picked up the pink princess phone, and punched in his number without pausing to think that I could be waking him. I wanted him to know that I knew now how I felt. I was sure.

"Merry Christmas," a soft female voice answered. "I woke up and you were gone," she said.

I froze, hanging on to the receiver. Wrong number, I thought, and started to hang up. But then I realized it was Carla Terrance's voice. There's just something about your boyfriend's ex-wife you don't forget.

"Hey, Carla," I said. "Merry Christmas. Is John around?"

Of course, on the other hand, leave it to an ex-wife not to forget the sound of her ex-husband's new girlfriend. "No," she purred, sounding just like a sex kitten sitting in a milk bath. "I don't know where he is. Maybe he went out to find breakfast for the two of us."

I didn't react. I wouldn't give her the satisfaction. I wouldn't ask why she was there or scream or give her anything but Sierra Lavotini, secure and content.

"Well, good. I'm glad things are going well." Yeah, that's it, I thought. Make her think you knew she was there.

"Are you really?" Carla asked, begging for it in my opinion.

"Yep. I know he wouldn't want you to be alone on Christmas. I'm just sorry I'm not there to join you. But I'll be back tomorrow, so don't worry."

It was weak, a lame attempt to sound like I had the plan and the key to John Nailor's heart, but what in the hell was she doing there?

"Oh, I don't know," Carla said, her voice getting huskier by the syllable. "By tomorrow he may have moved on. In fact, I do believe he said something about needing to call you."

I couldn't help myself. "Call me?" I echoed.

"Yes. He's not going to be able to pick you up tomorrow. He has plans."

The way she said "plans" made me envision her naked, stretched out in bed and beckoning for him to come to her. Suddenly the Lavotini temper took over and I found myself snapping.

"Just have him call me when he gets in, all right?" I said, and slammed the phone back onto the receiver.

There had to be a better explanation than the obvious. I punched in the number to my answering service and waited. Certainly he'd foreseen this, known I'd call him on Christmas Day. He was just caught up in a case, that's all. And as for Carla being there, well, it was Christmas, after all. She was stuck in Panama City, miles away from her South Florida home. What else could the poor sweetie do but invite her in for Christmas?

I looked at my reflection in the mirror, then over at Fluffy, who was staring at me with the same expression of disbelief.

"Yeah, and I'm the queen of fucking England!" I snapped at my reflection.

The monotone of the automated service reported only one call. "December twenty-fourth," the female automaton said, "eight forty-eight P.M." There was a click and then a voice began to speak, the same mysterious voice I had heard at the airport.

"Don't worry," it said. "I know how to find you."

Twenty

Pa insisted on driving me to the airport the day after Christmas. He wouldn't let any of my brothers come with us. He always took me to the airport alone, and this year, although everything else seemed to have been tossed upside down, he didn't vary this part of our tradition.

When he pulled into the Montrose Diner, intent on pie and coffee, I almost balked. I wanted to tell him to take me straight to the airport just this one time. I wanted to tell him that I wasn't sure I could keep up the act I'd been playing for an Oscar ever since I heard Carla Terrance answer John's phone, ever since I'd spent all day trying to call him back and hearing no answer and having no answering machine pick up. I wasn't sure I could sit across the booth from Pa and not burst out crying, and neither one of us needed a mess like that.

But I pulled it off anyway. I sat there with my thick white mug and my slab of pumpkin pie and smiled like the actress we all know me to be.

"Sierra," Pa said finally, "you can wipe that phony grin off your face any time now. It ain't cutting it with me. Is it your Ma?"

And suddenly the tears were right there, eating away at me. "Well, Pa, of course I'm worried," I said, "but Ma's gonna be fine. I just wish I weren't so far away." *And so all alone.*

"Baby," he said, covering my hand with his thick one, "I got your Ma taken care of. Don't you be worrying. You came home, you set me straight, and we're going on from here."

I smiled at him again.

"Okay," he said. "That's it. You got that same stupid smile going again. Is there anything else on your mind? I mean, obviously there must be."

I smiled more, like a fool I smiled. "Pa, I'm just not wanting to leave. I mean, usually I'm here another week, but this year there was so much going on and I didn't know what was happening up here . . ."

I was babbling, and Pa was watching me like a hawk and probably didn't believe one-tenth of what I was saying. He took a long sip of his coffee and looked at me.

"Sierra, I know when you're lying to me. I respect your right to have your own life. But if I find out something's bad wrong and you neglected to tell me about it, I'm coming down there." He reached in his wallet and threw some money on top of the check. "You don't want me coming down there and cleaning up a mess, do ya?" He stood up and waited to see what I was going to say.

"Pa," I lied, "there's no mess to clean up and nothing to worry about. I'm just stressing a little, that's all."

I could tell he didn't believe me. He let it go, but he didn't believe me. We drove the rest of the way to the airport with me lecturing him on the care of Ma and him reassuring me that he had it covered. When we got to the curbside check-in I turned in my seat and looked at him.

"Pa," I said, "I'm breaking with tradition." I looked at my watch. "Ma's been alone at the house with just the boys there for an hour. How about you drop me off right here this time." He started to object. "Really, Pa. You know how it is. They won't let you come down to the gate without a lot of fuss and badge flashing. Go home. I'll feel better about it, really I will."

I reached into the backseat and gathered Fluffy up into my arms, reluctant to crate her until I had to. Pa sighed, knowing this was a battle we didn't need to have.

"All right, sweetheart." He got out of the Lincoln and walked around to the trunk, pulled out my bag and Fluffy's crate, and set them down on the curb beside the car.

"I love you, honey," he said, hugging me so tight I almost couldn't breathe. Fluffy squirmed and yipped, forcing him to pull away before I lost it completely.

"I love you too, Pa." I stood watching as he slowly turned and walked back to the driver's side of the car. The past few days had aged Pa. For the first time I could see the vulnerable side of him, the side that would one day become an old man who needed me, the part of Pa that no one had ever seen before.

Neither one of us paid much attention to the limousine that pulled up and stopped just behind the Lincoln. I wouldn't have noticed it when Pa drove off had it not pulled immediately into the space where Pa's car had just been. I would've turned and walked away if the back door of the car hadn't flown open, blocking my path for a moment.

A suit, well-built with a bulge under his shoulder that meant gun, stood just in front of me. Before I could turn and walk around him, another suit emerged from the car, blocking me between the two of them. This was still not a problem, but the gun the second guy stuck between my ribs was. He did it in such a way that no one walking by would notice. He stood so casually that I almost figured I'd been mistaken, but then the first suit smiled and looked at me directly.

"Ms. Lavotini," he said, motioning me toward the backseat of the limo, "with Mr. Lavotini's compliments. He'd appreciate a brief moment of your time."

I froze. The only Mr. Lavotini I knew had just driven off in a powder-blue Lincoln Town Car. The only other Mr. Lavotini who would appear in a limousine looking for me was my alleged "uncle," Big Moose Lavotini of the Cape May, New Jersey, syndicate Lavotinis. In other words, I was up shit's creek.

I looked into the dark interior of the snow-white limo. It was all done in deep burgundy leather, with just enough red in the color to let you know it had been personally created for its owner. The leather you see on the showroom floor is always a deep wine color. This red was different. It looked like a booth in La Trattoria or any other Italian bistro in South Philly.

If the button-tufted leather wasn't enough to set it apart, the glasses sitting in the burled-wood rack that rimmed the custom-made bar were. I was sure I was staring at Waterford crystal.

I felt a little shove from the snub-nosed revolver that rested uncomfortably in my back and knew the moment of reckoning had arrived. After all, even in a town as small as Panama City, you cannot blindly invoke the name of a major mobster without expecting to one day deal with the ramifications of such blatant name-dropping. It was one thing to tell Vincent Gambuzzo that I was connected to "Big Moose." It was another to use his name to stem a bloodbath involving another northern mob family. I'd done that a mere two months ago, damn the consequences, and now it was time to pay the piper.

I bent, ducking to enter the back of the limo. I stepped awkwardly into the car and sat down on the seat directly behind the driver, facing the wide backseat. I stared at the man across from me and knew there had been a mistake. There was no way on earth that this man was "Big Moose" Lavotini. No way could this man have two adult sons and a reputation as one of the most heinous syndicate heads on the East Coast. There was no way. Was there?

The man leaned back in his seat and stared at me with dark, almost black eyes that seemed to bore right through me. As I watched, he turned away, exhaling a thin stream of smoke. He stubbed out his cigarette with a well-manicured hand and turned his attention back to me. He was tanned, the kind of tan you get when you have a winter home in South Florida. And he was tall. Even in the spacious limousine, he seemed folded up and cramped. If I had to guess, he was about six-foot-five. I studied him, taking into account the way his expensive suit fit his muscular body, and guessed there wasn't an ounce of fat on him.

His hair was thick and very black, without so much as a trace of gray. And here he was supposed to be sixty. Mob life couldn't be that good. He had a thick black mustache and a smile that, on anyone else, I would've found absolutely charismatic, except that this man allegedly killed people for a living. I stared at him, frozen. I guessed he was in his mid-thirties. Upon closer inspection, I figured he was perhaps the most dangerously attractive man I had ever seen. Something in the way he stared back at me communicated a warning, something that let you know that for all his sophistication and worldly manners, this guy would cut your heart out with a butter knife if you messed with him. I had no illusion that he would feel one shred of remorse at committing a crime like that, either.

"Well," he said, "you are more beautiful than the pictures they sent me." His eyes traveled the length of my body slowly, savoring each inch.

I shivered, but deep inside something stirred. Whatever that something was, it locked on like a homing device and began humming.

"You have pictures?" I said. The attempt to be casual was blown by Fluffy who yipped when I pinched her against my side.

"Hello, Fluffy," the man said softly. "My associates tell me you are one ferocious lapdog." He laughed, deep and warm.

"Wait a minute, here. I thought when your friends said a Mr. Lavotini wanted to talk to me that you were 'Big Moose' Lavotini, but you're not him, are you? I mean, 'Big Moose' Lavotini has grown sons. You're not old enough to have adult children. Does your father know you're here?"

Moose smiled. "Hardly. My father's been dead for over a year. It's a little business complication," he said. "You see, when my father died, we didn't want to risk a battle for the corporation. So we just let it slide."

"How do you let a death slide?" I asked, aware that he had me sitting on the edge of my seat.

"Well, it was a private burial, just the immediate family. And since no one had seen my father for many years, we just arranged to allow things to continue along as they had been. I do the talking, and everyone assumes I'm carrying out Pa's orders."

One of the suits slid into the back of the car, sitting just to my left. The other one closed the back door, then opened the front passenger door and climbed in beside the driver. Everyone but me and Mr. Lavotini was wearing shiny black sunglasses, the kind that reflect your own image back to you while telling you nothing at all about the person behind the lenses. In a moment the car was moving, leaving the curbside check-in area and pulling away from the airport.

"What are you doing?" I said, the panic creeping unchecked into my voice.

Moose stared at me, his eyes locking onto mine. The humming grew even louder and I started thinking maybe my ears were ringing. "I thought we should get acquainted. Like I said in my note, we need to talk."

"But my flight leaves in an hour," I said. I was totally freaked. This guy wasn't going to turn around just because I had to catch a plane. The fact that I had a nonrefundable, nonchangeable ticket would mean nothing to him. One look at his Armani suit told me that money meant nothing to the Moose.

Moose nodded to the suit next to me. The man turned to a built-in compartment, pulled out a bottle of wine, and with swift efficiency began to open it.

"Sierra," Moose said, "relax. No one's going to hurt you . . . unless I say so." He saw the terror on my face and laughed. "I'm kidding, honey. I'm not going to hurt you. After all," he said, his voice dropping to a seductive whisper, "I'm your uncle." He stared into my eyes, not breaking his gaze as the suit handed him a wineglass. "That is what you tell your friends, isn't it? That I'm your uncle?"

I could do little more than nod. Anything I might normally have done was erased when he stared at me. I was doing good to remember my name. I took the glass of wine that the suit offered and held it in my hand, willing it not to shake and give me away any more than I was already doing.

It was a red wine, more purple than the leather interior of Moose's limo. It didn't matter that it was still morning and too early to drink. This was an occasion that called for something stronger than chewing on my fingernails. I took a big swallow and felt the taste of oak and berry break over my tastebuds like a wave. It was drier than Pa's Chianti, with a hint of some spice I couldn't quite name.

"You like it, huh?" Moose asked.

I leaned back in my seat and stared at the man across from me. I forced myself to lift my chin a half an inch, to meet his eyes as if this were nothing more than a leisurely chat.

"Someone's meeting me at the airport on the other end," I said, wishing that were true and knowing it wasn't. "He's a police officer. If I don't show up, he'll know something's wrong. He'll find me."

Moose smiled softly. "Is that so?" he murmured. He looked at his "assistant," snapped his fingers softly, and waited as the suit pulled out a thin brown envelope from his inside jacket pocket. "I don't really think it's like that at all, Sierra."

He handed me a five-by-seven black-and-white photograph. It was obviously taken at night, and the image itself was grainy and slightly blurred, but not so much so that I couldn't make out John Nailor standing on his front porch, the key in the door, and Carla Terrance by his side, her hand gently touching his arm as she smiled at him. Across the bottom of the picture, in tiny white letters, a caption read, DECEMBER 24, 10 P.M.

I tried to feign uninterest. I handed back the picture, but I couldn't quit staring at it.

"You want to tell me about it, or don't we know each other well enough?" he asked.

I took another swallow of wine and found him watching me. "Where are you taking us?" I asked.

143

Lavotini nodded. "Fair enough," he said. "We're driving south on I-95. I need a winter vacation. I'd like to see where my niece is living. Besides, I have a little business to take care of in your home-town."

I jumped in my seat. "You can't do that!"

Moose smiled. The suit smiled. When I looked down at Fluffy, even she was smiling.

Moose leaned forward in his seat, his dark eyes boring into mine. "I think we have many things to discuss, the least of which is that boyfriend of yours. And besides," he said, "you got some large trouble down there. You ever think you might let your old 'uncle' help you out with that? I mean, I might take an interest. I might be useful."

Yeah, I thought, but at what cost to me? I felt the hum in my body grow steadily louder. I tried to ignore it, to look away from the dark shadow behind his eyes, and failed. I knew exactly what the price was going to be, and Sierra Lavotini didn't ante up like that.

This was one hell of a situation. I was receiving a personal escort back to Panama City, courtesy of the Cape May branch of the family. I had bikers waiting to talk to me, bikers that were not at all happy about doing it. I had no job to return to. And my boyfriend seemed to be sleeping with his ex-wife.

I looked over at the Moose. He hadn't taken his eyes off me, but his wineglass was nearly empty. I took a quick glance at his assistant and then a large swallow of my wine.

"All right," I said, "what do you want? I mean, a guy of your stature in the, um, community doesn't just decide to go for a joy ride to the Redneck Riviera. You must want something, and I'll admit I might owe you a little on account of me dropping your name a few times around town, but I didn't take any untoward advantage. I just told a couple of guys to lay off."

Lavotini was watching me, his eyes half-hooded as if he were contemplating sleep, but he didn't fool me. Moose Lavotini didn't sleep. He was taking notes.

"I don't know, Sierra. There may be a business situation in Panama City, an investment opportunity, so to speak. I may need you to smooth the way a little, introduce me around. Like you say, nothing big, no risk to you. These are people you know. It might help me in my negotiations if I had an insider's opinion."

"Mr. Lavotini," I said, "could we be a little less vague about whatever it is that's going on?"

He smiled. "Call me Moose," he said, not answering the question.

Six hours later, somewhere around Richmond, we had progressed no further. We spent the entire time slowly finishing one bottle of wine and opening another. One of us would start a line of questioning, the other would switch it to something else. We sparred, we smiled, and underneath it all, there was another conversation. The kind of conversation you have with someone you know is a match, someone you can't walk over or manipulate. It was clear: Moose Lavotini and I were cut from the same cloth.

Twenty-one

$\mathcal{B}$y the time I realized I should call Pa or be prepared for an invasion from Philly, Moose Lavotini had us seated at a table on the patio of San Genarro, a tiny Italian café in Atlanta with twinkle lights and red-checked tablecloths. We had the patio to ourselves, and a platter of fresh tomatoes seasoned with basil and capers had just arrived.

"Pa's gonna kill me!" I said, and reached for my cell phone.

Moose stretched out one big hand and grabbed me.

"Don't," he said. "I handled it. A friend of yours called to say your flight got delayed outside of Atlanta. You'll be calling them tomorrow."

"What about . . ."

I let my voice trail off. For a moment I'd forgotten that John Nailor could've cared less about my arrival back in town. Maybe I was just a complication to him now.

"Screw him!" Lavotini said. "Here you are, a beautiful woman, called out of town on a family emergency for Christmas, and the schmuck takes his ex-wife home with him? And you're still looking to give him an explanation? What is this?"

His eyes were moving across my body, flicking back up to my face and then starting their relentless journey again.

"You got a mirror at your house?" he asked. When I nodded,

147

he continued. "You ever look in it? I don't think you're seeing what I see. I see a beautiful woman whose man don't appreciate her."

I fingered Nailor's locket. There was an explanation. There had to be an explanation.

Moose picked up the vibe and dropped the line of questioning. "I want to talk about what happened at your club," he said.

"What about it?"

"Update me," he said softly. "I want to know who the new owner is. Who's the competition? And what's with the whack— accidental crossfire or your boy, Denny, got an enemy? And don't worry, I know Gambuzzo ain't got the cochones to hit somebody cold or otherwise."

So I told him. I gave him everything I had on all the rival club owners: Mike Riggs, the new owner of the Tiffany, and Izzy Rodriguez, the snake from the Beaver. I told him about the bikers and every other bit of information that had occurred to me in the days since Denny took the cap and Vincent lost the club. I told him about the dead biker at Dennis Watley's funeral, and how some guy named Turk seemed to be in charge of taking care of Denny. My presentation could've been more organized, but considering my blood alcohol level, I figured I was doing good to remember my name.

Lavotini nodded. He was tracking it all, keeping it logged in his brain without seeming to extend any effort. The food arrived and we hadn't even placed an order. Moose had merely nodded at the waiter and things had begun arriving at the table. The soup came first, carabaccia, rich with pancetta and onion, a thick slice of toasted focaccia covered with cheese floating in the rich chicken broth. This was followed by pasta allo scoglio, so full of seafood you almost overlooked the noodles.

I looked up at some point and saw him smiling.

"You like to eat," he said. "That's very good." His eyes were dark pools that seemed to reach inside my body, igniting it. "I like a woman who isn't afraid to dig in and take what she wants."

We were no longer discussing food, if indeed we ever had been.

I let the fork slide slowly out of my mouth, my eyes never leaving his. What in the hell was going on? I had a man who loved me waiting back at home — at least, I was pretty certain he loved me and half sure he was waiting. But here I was, making goo-goo eyes and speculating about touching a man I knew was mob connected. Still, I couldn't stop.

"Yeah," I said, letting my eyes drift across his shoulders and down over his chest, "I'm like that. I like new experiences and I like to taste new things." I looked him right in the eye even though I could feel my face start to flush and my nipples hardening underneath my shirt.

Lavotini didn't look away either. "Well, I guess I'll have to find out more about your tastes, won't I?" he said.

I believe that is when I dropped my fork with a clatter that rang against the white china dish and echoed across the patio.

Lavotini laughed. He motioned to the waiter, and coffee arrived at the table, accompanied by bomboloni, tiny cream puffs that melted in my mouth. It was maybe better than sex, but then I looked over at my dinner companion and wondered. The candlelight played off his dark Italian features and for a moment I was lulled into thinking he was merely intoxicatingly attractive. Then his cell phone rang and I saw the other side of Moose Lavotini.

He flipped open the tiny phone, held it to his ear, and began frowning almost immediately.

"Unacceptable," he said, his voice stiff.

"Not our problem," he said a moment later. Then, "Take care of it." He listened for another moment. "I think you know exactly what I'm telling you to do. Twelve hours. That's all. No compromise, no deals. I'll expect the contract tomorrow."

I don't know if the caller was suicidal or not, but there was a further period in which Moose listened. Then abruptly, he shot back. "Fuck that!" he said. "And fuck him! You tell him no deal, you got me? No fucking deal now." Then Lavotini lapsed into Italian and I was lost.

When he flipped the cell shut, he stood, pushing his chair behind him, clearly angry. He had entirely forgotten me.

The man who turned back to me a minute later was the charming Moose Lavotini, but the aftertaste of the other Moose lingered and I was on guard. When we reached the car, I had a moment where I thought of trying to run away. I looked at the darkened parking lot, now empty, and back out at the busy road that ran in front of it. I thought I could run out to the street, flag someone down, and this episode with Moose Lavotini would be over. But I also had no doubt he would pursue me.

I felt him watching me, looked up and saw the dark, inscrutable eyes soften.

"You wanna go, go now," he said. "This ain't a total hijacking. You aren't really a prisoner. You wanna walk, I'll call a cab."

I hesitated, thinking about it. My feet, however, had made up their mind because my body was moving toward the car, and my mouth was in on the decision.

"And turn down a chauffeur-driven limousine ride?" I was saying. "No, you're stuck with me." But I didn't mean it, did I?

I think he sensed my uncertainty because he ignored me the rest of the way. He sat across from me, accepted a steaming mug of coffee from the suit, and began reading through a file folder of typewritten pages. I continued to study him until I began to realize that perhaps I should reflect upon what I was learning with my eyes closed. When I woke up it was to the barest light of dawn. The white stretch was pulling up into the Lively Oaks Trailer Park and I was home.

Twenty-two

$\mathcal{M}$oose Lavotini looked at me as I stepped out of the limo. My bag and Fluffy's crate were on the sidewalk and Fluffy was already gone, having bolted up the steps and through the doggie door into the relative sanctuary of her kingdom.

"I'll be in touch," he said. "I don't want you talking to those bikers by yourself."

Right, like I was going to show up in a limo with mob enforcers for protection. Oh, that would really gain their confidence. They would just love to confide in me then.

"Sure," I lied. "It's set up for tomorrow. Call me." I peeked at my watch. In three hours, Frankie and I would be sitting at a picnic table at the Oyster Bar having a conversation with a guy named Dimitri. The syndicate was most cordially uninvited.

Moose smiled. "That a girl," he said. "Thomas is going to stay here and make sure nothing happens to you," he added, motioning to one of the suits.

I looked at him and saw he knew I had no intention of dealing him in on anything. In fact, the way he smiled, with his entire mouth and his eyes, let me know he was enjoying what he saw as a game.

"No, sorry. Thanks for the offer," I said. "I don't do butlers. I don't need protection. And I want my privacy."

Moose stopped smiling and gave me the look. It was the same look I'd seen him get when he was talking on his cell and he was displeased. It was dark and revealed an unwillingness to compromise.

"Sierra," he said, "that wasn't a request. Learn who's in charge, baby, and accept it. There are things I'm good at, areas where I have expertise and you have amateur status. Let me do what I'm good at. Let's not get you hurt."

Then he smiled, as if the sun had come out and we were all happy campers. The limo door closed and Thomas, all neck and no visible personality, stood on the sidewalk waiting for an invitation inside.

I sighed and reached for my suitcase. His hand covered mine in an attempt to get to it first. We were stuck there, head to head for a second, each one wanting to take charge.

"All right," I said. "Knock yourself out." He picked up the case and stood waiting for me to lead the way up the stairs and into the trailer. "Some people, they get stray cats left on their doorstep. Me, I get a stray gunman. Go figure."

I was yammering, but I was also trying to figure out how I was going to ditch this boy so's I could go meet Frankie. I led Thomas into my kitchen and took my suitcase out of his overstuffed hand.

"I'm going to change," I said. "It's been a long twenty-four hours. Why don't you get some rest? I've got a nice guest room."

Thomas seemed to be about out on his feet, but he just stood there, rigidly planted in my kitchen. I tried to figure out what a guy like him had for a weakness. He was well-built, nothing spectacular to look at, but if you took into account that he wore a suit, you might say he'd pass for good-looking. I smiled, giving him the Sierra thousand-watt turn-on treatment. He didn't flinch, so importing Tonya the Barbarian to distract him wasn't an option.

"Okie-doke, Thomas," I said, "I'm heading down the hallway. Make yourself at home."

Thomas didn't answer. I was starting to wonder if he even spoke English.

The idea came to me while I was taking a shower. It was born of bad movies and too much TV, but it was my only option. I stepped out, naked and dripping, and dialed Raydean's number.

"Comedy Central," she answered.

"I got a situation," I said.

"What you got is trouble," she answered. "New Jersey plates on that limo. Tinted windows. You think I didn't see *Men in Black*? Them aliens ain't registered. Now you got one taking over your house, am I right?"

I wrapped myself in a towel and shivered. "You're about as right as they get," I answered. "I was wondering, do those people at the mental health center give you anything to help you sleep?"

Raydean chuckled. "Honey, I could choke a horse with the medicine I got here. You want a cocktail or what?"

"How about coffee and rolls?"

I could hear the mental calculation going on across the street. "You want him dead or alive? I can put the boy in a coma or straight on to Jesus. Makes no nevermind to me. Gotta take into account an alien metabolism, but I figure I can bring it right close either whichever way you say."

"Alive and asleep and nowhere near dead."

"Uh-huh," she said, her tone clearly conveying her disappointment. "And I cain't shoot him?"

"No, not this time."

"Maybe later we can drive him out into the countryside and dump him. You know, see if he can find his way back."

"All right, that might work," I answered. "But do you think you could brew up something?"

"Already got it on the stove," she said.

I hung up and felt a little sorry for Thomas. I even went so far as to fix myself up a little extra and curl my hair as a diversionary tactic. We weren't in Jersey anymore. We were on my home turf, and losing a bodyguard was one of my specialties.

By the time Raydean arrived carrying a white carafe and a plate of sweet rolls, I was sitting in the kitchen with Thomas attempting to discuss political philosophy. It wasn't going well. I was talking and Thomas merely staring, blinking if I said something particularly controversial. I was sandwiching some subliminal suggestions into the conversation every minute or two. Things like: "Gee, it sure is hot in here, isn't it? The heat always makes me sleepy. You must really be wiped out, what with no sleep for over twenty-four hours."

Thomas wasn't answering me.

But once Raydean burst through the back door, Thomas was a goner.

She bustled around like she was my mother, all the while talking about aliens and the destruction of the universe. Thomas, whose face I could now read like a book, watched her and blinked. At one point I caught his eye and whispered, "She's completely insane. Don't eat the sweet rolls, they're terrible. Just drink the coffee and she'll go away happy. Otherwise . . ." I let my eyes widen and I shook my head as if we didn't even want to go there. "She'll never leave."

Thomas blinked and began drinking the coffee she put in front of him. He kept his eyes on her at all times, watching her sudden jerky movements as if he expected her to suddenly pull a weapon and shoot him. The fact that she wore a slick yellow raincoat over her housedress and had Marlena the Shotgun tucked into a specially made holster that stuck out of the thin raincoat lining seemed to only increase his vigilance.

"Look at this!" she commanded, while pouring more of the thick sludgy liquid into his cup. She set the carafe down in front of him and slowly pulled up the hem of her dress. Strapped to her white, wrinkled thigh was a small silver gun.

"Cool, huh?" she said. She looked up at Thomas, her bird eyes twinkling with a maniacal gleam. "They sneak up on me and I shoot their little gonads off."

Thomas reached for his cup and downed the coffee. Thirty minutes later he was snoring with his head on the table. Raydean smiled and high-fived me.

"I say we bury him out back when it gets dark," she said. "Fertilize the property."

"He ain't dead, Raydean."

Raydean nodded, grabbed a handful of his hair and pulled his head up, letting it fall back to the table with a loud thud.

"He would be after we buried him," she said, smiling.

Twenty-three

I pulled into a parking spot right in front of the Oyster Bar at eleven A.M. on the dot. The sun was glinting off the plate-glass window that showcased the interior of the tiny place, so it was impossible to see who or what was waiting for me as I stepped out of my Camaro. The row of chopped Harleys in various states of disrepair let me know I'd hit the right place at the correct time.

I took my time locking the car, hiding behind my sunglasses as I tried in vain to scope the place. I figured inside they were doing the same thing. I was dressed for success, wearing black spandex capri pants, little spiky slides, and a leopard-skin tank top underneath my own black leather motorcycle jacket. My hair was piled up high, with some curls escaping for effect. My mace was wedged in the back waistband of my pants for easy access, and my sweet little Spyderco knife was deep in my right front jacket pocket.

Make no mistake about it, I knew the odds of me successfully taking out a small cluster of bikers were about the same as me winning the lottery and receiving a proposal from Prince Charles, but a woman has to make the effort. I figured to take at least three of them down with me if the situation turned ugly.

I stepped up to the front door, pushed it open and stood just inside, letting my eyes adjust. The place wouldn't seat more than fifty at best, but I didn't have to worry about finding my party. They were sitting at a back table, close to the bar, and not one other soul sat at any other table.

I heard movement behind me and turned just in time to see a guy wearing a white apron and sporting an early-morning case of five-o'clock shadow. He was locking the door behind me and flipping the sign to read CLOSED. His arms looked like sledgehammers, and when he smiled, I could see he was missing a top front tooth.

The table in the back looked like a display at a tattoo convention, or a before picture for Weight Watchers. Frankie, sporting a new clean-shaven witness-protection-program disguise, looked up at me from his seat against the back wall. He was pinned on either side by two huge men and he did not look happy. In fact, he looked frightened. Great, I thought, another mess.

I started walking toward them, even before my brain could swing into action and figure out a plan A with a follow-up plan B. The deal is to look unafraid. Never let a big man see you sweat. In fact, never let any man see you sweat. Men are, in essence, like toddlers and dogs; they smell fear and they take advantage of it every time.

So I'm standing extra tall and I'm scoping them out to see who is likely to be Dimitri, the big man. It didn't take a brain surgeon to figure it out. Dimitri was the one who sat with his back to the wall and his eyes on the exit. He would be the first to spot trouble and the last to be openly attacked. He would be the one with the best shot at drawing a gun and blowing away half the people in his way before slipping out the kitchen exit. In a nutshell, Dimitri was the one who ensured his own safety, while at the same time commanding the attention of anyone walking into the bar.

He was leaning back in a plain wooden chair, watching me approach. He had one of those blue-black faces, the kind where his beard growth was so thick it made his skin look an inky bluish color. His eyes were black holes and his eyebrows almost met in the middle when he frowned. His chin had an ugly scar right down the center that divided it into a deep cleft. He had more tattoos than the others, and I found myself staring at his left arm. A snake slithered across his upper arm, twisting around the length of his forearm and across the back of his hand. The head sat, with bared fangs, just above the space where his little finger should've been. It was missing and I guess the implication was supposed to be that the snake had bitten it off. I shivered and reminded myself not to shake hands.

Dimitri pushed the sole chair out from the table with his black booted foot.

"Have a seat," he said, and his voice sounded like two slabs of concrete scraping against each other.

"Thank you," I said, and sat in the chair that would make me most vulnerable. I was across from Dimitri with my back to the exit and with two guys on either side of me who could've prevented me from leaving had I wanted to attempt such a foolish move.

"Thanks for seeing me," I said, smiling as if he was a friend of mine. Dimitri took it in and stared back at me without expression.

"You can thank Frankie," he said. "It was sort of a last request."

Frankie attempted a smile and failed. I'd never seen him look so frightened. In fact, I'd never seen him look frightened at all.

"Last request?" I said, shooting my eyebrow up like I wasn't sure I'd heard right.

"Yeah," Dimitri said, starting to smile softly, like a cat with a big secret. "He's retiring from our organization. In fact, we'd pretty much written him off as lost to us when he turned up. Now we get to say the real good-bye."

I looked around the table and couldn't read one face. Some of them looked at Frankie, working to make sure they made eye contact. Some of them were watching Dimitri. I couldn't figure what was going on, but it didn't look good for Frankie. Why had he gone to the trouble to hook me up if this was going to be the end result?

"Whatever," I said. "I guess he gave you the picture?"

Dimitri nodded, but said nothing.

"Okay, then. You know that I got no interest in what was going down with you people. All I want is information. I want to know what you saw. I want to know who shot that little pissant, because I know it wasn't Vincent."

Dimitri's eyebrows thickened. "I don't give a fuck who did it. It wasn't us, that's all you got to know."

All right, I'm thinking here that Dimitri is certifiable. What, I'm supposed to believe him because he says so? His guys didn't kill Denny because *they* say so? Right.

"Frankie says you got a member of your team who saw the shooter. Is that right?"

That's when the entire table seemed to stiffen and become uncomfortable. Dimitri looked at me, his eyes boring into mine.

"That would be true," he said.

"Okay." I looked around the table. "Which one of you saw Denny's killer?"

Dimitri didn't even look at them. His eyes remained fixed on me, as if he were absolutely confident that not one of them would speak. And they didn't.

"Well, now," Dimitri said, "that's unfortunate. You see, Tinky is no longer with our organization."

I guess I lost it here. I looked at Dimitri and before I could stop it, my mouth was in gear and my brain had fallen into a shocked stupor.

"Organization? No longer with your organization? What is this shit? You're bikers. You don't have an organization. You have a gang. You rob and murder people. There's no organization. No 401(k). No dental plans and vacation days. What is this shit? Now where is Tinky and how can I talk to him?"

Frankie slowly lowered his head, shading his eyes with his hand and looking as if it were all over now. That's when the connection hit me and I began to realize where Tinky was, or, at least, where he had been—in Dennis the Whiner's garage. Nailor had told me his nickname, but I'd temporarily forgotten.

Dimitri leaned in toward the center of the table and rested his elbows on the slick wooden surface.

"What I mean by 'no longer with us' is this: He is literally no longer with us. Tinky didn't retire or get fired. He got his ass shot while paying his last respects to a punk-ass wanna-be and gathering some information we thought we needed to have. He can't talk with you now on account of he's laid out down in Port St. Joe, awaiting burial."

I sighed. "Then why am I here? Why didn't you just call and tell me this over the phone?"

Dimitri smiled. "Because now we have a problem." He leaned back and looked from me to Frankie. "You see, Frankie here fucked up and he knows it. He told you that we robbed your club. Now whether that matters to you or not is no concern of mine. The problem at hand is now you can identify us to the police. That," he said, shaking his head slowly, "is unfortunate."

I leaned back against my chair, stretched my legs out in front of me, and jammed my hands into the pockets of my leather jacket. I felt the canister of mace press against my back and curled my fingers around the knife in my right pocket.

"I'm sure Frankie came to you thinking he had a professional relationship and that he was helping you out. So this is how you reward his loyalty? You don't keep the information to yourself, and instead you run to the police. You not only betray me and my people, but you fuck your friend Frankie here."

Dimitri stared at me. I looked at the others around the table. My act wasn't selling, so I worked it harder.

"Frankie didn't have to come to any of us with a plan, but he did. I suppose he thought you'd be smart enough to take the chance to throw the heat off your group." I shrugged. "Oh, well, I guess he was wrong. You see, somebody else could take the entire fall, but youse guys have overlooked your opportunity."

Dimitri's eyebrows twitched slightly. He was listening.

"You could've set up the real killer, made it look like he hired people to fake a robbery, or actually do the robbery. It could've been golden. Now you're right, you do have a problem, but me and Frankie ain't it."

Dimitri started to smile. "Maybe I have another opportunity," he said. "Maybe *you* hired the gunmen to rob the place. After all, who better than an insider? Who better to make it look like the boss did the job and you're just a bystander?"

Dimitri leaned forward. "Maybe the payoff went wrong. Maybe Frankie didn't like that his team didn't get no money and you haven't paid him off yet. Maybe you and him go out to the landfill and somebody gets shot. Maybe two somebodies get shot, only one body is never recovered." His smile broadened. "Maybe my opportunities are endless. And maybe you thought all bikers are stupid. Your downfall," he said, "is stereotyping people."

He was looking at the others like there was a prearranged ending to our meeting, giving them the nonverbal cue that our fun was about to turn deadly. I gripped the knife, drew my legs back and prepared to react if they came for me. It was stupid. Me against them.

"Okay," Dimitri said, pushing back from the table and starting to stand. "I think I have other places to be and things to do." He looked down at me. "I'm sorry," he said, "I would've liked to have seen you dance." He looked at Frankie and his eyes darkened. He didn't say a word to him. He didn't have to say anything.

None of us saw the hit coming. One moment Dimitri was talking and the next his right shoulder was exploding in a burst of red and bone. It happened before the others could go for their guns. It came from nowhere and continued, a spray of bullets peppering the wall above our heads.

I hit the floor, scooting for security under the table.

"Don't move," a deep voice said. "I can kill every one of you."

I froze. Then I heard something that disturbed me far more than anything else.

"Chief," Raydean said, "just let me get his other shoulder for you, even it up." I peaked out from under the table. Raydean and Moose Lavotini stood side by side, only Moose was looking irritated and Raydean was looking smug. Moose had a big black gun trained on the bikers, and while he was frowning, he wasn't directly looking at Raydean.

"I thought you were going to stay in the car," he said. "I thought those were the conditions."

Raydean shrugged. "Desperate times call for desperate doin's," she answered. "Besides, Marlena here heard the shooting and just couldn't resist the fun."

There was a huge explosion as Raydean fired her gun into the wall above Dimitri's head. He screamed and slid further down, an angry trail of blood covering the wall behind him.

I slowly crawled out from under the table. Raydean was shoving Marlena back into the inside pocket of her yellow slicker and breaking into a broad grin at the sight of me standing before her.

She reached into one pocket and brought out a round box of snuff. She opened the lid, reached inside, and looked up to see me frowning.

"Raydean! What are you doing? You know that's bad for you!"

She smiled and showed me the inside of the little box. "Watermelon bubblegum," she said. "It's a turrible habit to break. I got me off the hard stuff, but this bubblegum'll slam you into the DTs if'n you try and cut it cold turkey."

Two men stepped up to join Moose, their guns drawn and trained on the crew of frightened bikers.

Moose slowly lowered his gun and turned to look at me. "I thought we had an agreement," he said.

"You had an agreement," I corrected. "I was along for the ride, remember? You weren't offering any terms or options. You were pretty much sliding the contract over and telling me to sign. You left me with a babysitter, remember?"

I looked at the bikers, all of them aching to kill us.

"You think I couldn't have handled this?" I asked. "I could've handled this. What do you think this does for my self-esteem, you stepping in here like this? It says you have no confidence in me. I could have to go back into therapy for this kind of shit."

Moose was looking at me like I had two heads, and then he laughed.

"You're fuckin' nuts, you know that?" he said. "Let's get out of here."

I looked back at Frankie. "Can I bring my friend?" I asked.

Moose looked like maybe he didn't understand, but when Frankie started to stand, he nodded. "The more the merrier." He looked at Dimitri, now unconscious from pain and blood loss. He made sure he made eye contact with each of the others, and then he spoke.

"It's like this," he said, his voice pleasant and neutral. "My organization is extensive and powerful. I believe all of you can remember a certain, shall we say, transgression that occurred in Fort Lauderdale last year after the Daytona Rally? That was me, my people. Don't make me repeat that lesson here. There are fewer of you. You don't have the manpower or the firepower to be more than a blip on our radar screen, so be forewarned. If you make life anything other than exceedingly pleasant for any of my friends"— and here he gestured to the three of us—"I will demolish you."

Moose paused for a moment, waiting to see if his words were sinking in. Apparently satisfied, he continued.

"Think about Fort Lauderdale. Look up the pictures from the local news coverage if you need a refresher, and then think of your own situation. Do you really want that kind of hell unleashed on your club?"

No one tried to speak. Lavotini motioned to his men, then gestured us out through the kitchen to the waiting limo. We stepped over three bodies on our way out, one of which was the man in the apron who'd locked us in. I looked at them as we went by and figured they weren't dead, but whatever Moose and his men had done, it had rendered these three very deeply unconscious.

When we got out to the parking lot, Moose turned to Frankie. "You got a weapon?"

Frankie was still scared. I could tell on account of his face was

164

closed and his eyes glittery-hard with anger and fear. All he did was nod at Moose. He couldn't even get words out.

"Good," Moose said. "Cover the lot until them guys get out here, then they'll take you where you want to go."

Frankie looked at me for a brief instant, then reached inside his jacket and pulled out a gun. This apparently satisfied Moose, who turned his back on Frankie and led me and Raydean to the limo. I looked over my shoulder at Frankie and tried to smile, but all I could do was stare into his eyes and hope he got the message that I was sorry. I barely saw his head move in an acknowledgment as he turned his attention to the back entrance. It was going to be a tricky leave-taking for the men inside. Frankie was ready.

The yelling didn't commence until the limousine door was closed and we were pulling away from the back entrance of the Oyster Bar.

"What were you thinking?" Moose yelled. "Were you thinking 'let me get my ass killed and take out some other innocent victims while I'm at it'? Because you had to know he was going to try and kill you. I mean, even a child would've known that!"

I wouldn't look away from him. I just sat there, aware that I was blinking and suddenly feeling like a kid getting yelled at by Pa. Being yelled at by Pa was different than being yelled at by a nun. When Pa yelled it was because he was right and because he was scared, scared for his kids or his wife. Moose was yelling just like Pa and I felt myself starting to feel really, really bad. I hadn't thought about endangering myself or others when I set it up to meet with Dimitri. I'd just been thinking about Vincent.

Raydean had started rocking, back and forth, trying to pull herself away from us and into some alternate reality where there was harmony. I looked at Moose, hearing the words come out of his mouth, not even listening. I was pulling a Raydean, taking myself out of the picture and running far, far away. This was made worse by me starting to cry. I really hate it when I do that.

"What are you crying for?" Moose asked. He stopped yelling

and leaned forward, genuinely puzzled. "What's with the crying? I'm pointing something out to you and you're crying? Stop that!"

Believe me, I was trying, but the tears just came faster and Raydean's rocking grew more frenzied.

"I could've handled it," I said, but my voice wouldn't squeak out any louder than a whisper. "I didn't know they were going to make a mess. I thought . . ."

"No," Moose said, his voice dead even, "you didn't think." He smiled gently and leaned back in his seat. "That's why I'm here, to help you think."

I wasn't thinking anything except that Moose was a complication. He was a complication that needed to go. He was large and handsome and dangerous—very, very dangerous. I didn't need a complication like that in my life. I closed my eyes and envisioned Dimitri's shoulder exploding. I shivered. If Moose hadn't intervened, Frankie and I would've been out at the landfill, fertilizing trash. But did he have to shoot Dimitri?

The answer was probably yes. Pure force had been necessary in order to take us out. Dimitri had been holding a gun in his hand, pointing at me. Moose really had had no other option, but he hadn't even hesitated. His facial expression had never changed. He'd fired his gun as if it were an extension of his arm, without conscious thought, it seemed. He had saved us, but all I wanted was to be away from him. His force was now directed at me and I didn't like that. He was scaring me.

"Okay," Moose said, breaking into a broader smile, "that's that. What happened is now in the past. We've all learned something here."

Yeah, right. I'd learned something all right. I looked at Moose and smiled, but inside I was a hundred-thousand miles away. I'd ease him off of us and send him back to Jersey. This was one volatile man.

I thought about it a little more. I'd learned some useful information, or rather, confirmed what Frankie had told me. The bikers hadn't killed Denny. There was no real payoff in them lying. There were a lot of other stories they could've told to make themselves look better or come out cleaner. Having an eyewitness biker wasn't one of them.

So Denny had been killed by someone at the table, someone who wanted Vincent to look like a killer or wanted Denny out of the picture. If Vincent went down on Murder One, he wouldn't be able to return and pay off his debt or take his club back. I thought about what Nailor taught me about homicide.

"People kill for three reasons," he'd said, "greed, revenge, or lust." I could not imagine anyone killing Denny to frame Vincent out of a lust motive, so it had to be greed or revenge. A lot of people thought Vincent was an asshole, but I didn't think anyone took him seriously enough to want him locked up for life in a Florida penitentiary.

That left greed. Someone had killed Denny with Vincent's gun in order to frame Vincent for murder and effectively get rid of him so they'd have a clear shot at Vincent's club. After all, the Tiffany was the only thing Vincent had that anyone else could possibly covet. It was, without a doubt, the best exotic dance club in Northwest Florida, perhaps even in the whole Southeast.

"All right," Moose said, "you're home, ladies."

We had pulled into my driveway and I hadn't even noticed. I looked at Moose Lavotini. He was staring at me, his face still and thoughtful. He was reading me, and whatever he saw in my face, it didn't make him happy. His eyes were pure black pools, and the smile that always seemed to change his face into something human and kind was gone.

"Sierra," he said, "I didn't mean to hurt your feelings. I just want you to understand that those people are dangerous. You can't go busting in on them with bravado and think that's enough to carry the day. You're in the big leagues now, honey. It don't work on bluster."

I nodded, hoping I could find my voice and realizing I didn't have a comeback for what was probably the truth.

"I'm leaving a couple of guys here," he said. "Outside." He

raised his hands, palms outward in mock surrender. "I won't put a man inside again, I promise. You two are dangerous." He seemed to notice Raydean rocking for the first time. "She all right?"

"No, she is not all right," I said, frowning. "You scared her, yelling like that. Don't you have any self-control? You know, anger can rule you if you don't rule it."

I took Raydean by the hand and tugged her out of the limo. I walked her over to my steps, sat her down, and returned to speak to Moose. I leaned down, ducked my head inside the car and looked right at him, aware that he was getting a clear shot at the cleavage that made the Tiffany famous.

"I'm grateful to you for pulling my ass out of the fire," I said softly, "but I want you to go away."

Moose frowned slightly and looked like he was about to say something but I wasn't giving him another shot.

"Thanks, but I can handle it from here on out."

"I frightened you," he said.

That was perhaps true, but there was a swirl of other emotions buzzing around my head like flies and I couldn't tell him what I hadn't yet worked out into words, so I shrugged.

"I run my own show," I said. "Thus far, I have kept myself alive. Today it might've gone down differently, but who's to say? I am grateful, but I like to work alone."

Moose smiled. "I can understand that," he said. "I work alone most of the time, too. But I'm thinking you and me do good part-nered up. So thanks for the brush-off, but I'll be keeping an eye out for you."

"No, thank you," I said, taking my time with each word and looking him in the eye.

"You're afraid, Sierra," he said.

"Bikers don't scare me."

"No," he said, "but I do. It's not that I shot Dimitri, or that I took charge of a bad situation. It's what's between us that you can't deal with, that something deep in the pit of your stomach that reacts whenever you look at me. I make you feel, and you don't like that. You like to run the show, but you can't run me, can you?"

I was out of the car doorway and up the stairs with Raydean before I could even allow myself to think about what he'd said.

Twenty-four

I started to make tea for Raydean and tried to take stock of the situation. I leaned against the kitchen counter and stared out the window, lost in thought, barely tracking the black sedan that sat like an armored tank at the end of my street. Thomas was gone, but Moose had us covered. I had to wonder how a syndicate boss from Jersey was so well connected in Panama City, but I knew he wouldn't have picked me up at the Philly airport without a complete plan and the manpower to back it.

"Sierra," Raydean said, "that pot's just a'boilin' away. You making tea, or are you trying to humidify the trailer?"

I jumped at the sound of her voice. When Raydean went into one of her noncommunicative states, she usually stayed that way for a day or two. Raydean was tough, but violence made her fragile.

"I forgot, I guess," I said. "I'm making you some tea."

She was standing by the bay window, staring down the street and shaking her head.

"Girl, I'm thinking you'd better opt for something stronger. We got us a situation here and I think it calls for Wild Turkey, not tea."

I reached for two mugs, ignoring her suggestion. The last thing Raydean needed was liquor.

"I know," I said, "it's a bit of a mess, but at least we've narrowed the field a little. The cops'll be looking for bikers and we'll be looking in the right direction."

"The cops won't be looking for bikers, Sierra," Raydean said. "They'll be looking for you. Honey, didn't you leave your car in front of the Oyster Bar?"

A cold chill spread over me. Stupid, stupid, stupid . . . again.

"And don't think about going to get it now, 'cause it's too late."

I poured the steaming water into two mugs and attempted to put tea bags into the cups, but now my hands were shaking. So what? My car was parked in front of the Oyster Bar. There're a thousand reasons to be on Beck Avenue. I didn't have to be in that bar. I tried to relax, but Raydean went on.

"You talked to that boyfriend of yours today?" she asked.

The wave of sadness I'd been fighting swept over me. For a few short hours I'd managed to push him out of my mind, but now it was back, stronger and harder than ever.

"I'm thinking he might not be my boyfriend much longer," I said, my voice cracking as I spoke.

Raydean turned from her spot by the window and looked at me, her face wrinkling with a pained expression.

"What're you saying, honey?" she asked.

"I'm saying that his ex-wife is in town and she spent Christmas with him."

Raydean turned away, peered back out at the street and then looked back at me. "Where?" she asked.

"At his house."

Raydean smiled. "Honey, that don't mean nothin'. They were alone. It was Christmas. Maybe he was bein' charitable."

What? By letting her sleep in his bed? I couldn't say it. I couldn't tell her what I was thinking. The hurt sealed my throat and I couldn't speak.

"Men are creatures," she said. "They sniff over the traces, like dogs. It don't mean much. I mean, face it, he buried that bone a long time ago. You don't go sticking your treasure in a place what burned you. You move on. Honey, I seen the way he looks at you.

You're bone-hidin' material. You're where he wants to keep his treasure."

I placed the mugs of tea on the table and sat down.

"Why don't you quit looking out the window and come drink your tea, Raydean? We can't do a thing about Lavotini watching us."

Raydean turned and smiled, her eyes twinkling.

"No, babe, that we can't. However, you'd best be prepared for a little bone burying, 'cause that dog of a boyfriend of yours is making his way to the door. In fact," she said, stepping over to the door, "I'll be letting him in on my way out!"

Raydean picked up her mug and stepped over to the door. She opened it wide and poked her head out.

"You ain't got the sense God gave a dog," she said. "Look at you! No coat, no hat, and your ears flapping in the wind. Child, it's gotta be forty degrees out here and you're dressed for a summer afternoon."

Nailor murmured something in response, something heard only by Raydean.

"You trackin' them hired killers we got in that sedan?" she asked.

I stood up, hoping to intervene before Raydean blew the whole deal wide open, but Nailor was too quick.

"Same ones as gave her a ride home from the Oyster Bar?" he asked casually.

Raydean shook her head and smiled. Nailor was standing on the stoop, watching Raydean evade the question.

"What oyster bar?" she asked. "Sierra, you been to an oyster bar and ain't told me? You go last night or what?" Raydean shook her head, her frizzy gray hair never moving under the weight of all the hair spray she'd used to hold her pin curls in place.

She looked back up at Nailor. "You mean to tell me that girl snuck off again and went to eating aphrodisiacs alone?" She turned her head in my direction. "You mean we've been sitting here the better part of all day and you ain't told me about them oysters?"

Smooth operator that she was, Raydean had alibied me and attempted to distract Nailor, all with one movement. Too bad Nailor wasn't biting. He stepped past her, cool as the proverbial cucumber, and stood in the doorway. Raydean looked at me and shrugged.

"Well, I'll leave you kids to it," she said slowly. "But let me tell you one damn thing, Detective."

Nailor turned in time to catch Raydean's sudden change in expression. She looked angry now, ferocious even.

"What's that, Raydean?" he asked.

"You hurt my girl any more than you have and I'll come hunting you. I'll scalp that little ass of yours and pin it to my birdbath, just so's the others can see what we do to them what causes undue hardship."

To anyone who didn't know him, Nailor looked puzzled. But I caught the sideways glance he shot in my direction, the little question of "do you know about Christmas?" I saw the flicker of doubt and the quick return to a neutral, open expression that gave nothing away. I'd learned to read him all right, only now it was too late. It didn't matter how well you read someone if his heart belonged to someone else.

"Well, Raydean," he said, "I thought you knew me better." Nailor was acting hurt. "I wouldn't harm Sierra. The only people who get on the wrong side of me are the ones who don't tell me the truth."

He was staring at Raydean like she might understand this, like she might have been tempted to lie to him. His face seemed to say he was sure she and I weren't liars. Too bad I couldn't say the same for him.

Raydean walked past him, down the steps, her back stiff and her head held high. "Be careful what you ask for, Detective. You just might get more than you bargained for." She marched on across the street, stopped at the edge of her booby-trapped front yard, and stared back at the two of us. Her eyes focused on me and she smiled. "Remember honey, the Lord loveth a cheerful giver."

Her attention switched to Nailor. "But let he who is without sin cast the first stone," she said. Her voice thundered out across the silent trailer park, bouncing off the metal trailers and echoing down the narrow street. Raydean had spoken.

Nailor turned and looked at me. His eyes darkened, his face remained neutral, but I knew we were headed for trouble and if he didn't start it, I would.

"I thought you were going to call me and let me know when you were flying back in," he said. His voice was husky and controlled.

I stood blocking the doorway, letting him shiver in the cool December air.

"I did call you," I said.

"When?"

I just looked at him and then I stepped backward, closing the door as I went. He stuck his foot out and blocked the door, and the next thing I knew we were in a full-out battle.

I pushed the door against his foot, not caring that it had to hurt, in fact, wanting it to hurt. He stuck his hand out, gripping the frame and calmly exerting pressure until I could hold the door no longer.

"What the hell is going on, Sierra?" he asked.

"What the fuck do you think?" I turned away from him. "You think I don't keep my word? You think I don't call? I called. I called and called all day on Christmas."

Nailor knew. I knew he had to know, and yet he persisted in playing dumb.

"There was no message on my machine."

That's when I lost it. I whirled back around, facing him. I could feel the heat staining my face. My eyes were blurring with the kind of tears that come from anger and pain and, worse than that, betrayal.

"There was no message because the machine wasn't on. I didn't figure Carla would tell you I called, so I tried over and over again," I said. "I called until I knew for certain you weren't going to answer. I paged you, too."

He reacted then. The color drained from his face and he looked as if I'd punched him right in the gut.

"When did you call my house?" he asked, his voice almost a whisper.

"Christmas morning, about seven."

"And Carla answered?"

"You could say that," I said. "She thought it was you. She wanted to know why you left. She said she woke up and you were gone."

Nailor sighed, an explosion of spent air whooshing out into the room. It was as if all the hope he had left in the world was leaving with that used-up air.

"I'm sorry," he said.

"Yeah, well, me too."

We were staring at each other, looking into each other's hearts and trying to sort it out, but the words weren't there. There was no decent explanation.

"Sierra," he said at last, "it's not like what you're thinking. She was—"

I interrupted. "You don't know what I'm thinking," I said. "And it doesn't matter what she was, it's what *you* were that courts. You were with her. The rest is just window dressing. Bottom line: You were with Carla."

His shoulders drooped. "But not like that," he said. "She was alone. She was stuck in Tallahassee working a case. It was late. She couldn't get back to Miami and it wouldn't have mattered anyway, because she doesn't have anyone there."

I just looked at him, my face frozen into a neutral mask that said nothing, gave nothing, and expected less.

"I was alone. She was alone. It wasn't anything other than—"

"No," I said, "it was just exactly what it was. Here's a woman who's done nothing but dump on you and you take her in? You offer her Christmas Eve because you don't want her to be alone? Well, here's how I see it."

I took a deep breath and launched in. There was no stopping it now. I was out of control.

"I know you didn't sleep with her; that's not the issue. But if she can treat you like she has, try to ruin your career, leave you, and you still take her back in, then you're not finished. You and Carla aren't a done deal. You've got feelings for her in the face of her treating you like a dog. And you want me to believe that you and I have something here?"

I shook my head. "I don't know that you have room in your heart for another relationship right now. You can't double park love, big man. It just don't work that way."

Nailor's eyes were still dark, deepening as I spoke. I was hurting him, chipping away at what we had and I knew it.

"And I suppose you're an expert at availability?" he asked. The darkness had been replaced by an angry glint.

"I was trying to be," I said.

His shoulders sagged again. "So was I." He took another deep breath, looking like he was gearing up to tell me something I wouldn't possibly believe. "Honey, there wasn't anything to Carla staying at my house, can't you see that? Sierra, don't you know that I love you? Why would I try so hard to get past those thick walls of yours if I didn't love you?"

I shifted my weight, leaning against the counter and studying him. The truth was, I did sort of believe him, but wasn't that always my problem? Didn't I just always believe them when they told me something, and didn't I just always end up wrong? Was it any different this time?

Nailor's pager went off before I could answer him. He swore under his breath and reached for the wall phone, dialing the number to the police department without thinking, still looking at me, reaching for me with his eyes. Trouble was, I was falling for it, stepping toward him, watching my body move and respond to that unspoken thing that ran between us like a hot current.

By the time he reached the dispatcher, I was in the circle of his arms, my head on his shoulder, my heart in his hip pocket, and my mind going ballistic with the unreality of it all.

"Uh-huh," he said, his voice rumbling through his chest, his arms tightening around me. "When will I be able to interview him?"

Nailor listened, silently kissing the top of my head. I leaned into him, missing him, missing the way it was before it all got so complicated. I was mourning the way it was when I didn't know and didn't care if he still harbored feelings for his ex-wife. But I knew now. I knew that despite what he said, he couldn't be ready for me until he was through with her.

And in a way I felt relieved. After all, I didn't have to deal with the big question, the "what next?" that always comes when you know you love each other and you want to spend all your time together. We didn't have a "what next?" yet, and that was fine by me.

But in another way, I was hurt, pretending to be relieved. Wasn't I special enough to drive Carla out of his heart? Or was it even me? Maybe it wasn't all about me. I shook my head slightly and nuzzled closer to him, smelling the leathery scent of his cologne, closing my eyes and recalling the way it was to lie in bed with him, skin touching skin.

Nailor said, "Post someone outside the room. Notify me when he's awake and I'll be down." He listened for another moment, then hung up. He didn't move, didn't try to release me. He just stood there, barely breathing, his breath warm against my hair.

"It will be all right," he said, his voice soft and deep. "We'll get this sorted out and we'll get through it."

I didn't say anything. I couldn't say anything because what was there to say? I couldn't agree or disagree because this was all new to me. Where I came from, you didn't work it out, you moved on or you got plowed under.

"Sierra?" he said, pushing me away ever so slightly.

I looked up at him.

"I need to ask you about the shooting at the Oyster Bar."

We were back on familiar turf—his turf—only this time I had the urge to turn it around. On any other day I would've played it closer to my chest, left out significant pieces of information, just in case he decided not to believe me and use what I told him against someone I knew was innocent. But for some reason I couldn't yet figure completely, I decided truth might be the correct flavor of the day for us.

"All right," I said. "I went to meet with that particular crew of lovelies because they robbed the Tiffany. I didn't so much care about that because they had information I needed. They had a guy who saw Denny get capped. We figured it to be mutually beneficial for me to know more about that on account of it would take the heat off them and put it more on the guy who committed the murder."

This was a little too large for Nailor to handle. He let go of me, took my hand, and led me to my kitchen table. He sat me down, pulled up his own bar stool right between my legs almost, and looked me in the eyes.

"You're trying to tell me that you were dumb enough to walk into a setup like that without backup? You really thought they'd tell you something?" He shook his head in disbelief.

"Hey," I said, "I'm here, aren't I? And who got fucked up over it? Not me." I made a point of examining my body while he watched. "Nope, I seem to be A-okay."

Nailor was fuming. "So you walked away knowing who killed Denny and it wasn't Vincent?"

"Not exactly."

"Not exactly you don't know who killed Denny or not exactly it wasn't Vincent?" The little twitch in Nailor's jaw started up. He was about to blow and I was almost enjoying it.

"The former not the latter," I answered. "I know who saw Denny get shot, but now he's dead too."

"What are you talking about, Sierra?" Nailor asked.

"The biker that got his neck broken at Denny Watley's house, Tinky. He was the witness."

Nailor shook his head like he was clearing it out, like I'd overloaded him. "I don't understand. What was he doing at Watley's house?"

I shrugged and touched his arm. "They said he was there to gather some information, but I didn't get to find out what kind of information."

"All right, then who shot Dimitri Logos?" he asked.

"Well, there was a small problem." I shifted in my seat, moving away from him.

"Problem? You're damn right there was a problem!"

I sighed. "It's like this: Dimitri didn't exactly think I was so trustworthy after all, and he didn't like it that someone told me all about the robbery. He decided the world would be a better place without me and—" I stopped right there, swallowed, unwilling to give up Frankie, and went on. "Well, without me and my friend in it. He was going to kill us." I smiled at Nailor like it was a big party and he was invited. "But another friend of mine showed up and convinced him otherwise."

"Names, Sierra," Nailor said.

"It really was shoot or be shot," I said.

"Names." Nailor wasn't coming off of it. I thought what the heck? It wouldn't really be the end of the world. It was self-defense after all; Moose wouldn't pull time or even go to trial. And it might get the mob off my tail long enough for me to figure out who was trying to frame Vincent.

"All right, all right," I said, throwing my hands up. "I'll tell you." I looked straight at him. "It was 'Big Moose' Lavotini."

Nailor shook his head, stuck his tongue down in his jaw like he was really pissed, and looked back at me. "Yeah, right. Try again. It's not like I'm Vincent Gambuzzo believing every little word you say. You are not related to that gangster and I am not buying that a New Jersey mobster suddenly appeared and shot a biker who was threatening you. Now come on."

I shrugged. "Well, it wasn't like he was alone. Raydean was with him."

Nailor pushed back his bar stool and stood up. His face was hot with anger and his eyes glittered. "You know, I keep thinking it's going to change. I think maybe this time you'll grow up and realize this isn't a game, but no, you're still on planet Neptune, laughing at the police. It's juvenile, Sierra. Don't mess with an investigation because you're mad at me."

Part of me wanted to laugh, but the rest of me went off.

"You know, I didn't have to give you that information," I said. "I told you the truth and you chose not to look at it. So in the days to come, when I prove you wrong, don't forget I was straight up with you."

Nailor was already headed for the door. He stopped when he reached it, pulling it open wide and ushering in a blast of cold air.

"Relationships are about communication, Sierra, not games. I was straight up with you about Carla, but obviously you're not ready to see past being petty. I don't think I'm the one looking to avoid a commitment. Call me when you're ready to get honest, and I don't just mean about this investigation."

He was gone then, slamming the door behind him, leaving me speechless, amused, and horrified all in one. What in the hell was happening to us?

Fluffy picked this moment to wake up from her nap. She wandered out into the kitchen, sniffed my foot, and sauntered over to her dish. She leaned over to eat and farted.

"If only it were all that easy," I told her.

She dug in farther, half burying her face in the bowl, chowing down without a care in the world.

"You know," I said to her, "Nailor thinks I'm holding out on him. Isn't that funny? I tell him the truth and he doesn't believe me. What's that? And I'm the one feeling defensive."

Fluffy stopped eating long enough to look back in my direction.

"I know, I know. I've got to go with my gut and not my heart."

Fluffy turned back to her dish, lost in the pleasure of fine doggy dining.

"You gotta admit this," I said. "They're all the same. Same man, different address. And they think we're hard to live with!"

Fluffy sighed and continued eating. It wasn't anything she hadn't heard before.

"I say we move on," I said.

Fluffy liked this. It implied a car ride, or so she thought. She liked anything that involved sticking her head out the window and taking in the new scents of the day.

"You're right, girl," I said. "We need to go talk to the others. One of them killed Denny." Fluffy was practically prancing now. "And we oughta go see the widow, too. You know, just on the outside chance she'd know why her husband got whacked. Maybe we attack it from both those angles and we'll find something. Maybe I'll get my head back in focus. You know men can mess you up, girl. You let a man crawl inside your head and the next thing you know, you're lost, wandering around in a daze."

Fluffy was standing by the door, wiggling with impatience. Fluffy was past the point of caring about a man. She had her shit together.

I would've been right behind her, but the phone started shrieking just as I found the car keys, just as I realized I had no car. It was Raydean.

"The Lord works in mysterious ways," she said.

Sometimes I wonder if Raydean can read my mind. I mean, it is my experience that crazy people on the whole are a lot smarter than the rest of us. Raydean is a case in point. She always knows when I'm planning to go somewhere. Now, either Fluffy alerts her, or it's her psycho-ESP swinging into overdrive. At least that's the assumption I made.

"I need to borrow your car, but I can't take you," I said.

"Well, you ain't going anywhere no how, so it don't matter."

I figured her for stubborn.

"Really, honey, I'd take you, but I'm only going to talk to a couple of people. And if you think I can't get past Moose's men, well . . ."

Raydean cackled. "No baby, you don't get it. I mean you are stuck. The Lord giveth and the Lord taketh away. You read me?"

At that moment someone began banging on the door and Fluffy started barking and growling.

"See what I mean?" Raydean said. "You ain't goin' nowhere."

Twenty-five

$\mathcal{O}$pportunity stood waiting for me to open the door, and when I did, she smiled a big, fat Barbie-doll grin that had all the sincerity of a drunken husband on payday.

"Well, look who it is," I said, smiling back with my own version of a fatuous grin. "Fortune smiles on them what wait around long enough for hell to freeze over." I shifted a little. "If you're looking to switch professions, I might have a few tips for you. Otherwise, I'm open to suggestions."

The blonde from the deadly poker game that cost one man his life and another man his livelihood stood on my stoop. She looked unchanged from the last time I'd seen her, except her mouth wasn't open, screaming, as she ran past me and away from the shooting.

She was wearing a low-cut baby-blue sweater, and if you looked or, in my case, couldn't avoid looking, you could see the edge of her little angel tattoo peaking out over the crest of her breasts. Her hair was still spun cotton candy, blond with a pink cast to it, and her lipstick was tinted to match. You'd have thought she was making a professional call and not looking for a favor. And I knew she was looking for something because nobody like her comes looking to socialize without an angle.

"I didn't think you'd remember me," she said. "My nonstage name is Yolanda, but everyone else calls me Angel. I just need a little minute of your time."

There was a glint to her steel-blue eyes, a hint of determination and street-wise, alley-cat toughness.

"And what's that to me?" I said. I was still seeing the way she ran away when the gunplay started, still remembering that it wasn't her who ended up calling for help or even trying to aid anyone hurt in the shooting. No, this girl was strictly in the game to help herself.

"I want to talk to you because I hear you've got an in with the lead investigator on this case and I've got something to say that don't necessarily need to be said in a police station."

"So call him and tell him to meet you in the park," I said.

She looked anxious, bobbing her head back and forth in either direction, scanning the street, looking for something or someone that seemed to be breathing right down her neck.

"Could you just let me come in for a minute?"

Fluffy sniffed her foot and looked up at me. She was giving Yolanda the clearance to come inside.

"Fine," I said. "But I don't have all day, so let's cut to the chase, shall we?"

Yolanda stepped into my kitchen, looking back over her shoulder as she crossed the threshold, checking the perimeter one more time before the door closed behind her.

"It's like this," she said. "I was there at the game for a reason. I was working."

"Hired by who?"

She smiled, but not an anxious I-want-you-to-like-me smile. This was a canny, business smile, a let's-make-a-deal smile that curved at the edges of her mouth but didn't quite carry through to the middle of her lips.

"Listen," she said, "I'm not going to lay it all out and take the risk of getting hurt, or worse, without some financial consideration. If I talk, my business takes a hit. People come to me in confidence. If it gets out I rat on my customers, I'm out of business."

"Yeah," I said, "flat-backing's like that. They like to know they can drop a dime in the bucket without hearing it echo."

"Exactly," she said. "I'm like a priest."

I rolled my eyes at Fluffy. Pros are not confessors. Pros are working one angle and one head at a time, not like exotic dancers. We're your more holistic healers. We trade on illusion and talent, but the difference is, we really care about our customers. We know them. A lot of the guys are regulars. We know about their kids, their wives, and their failures. We know where it hurts and we listen. We don't gotta lay a hand on someone to make their every dream come true.

"Anyway," Yolanda said, "I want you to tell your detective something and then get back to me. You tell him I'm talking to him and only him. Tell him it's that way or I don't tell nothing. It's him. Alone. He can't tell another living soul, you hear? You tell him I got hired to keep certain individuals from thinking too carefully or noticing too much. Tell him I didn't do nothing wrong, but I saw plenty. Tell him I think it's worth setup money for me to start over somewhere profitable, like Texas."

I smiled right back at her. "So why are you coming to the police? Why not go directly to your customer?"

I saw the flicker in her eyes before she could hide it. She was playing both ends against the middle. What a stupid, risky thing to do.

"Listen, Yolanda," I said. "I hate to intrude on your business know-how here, but you might not want to piss this guy off. I mean, if you know something, have you considered you might be at risk?"

Yolanda laughed. "I can handle myself. I just want you to pass along my message: I know something and I'm not telling anyone a thing until I have some guarantees."

I shook my head. "Honey, the po-lice don't work like that."

Yolanda cocked her head and smiled, making her look like a pink and blue parrot. "Well, I'm ready to bet that they've got the wrong suspect and I got the right one. I'm marketable. I'm gonna sew this whole thing up, and cops just love shit like that."

It was driving me nuts. I wanted to jump across the three feet between us, grab her by the neck, and shake her until she gave in, but somehow she didn't look like the type to cave. There was a hard, brittle edge to her. No, she needed to be played.

"All right," I said. "Be back here tonight at eight. I'll have an answer."

"Bring the cop," she said. "And tell him to bring cash, and I don't mean petty cash. Oh, and tell him I want witness protection. You know," she said, nodding toward the exterior walls of the trailer, "like a house, a car, and an identity."

I laughed. "Unless you're talking offering up tapes and a confession, I don't think the Panama City Police Department can deliver on all that."

Yolanda looked at me, her eyes darkening to a deep, almost navy blue. "I think what I got is good, but remember, it vanishes like the wind if he talks or comes bringing a flock of police with him."

"Then stay out of sight. If you're holding a murderer by the tail, your ass is gonna get bitten."

Yolanda shifted her weight and looked toward the door. She reached in her huge leopard-skin tote bag and drew out a long-barreled gun. It glinted in the sunlight that bounced in through the kitchen window. It was a freaking cannon.

"Girl," she said, "I grew up on the street in Detroit. Don't no little low-life punk rattle my cage."

Whatever.

I watched as she stuck the gun back in her bag and turned to go.

"Eight o'clock," I said. "Here."

"Gotcha." She opened the door and walked outside. Fluffy stood looking after her, not at all inclined to follow her like she would any other visitor. Fluffy had made her mind up that this girl was trouble and it didn't bear risking her own little hide to be associated with her. Fluffy didn't do complicated either.

Twenty-six

I was a coward. I left Nailor a voice mail at his office. It was simple. I told him he could hook up with a potential witness at eight o'clock at my place. I told him the conditions and I told him she promised to have the real goods for him. I told him that, should I be absent, the key was under the doormat. But I couldn't say, "Make yourself at home." The words just wouldn't come out of my mouth. I didn't want him comfortable and I didn't want him to think of my place as his home. Not now. Not in light of everything that had happened.

After I'd left my message and disconnected, I just stood there, staring at the receiver like an idiot.

"Fluff," I said, waking her from her twilight sleep, "let's ride." I picked a name from the hat of suspects and decided to start investigating. After all, a bimbo like Yolanda was probably looking to work an angle. Just because she said she could wrap up and bag the case didn't mean she could bag it with the right guy. No, it only meant that she felt she could produce something that would advance her own lowlife career.

I walked across the narrow street to Raydean's house. As usual, Raydean opened the front door before I could knock the secret it's-just-me knock. She handed me the keys to her ancient 1962 Plymouth Fury and looked back over her shoulder.

"You need me?" she asked. "I'm receiving a message and it

might be important." In the background the TV was blaring and Oprah was talking about finding her spirit. I stared at it for a second then looked back at Raydean.

"You got a message coming in from Oprah?" I asked.

Raydean looked at me as if I'd lost my mind. "No, honey! What do you take me for, a soccer mom?" She snorted. "I'm waiting on my stockbroker to call. He was checking out this new biotech company, gonna let me know was it worthwhile." She laughed. "Oprah! What? Are you the last to know?"

I raised a puzzled eyebrow.

"Oprah's the Defender of the Universe," she said. "She's got one eye on the Flemish and the other on God. And honey, ain't a one of 'em gonna make a move in the wrong direction while she's at the helm!" She looked back at the set. "Now," she said, turning back to me, "git on with it. I got to wait by the phone. Just call me if you need reinforcements. I'm sure you can handle whatever comes up. They're only humans after all."

Before I could answer, she closed the door, leaving me on the outside and her on the inside receiving the true message. It was amazing.

Fluffy and I pulled the gray tarp off of the Fury, backed it out of Raydean's leaning garage, and started on the road toward the beach. A little pine-tree air freshener hung from the rearview mirror, swinging back and forth like a metronome. Fluffy watched it, her head gently swaying in time with the tree.

"You are getting sleepy," I said to her. "Very sleepy."

Fluffy ignored me.

"When I count to three, you will become a German shepherd." Still no response. "One . . . two . . . three," I said, my voice a perfect monotone.

Fluffy barked, startling me. I looked over and she was smiling.

"You are a ferocious German shepherd," I said.

Fluffy's grin grew broader.

"I could use a dog like you in my outfit. I am on the trail of a vicious killer and the only troop I have is a little pissant dog named Fluffy."

Fluffy snarled. Apparently the word "pissant" had thrown her off.

"A dog like you, Fritz, is a dog to take into battle. We will defeat the enemy! We will defend the lives and reputations of our fellow countrymen!"

Fluffy jumped to a standing position now, swaying against me as she yapped at the tiny pine tree. Maybe there was something to this hypnosis junk. Or maybe Fluffy had a phobia of air fresheners.

I pulled into the parking lot of the Busted Beaver and prepared to do battle. I looked over at the Fluff. She was snarling now, rehearsing her lines as a vicious attack dog, or more likely, feeling carsick from having stared at a swaying pine tree the entire ride over to the beach.

"I shall return. If I am not back by nightfall, go on without me," I said. "Don't look back on this chapter of our lives together," I said solemnly. "It is enough to know that we served side by side in the valiant campaign that was Vincent Gambuzzo's murder rap."

I pulled the rearview mirror over where I could look into it to adjust my hair and put on more Passionate Red lipstick. When invading enemy turf, it never hurt to use all the weapons at one's disposal. And Izzy Rodriguez was not an enemy to be taken lightly.

Izzy's place was a slum, a low-slung pink concrete cinder-block ghetto of a strip joint. I wouldn't dignify it by calling it a club. A club connotes class, and the Busted Beaver was as close to low class as you could get without being illegal. It was a dirty, sleazy bar that found itself haunted by the liquor control board and the police.

Izzy's girls were the worst in the business. They did what he said, not because they wanted to, but because they were doped-up, strung-out victims. They wore cheap polyester baby-doll negligees trimmed with fuzzy marabou that had flattened with age and the grime of greasy makeup and cigarette smoke. Some of Izzy's girls were no more than seventeen, maybe younger, and the rest were too old and too out of shape to be naked anywhere but in the privacy of their own homes.

I shivered as I stepped into the dark interior of the Busted Beaver, and it wasn't because the air-conditioning was set ten degrees below comfortable. Izzy's club reeked of abuse, physical and mental.

There was a stage against the far wall. A disco ball strobed colored lights in all directions, camouflaging everything about the dancers but their most basic body outlines. In the darkened room, by fractured, gyrating light, you couldn't see tattoos or scars or stretchmarks. But then, the customers in the Busted Beaver could've cared less. They looked for raunch, not style.

Izzy Rodriguez was sitting at the far end of the bar, smoking a cigar and watching me. When my eyes met his, there was no surprise. It was as if he expected me, as if he knew I would come to him.

I was more than tempted to turn around and walk back outside into the daylight, to draw a deep breath of fresh air and walk away, but I couldn't. This was something that needed to be done.

I kept my eyes on his, walking toward him at a slow deliberate pace, aware of the men who swiveled on their stools to watch me, aware of the strippers' malevolent glares from the stage. I was cutting into their tip money, distracting the few excuses for customers that might be so inclined as to reach into their pockets to produce a greasy dollar or two.

When I stood in front of him, he gestured to the bartender. "Hey, anything she wants, all right?"

The bartender nodded and I smiled. "I know alcohol is used to disinfect," I said, "but I doubt I'll be here long enough to become contaminated."

Izzy's face darkened, and a drunk sitting behind me snickered.

"What can I do for you, Sierra?" Izzy asked. "You can't be looking for work with that attitude."

I leaned my back against the smooth wooden lip of the bar

and stared at Izzy for a moment, trying to gauge the best way to crawl under his lizard-like skin.

"No, Iz, I'm not shopping for work, and if I was it wouldn't be here. No," I said, looking up at the stage then back to him, "I'm hoping to figure you out."

"Figure me out?" he echoed.

"Yeah, I'm just curious what a guy like you's gotta do to get a pro like Yolanda to shill a poker game."

Izzy's facial expression remained empty, but I thought I saw something flicker behind his eyes.

"I'm at a loss here," he said. "I don't know this Yolanda person. I believe you are trying to imply that I need to cheat to play poker, and I must assure you that I don't care enough to do that. What would be the point?"

As he said this, he appealed to the bartender and the few customers who were watching our exchange. He even managed a brief chuckle, but as I watched his hands, they began a nervous drumming pattern on the bar in front of him.

"Yolanda," I said, as if speaking to a child. "The blonde who was at the game where Denny Watley got capped."

Izzy smiled. "Ah," he said, with a knowing nod. "Angel, the tits with a body attached." Then he stared pointedly at my chest.

"You hired Yolanda. Why?"

Izzy turned and signaled the bartender to bring him another drink, then looked back at me.

"I don't need no pro," he said. "If I want somebody, I got a crew ready, willing, and very able." He looked at the girls lining the stage, all of them completely naked and working the poles. "See what I mean?" he asked.

"I'm thinking maybe you were looking for real talent that night, someone with half a brain, someone to keep the players distracted while you set up Vincent."

"That's nuts," he said, but now he was angry. His face reddened and his eyes glowed when he looked at me. "I'm a patient man,

Sierra. I put up with your shit when I came to offer Vincent's dancers some work. I figured you were just overwrought. But you're stepping outside of what I can tolerate now."

His hand tightened into a fist and he stepped down off of his bar stool, thus becoming a good four inches shorter than me. I was aware of a presence behind me, and when I turned I saw that two huge bouncers had materialized from the darkness.

"You don't come skipping into my club and call me everything but a murderer," he said. "You have overstepped the boundaries by a mile."

"Oh, did I leave that part out?" I said. "I beg your pardon. You are most certainly a murderer. I don't know if you whacked Denny or not, but I do know this—every time one of your girls dies from AIDS or a drug overdose, it's you. You're the one that takes in runaways and women too lost to figure out any option but getting naked. You're the one who sets them up and gives them drugs so they don't have to think about where they are and what they're doing, so they can offer themselves to anyone with a dollar to spare. You're the one gets them so strung out they can't do anything but flat-back it for their next fix." I sneered at him. "Yeah, I'm sorry, all right, I left out murderer."

I felt the bouncers on either side of me grab my arms and pull me backward. I fought to break loose, but their grips were like iron vises and I was powerless to get away. The only part of my body I could move was my mouth, and it was making up for the rest of me.

"How's it feel to deal in flesh, Izzy? What's it like to force women into slavery because they're craving a drug you put into their bodies?"

"Shut up!" he yelled. "You're nothing but a whore your-self!"

"Oh no, don't mistake me for a woman without a choice," I yelled back. "That's the thing about dancers, we choose. That's the thing about Gambuzzo, he don't take children. He don't take any-body that comes to him because she has to. And he don't take their souls by giving them drugs. He ain't you, Rodriguez. On his worst day, he ain't you on your best."

We hurtled through the doors and out into the parking lot. The two bouncers still had me in a death grip, but now they were out for fun.

"I bet you like it rough," one whispered in my ear.

The other one didn't say a word. Instead he screamed and dropped my arm. Fluffy, or maybe I should say Fritz, had galvanized into action. She had come at a dead run and launched herself right into the man's very core. When you're a chihuahua and vertically challenged in the powerhouse realm, you go for all the gusto you can get. Fluffy had tapped the mother lode. She sank her teeth into the man's crotch and shook her head back and forth, clinging to her prey like cheap cologne.

I kicked my one remaining restrainer with the sharpest point of my stilettos and reached into the back pocket of my jeans for my knife. I was on autopilot. I didn't think about what I was doing, I reacted. In a moment the knife was open and aimed at his heart.

I held it, weaving it back and forth in front of him, never giving him a solid target to aim for.

"You think I like it rough, asshole? Why don't you come on and try me?"

"Jesus, Sierra," a now-familiar male voice said, "do you ever give it a rest?" I took a quick glimpse over my shoulder and there he was: Moose Lavotini, accompanied by his entourage and one very sleepy Thomas.

"This don't involve you," I said. "This one I can handle on my own."

Moose was smiling, amused. "Looks like you and the mutt have it covered." He turned and started walking away toward his waiting sedan. "Come on, fellas," he said, "she's got it covered."

They were leaving. I looked back at the two bouncers and took a quick inventory. One lay on the ground and one was still standing, but backing away. Fluff was standing beside me growling like a German shepherd. Did I have it covered? I figured yes.

I looked at Fluffy and decided our work at the Busted Beaver was finished. "Come on, honey," I said, stepping slowly toward the car, keeping my eyes on my new friends. "Let's blow this pop stand."

Fluffy ran ahead of me, leaped up and through the open driver's side window, and waited for me to follow. The guy on the ground was struggling to stand, assisted by the other. The two of them looked like they were thinking about following up, but then they saw the Moose's car hovering on the edge of the parking lot and decided it wasn't worth the risk.

I cranked the Plymouth and pulled out of the lot and into traffic, the Mafia staff car right behind me.

"Fluff," I said, "this is not conducive to me conducting business. I can't hardly detect with a crowd following my every move."

Fluffy understood. At first I thought she was looking in the rearview mirror to track our followers, but then I realized she was hooked back up in her love affair with the scented pine tree.

Maybe it was time to check in with Vincent Gambuzzo.

Twenty-seven

Gambuzzo didn't look good in prison orange. He shuffled into the visitors' area, took a hard wooden chair behind a thick Plexiglas screen, and favored me with his best scowl. Without black sunglasses and a silk shirt, Vincent looked a lot more like his used-car-dealer genetic history than usual. The stubble on his chin wasn't helping either.

There was something else about Vincent. He looked beaten, defeated by his situation and left to hang, alone. His eyes had deep circles underneath the thick lids and his overall color was a pasty gray. He looked as if he didn't care and no longer expected to beat life at its own game.

I picked up the phone and leaned in toward him. "Big guy," I said, "how you doin'?"

He held the receiver against his ear and chuckled dryly. "How the fuck you think?" he said. But it was a weak response, not at all like him when he's pissed. "They got me locked in here eating prison food with a bunch of loser junkies and cons and you want to know how am I doin'?" He shrugged. "I'm fine."

"I'm working on it. Ernie's working on it. How's come you're still in here? Ernie didn't spring you yet?"

Gambuzzo stared at me, like maybe this was class and I'd been absent when they gave out the test information.

"Judge denied bail. Says I'm a flight risk. Me, a flight risk!" His lip curled, a tiny sign that the old Vincent was in there somewhere, lurking. "You know what it is," he said, leaning in toward me. "It's that damn DEA agent, and that," he declared, leaning back in his chair, "is your fault."

"Mine?"

"Yep, and don't we both know it. She knows you're knocking back the nasty with her ex. She's gunning for anybody you know. That's how's come they're looking to frame me on illegal gambling and dope dealing."

I shook my head. The drug angle and Vincent was all wrong. Vincent was about as anti-drug as anybody I knew, but the gambling charge, well, that was Vincent's karma kicking him in the ass. Still, why else would Carla get involved?

"Maybe they got you here on account of the murder charge and it was your gun with your fingerprints."

Vincent shrugged, like he no longer cared.

"Lookit," I said, "you gotta work with me here if you want me to help. Who's after you, big man? Who wants the club or you out of business?"

Vincent smiled. "Take a number," he said.

"All right, try this," I said. "Who among the guests at your game would possibly be looking to take you out?"

Vincent pretended to think this over. "Joe Nolowicki, the vice cop," he said sarcastically. "He was the arresting officer, but I guess he didn't want me bad enough to set me up. Now, Denny Watley was a nutcase, but I don't think he was looking for nothing. Besides, the victim couldn't shoot himself between the eyes with my gun just to frame me. That would be too damn good. Talk about cutting off your nose to spite your face!" Gambuzzo laughed.

"Get serious, would you?" I said. He wasn't even trying to help himself. "Tell me about your gun. If someone else shot Denny, when did they get your gun?"

Vincent shrugged again. "I guess when I dropped it. I was ducked down behind the table when Eugene and Bruno were shooting. I figured they was better shots than me, so I just dropped it down beside Eugene and kept my head low. I didn't see nobody else grab it, but then, who the hell was looking? I was trying to save my ass."

He looked sad, and I figured he was thinking back over that night. He shook it off and looked at me.

"Okay," he said, "Mike Riggs had already won the club, so he didn't need to set me up. Denny's friend was a first-timer. He was busy trying to keep a check on Denny, so that ain't no help." Vincent shook his head. "No, I figure you got to look at Rodriguez."

"Vincent, how'd these people get into the game?" I asked.

"Same as usual. They were mostly regulars, so that's why I didn't look to figure at Nolowicki as being a vice cop."

"How'd he get in?"

In the background I noticed a guard checking his watch and eyeing us. I was figuring visiting hours ended soon. We had to hurry.

"The vice guy got in on account of coming into the club and slinging money around on several occasions. He was slick about it, too. It wasn't no bum rush. The guy came in every two weeks, dropped a load, then left. You know, like he was traveling and only around every so often." Vincent looked disgusted. "They set me up good, all right. Even got me to invite my own cop to the game."

I wasn't going to risk letting Vincent slip back into his sludge pond of self-pity, not with time running out and the clock ticking.

"The rest were regulars?"

"Been knowing them for a long time," he said. "Except for that pro."

This was what I was looking for. "And who brought her?" I asked. I was aware of holding on to the sides of my chair, waiting.

Vincent laughed. "I don't recall. One minute we was all playing, the next a set of tits walked in the door. Eugene brought her back. I figured it must've been okay. Eugene don't let just anybody crash a game."

Now the guard was moving, walking slowly toward us, tapping the face of his wristwatch and looking at me like I should get the hint.

"Looks like I gotta go," I said, and stood up, the receiver pressed against my ear.

Vincent took a quick glance over his shoulder and turned back to me. "Get me out of here, honey," he said.

I looked back at him and nodded on account of I didn't think I could speak. Vincent begging. It had come to Vincent feeling like he had to beg, and beg me no less. What were we all coming to?

I left the jail with its shiny linoleum floors and its too-bright white walls, planning on making a beeline for the hospital. I knew I could find Eugene there, and maybe Bruno was feeling like talking.

I stepped out into the late-December afternoon and sucked in a lungful of freedom. Jails give me the creeps. I pulled my coat around myself and tucked my head down, heading for the Plymouth and Fluffy and a heater that worked like a charm.

Joe Nolowicki didn't see me. He was standing beside his unmarked car, talking into his cell phone and chewing on what appeared to be the same unlit cigar. I stood there for a second studying him. He looked like a run-of-the-mill high school algebra teacher, a little needy, a little like he sat in a recliner all weekend watching the college games and yelling at the players, loud, like they could hear him, like his advice could be in any way valuable.

I watched him for a little while longer, wondering what it was about him that made him such a good vice cop. How did he bust drug dealers? How could a guy who looked as out of it as Nolowicki get informants to give up their suppliers?

But then he turned and saw me, and I caught a little glimpse of the salesman in Nolowicki. He smiled at me like I was just the person he'd been looking to see, and I knew right then that Joe Nolowicki made his reputation off conning the cons better than they could con him.

"Sierra," he said, smiling. "What are you doing here?"

I pulled my sweat jacket tighter around my torso and crossed my arms. Had he forgotten our last encounter?

Nolowicki got it instantly. He dropped the smile and started over, backing up, revising his approach.

"Listen, I know you probably don't like me too much and I'm sorry about that. I had no idea."

"No idea?" Funny, I thought I'd made my feelings known.

"Yeah," Nolowicki pulled the cigar stump out of his mouth. "I didn't know you were hooked up with Detective Nailor and I treated you bad. I thought you were, well, I didn't know, and I want you to know I'm sorry."

He looked right into my eyes and I liked that about him. He was wrong, he was admitting it, and he wasn't afraid to ask me to ease up.

"Thanks," I said.

Nolowicki looked out at the water for a second then back at me. "Listen, I like your guy. He's a stand-up detective, but I know he doesn't know what to make of me. In fact, it wouldn't surprise me if he told you he doesn't like me too much. I come off that way, you know?"

His eyes looked like a basset hound's, big and pleading, so I cut him a break. "He hasn't said a word to me." Of course, he didn't have to say anything. I could tell Nailor didn't like him.

"They tell me I gotta work on it, quit coming on like a big know-it-all from the Windy City." Nolowicki sighed and let his hands flop to his sides. "You know, maybe that's why the wife didn't stick around."

I didn't know what to do now. I wanted to get going, but the man was spilling his guts. What was I supposed to do? I decided not to waste the opportunity. I could work him as good as he was probably gonna try to work me, that's what I could do.

"Come sit in my car," I said, giving him the Lavotini thousand-watt smile. "It's freezing out here. Let's talk." I led him over to Raydean's car, settled him into the passenger seat, and when Fluffy growled like a German shepherd, I gave her the back-off look, all the while smiling sweetly at my newfound informant.

"You know," I said, my voice honey, "you and John have been working like dogs on this case. The tension's bound to get to you."

Nolowicki nodded but didn't say anything. I waited, almost forgetting to breathe, waiting for him to toss me a bone, any bone that involved the police investigation. It only took a minute.

"I'm thinking out loud here," he said, "but I'm thinking that maybe this isn't about Gambuzzo and the club. Maybe somebody wanted that Watley guy dead and picked the chaos of the robbery as his moment. Maybe it was sheer chance that it happened the way it did, you know, like a lucky opportunity."

I raised an eyebrow like I was thinking it unlikely, but inside I was working it around in my head.

"Only trouble is," Nolowicki continued, "almost everybody hated Dennis Watley. He was just a little pissant pain in the ass that nobody liked and nobody wanted around."

I was waiting for the heater to warm up in the car, knowing it would be another five minutes and wishing it wasn't so cold outside. As the sun vanished, the little bit of warmth in the air seemed to go with it.

"Denny," I said. "Now, granted, he was an asshole, but why kill him just because of that? What is it John always says? People murder for greed, lust, or revenge. Now what has Denny got hanging him up by the balls?"

Nolowicki had started staring at the pine-tree air freshener, as seemingly transfixed as Fluffy had been, but he turned his attention away from it long enough to make eye contact as he spoke.

"Well, for one thing, him and Mike Riggs got into it on the dock last week. From what I can gather, Riggs pulled a fillet knife and promised to kill him."

I kept my face neutral and accepting. I wasn't about to let him know that this was such an unusual occurrence, him telling me something about an open investigation. Let him think Nailor and I talked this way all the time.

"Why was Riggs going to kill him?" I asked.

"Dunno. He denied it ever happened when Nailor and I asked him, and no one else seems to know." Nolowicki sighed. "And then there's Watley's friend, Turk Akins. Two years back Watley had a little fling with Turk's wife. Near as we can tell, Turk seems to have let it go. His wife was an alcoholic, pretty much of an albatross around his neck. She got herself killed driving drunk about a year ago. Only trouble is, we can't find Mr. Akins to ask him. He took off after we found that biker in Watley's garage, and not one person in town is willing to help us find him. Seems old Turk's the neighborhood nice guy. Everybody loves Turk, maybe most especially the Widow Watley."

"You think Turk maybe killed that biker because he knew he'd seen him kill Denny?" I asked.

"Now your honey says no, but right now, Sierra, we just ain't got a clue. I don't know. I figure if Turk was going to kill Watley, he'd have done it when Watley plugged his wife."

"I don't know, Joe, Vincent's looking better to me," I said. "There's more people looking to set him up than to do Watley."

Nolowicki thought it over. "Yeah, Watley could've been an accidental hit, just gravy on top of a bad situation. But it's not like you needed murder to pull Gambuzzo down. We had him on racketeering. And now there's the dope charges."

"You're wrong there, Joe," I said. "Vincent Gambuzzo is not a dope dealer."

Nolowicki looked at me and shook his head. "Well, I got him cold. He was dealing, Sierra, and you'll just have to make peace with that." He saw I wasn't going to back down. "All right, I guess we'll just have to disagree on that little point." His hand was reaching for the door handle and in a moment he'd be gone. I homed in on my last objective.

"So, you work much with Carla Terrance, you being in vice and all?" I tried to sound casual, but I knew the anxiety was right there on the edge of my voice.

Nolowicki gave me a strange look and then smiled. "Can't say as I do," he answered. "She's a little bit high-toned for my taste. Snooty. DEA and gotta do it all by the books. She's got an attitude, like she's entitled."

"What do you mean?"

"Well, you know, her being female and African-American. It's how they are."

I felt my entire body stiffen. Me hating Carla for being a manipulative bitch was one thing, but Nolowicki classing her as one of "them" and looking like it gave him a bad taste in his mouth was another.

"No," I said, "I don't know what you mean."

Nolowicki knew. He heard the tone and knew what would come next. With one fluid movement he opened the car door and stepped out into the early-evening air.

"I've gotta go," he said. "Nice talking to you." He left and the little pine tree started to sway with the vibration from the slamming car door. Fluffy stared after him for a second and then returned to staring at the pine tree. She growled, as if to remind me that she'd warned me about trying to manipulate for my own personal reasons.

"It was just business, Fluff," I said, but she ignored me.

I dropped the car down into reverse and pulled away from the jail. Nolowicki was sitting in his car, talking on the cell phone again. We drove past like we didn't see him.

"Okay," I told Fluff, "so you were right, he's an idiot. But we did score in the information department, didn't we? Now we have another angle to work. Mike Riggs threatened to kill Watley."

Fluffy barked once and then growled deep in her throat. It was suppertime. Even better, it was almost time to give Nailor the one thing he seemed to be looking for: a break in his investigation. Maybe after he talked to Yolanda he'd start thinking about me, or even better, me and him.

"Okay, girl," I called. "One more stop and then on to our just rewards."

Fluffy was staring at the pine tree again. She looked more like she was hungry rather than as if she were envisioning herself as a huge attack dog.

"Baby," I said, "don't fall for the two-dimensional fantasy. Hold out for the real thing."

But Fluffy didn't seem to hear me. I was talking to myself.

Twenty-eight

$\mathcal{E}$ugene was sitting with Bruno, the vinyl armchair pulled up close to the hospital bed. Having spent nearly a week in the hospital, Bruno was pale with a beard that had grown in the absence of the strength to shave, thinner than I'd ever seen him, changed by the opportunity to cheat death.

Eugene looked the same as he always did, tough and vulnerable, a Papa Bear in gangster clothing.

I walked around Eugene, leaned in over the rail, past the IV pole, and right down over Bruno's face.

"Recognize these?" I asked.

Bruno smiled. "I dunno," he said. "Here, let me check." And before I could move, he reached up and squeezed the girls, gently but with a firm, familiar touch, like they were friends. His eyes were closed and he was smiling.

"Yeah," he said, his voice a deep caress. "I remember them now." He lay there for a moment and then a look crossed his face and his eyes popped open. "I thought I was dying, Sierra."

"You were, big man," I whispered.

"Hey," Eugene said. "Is it enough with the emoting? I'm in the middle of this and I ain't got my hands on shit and I gotta watch this?"

I straightened up and Bruno sighed, the moment broken. "The real thing," I heard him whisper. "Not an implant in the house."

I grinned. "No shit, Sherlock."

I looked at Eugene. He was actually looking a little worse than Bruno.

"Have you slept? Have you eaten? Have you even gone home this week?" I looked around the room. A tiny Christmas tree sat on the dresser across from Bruno's bed, against the far wall, under the TV that perched like a bird on a stand above everybody's head.

Bruno answered for him. "He's my fuckin' mother," he said. "He only left when my real mother showed up, and that was only because Tonya grabbed him by the short hairs and took him home for a little R and R."

Eugene attempted to put on his game face and failed, a small smile creeping out at the mention of Tonya the Barbarian.

"So that's how it is, huh?" I said. "Amazing what comes out of tragedy." I looked back at Bruno. "When they springing you?"

Bruno smiled again. "I got me a private-duty nurse," he said. "Gonna come to my house. Her name is Cheryl."

I shook my head. There was an overload of testosterone in the room, but on the positive side, Bruno was back in the game. The tent forming under his blanket was a sure sign that my friend was on the mend.

I turned away from Bruno and locked on to Eugene. "I need to ask you something."

Eugene raised his eyebrows in a question. "Yeah?"

"Vincent says you brought that pro into the game, led her into the back room, I mean. I figure you wouldn't do that without knowing who she was or what the deal was. I need to know about her."

Eugene's face hardened; he was working, thinking back in his mind to the night and the lead up, seeing it happen before his eyes.

"Big Tits Walking," he said. "That's all I could think when I saw her. She came right up to the door, stepped out of a taxi, looked at me like I should know her and said, 'I'm here for the game.' "

Eugene smiled his warrior smile, his I-don't-give-a-fuck-what-you-say-you're-here-for-I-need-proof smile.

"I knew she was on the clock, but I wasn't sure. Then she says someone placed the call to her escort service and told her to show up here. She said the big man was looking for her, so I figured Mr. Gambuzzo called her in. I don't know why, because we got talent, but I was thinking maybe someone requested full service and not a lap dance." Eugene shrugged. "It could happen," he said.

I looked at him. It wasn't like Eugene to be stupid. I could see him falling for it on account of she had all the information, but to think Vincent would call a service for a customer? Still, it was an unusual circumstance, and he was losing his shirt, not to mention the house. But no, Vincent told me he didn't know her.

"So you let her in?"

Eugene shrugged. "She knew the stupid fucking password. You know that thing Vincent made up. Turtle."

I shook my head. "Vincent told you to bring back all the guests who gave you a password?"

Eugene smiled. "Ain't that just like him? Dumb fuck."

Dumb fuck, indeed. But at least I knew someone had called Yolanda, someone in the game, someone with the password. It narrowed it down for me; it was only the same old crew of suspects, but at least it wasn't the entire free world.

I wanted to give Eugene the business, to set him straight about S.O.P. at the Tiffany, but it wasn't in the cards. The door to the room swung open and we were all treated to a visual that I will carry with me for years.

Dr. Thrasher, small and looking like a virgin sacrifice, stood just inside the doorway with two of Tiffany's finest and most fully endowed on either arm. He looked like a kid in a candy shop, and there were lipstick marks on his cheeks and on the collar of his white shirt.

The girls were decked out like twins, wearing red-and-green sequined dresses that hit about mid-hip, and Santa hats with white pom-poms on the ends. One was a bleached blonde and the other was a deep redhead. Dr. Thrasher was about one-third in the bag unless I missed my guess.

"Bruno, my man," he said. "You win. I will release you tomorrow morning."

The girls giggled and tucked themselves in a little closer to the good doctor.

"Come on, honey," the redhead said, "I wanna go back to your place and play doctor."

Thrasher had the good grace to turn three shades of red. "Meg," he said, his voice cracking in his effort to remain professional, "I have to make rounds first."

The blonde tittered. "Ummm," she said, "if I put on one of those open-backed gowns, will you make rounds on me?"

I looked at the men. They were smirking.

"So what is this?" I said. "You guys bribed him to let you out early?"

Bruno hit the button on his bed control and raised himself up a little farther so he was eye to eye, so to speak, with the doctor and the girls.

"No, Sierra, the doc was gonna spring me. I just wanted him to feel my deep appreciation. All the girls are very thankful. They've been plaguing the good doctor. They all want to show their appreciation." Bruno smiled and Eugene outright laughed. "I had to work out a schedule so's we don't wear the doc out."

Bruno looked at Dr. Thrasher. "Take two every night at bedtime," he said, "and you won't have a headache in the morning."

Dr. Thrasher nodded seriously. "Ladies," he said, "I believe our work here is done."

And with that, they departed, wagging their tails behind them.

I looked back at Bruno and Eugene. "You two are pitiful," I said. "Effective, perhaps brilliant, generous to a fault, but pitiful."

Eugene smiled. "Fully automatic," he said. "It just comes to us, like brilliance."

Yeah, like brilliance, I thought, but not quite.

Twenty-nine

*I*t's dark by seven in Panama City. I was busting it to make it back to my trailer before Nailor. I had it in mind to take a shower and maybe look a little extra special by the time he arrived. I needn't have bothered. Eight o'clock came and went. No Nailor and no Yolanda. By nine, I was starting to feel like a prom date who'd been stood up.

It was after ten when I got the first alert from the guard dog. Fluffy was standing on the futon, growling. I sprang for the door, figuring for sure it was Nailor, guessing maybe I'd missed him and Yolanda, that maybe they'd rearranged the meet and had no time to tell me. But when I opened the door, I realized I'd made a serious tactical error. Izzy Rodriguez and Mike Riggs stood there. Mike was smiling, but unless I missed my guess and misread the fidgeting, he was nervous. Izzy, on the other hand, was your pro-verbial bird-eating cat, grinning like he had good teeth and fresh breath.

Fluffy was in full-tilt watch-dog mode now, growling, barking, and baring her teeth at my gentleman callers. In another chihua-hua, this might've been ineffective, but I knew what she was do-ing, she was calling in her red-dog mad-assassin squad, her backup, Raydean.

Between Raydean's outdoor baby monitor system and Fluffy's angry alert, it would be only a matter of moments before my callers lost their innocent illusions about threatening or harming me. Of course, I didn't count out what I was seeing from the corner of my eye, over their shoulders. A black sedan was creeping slowly down my street, lights out. The Moose patrol was on alert status too, or at least I hoped they were.

"So, youse guys are out looking for trouble or what?"

Mike glanced nervously at Izzy and then took the lead. "Sierra," he said, "we got off to a bad start and I can understand why you're mad."

I jumped in. "No, I don't think you could possibly understand. You see, understanding means you have sensitivity to the situation. What kind of sensitive man would come calling on a lady when accompanied by a slime-sucking snake?"

Mike's eyes widened but Izzy didn't react. He stood there staring back at me with a benign expression on his face. For some reason he had no concern. As short as he was and out without his protection, I figured he'd be at least watching his family jewels, but no, he was standing there like we were discussing another slime-sucking snake.

Mike Riggs shoved his grimy white captain's hat farther back on his head and scratched his scalp.

"I'm here to give you an opportunity," he said. He was hardening up a bit, trying to stand taller and look more like I should take him seriously, which I didn't.

"You're giving *me* an opportunity?"

Riggs looked over my shoulder, into the warm, inviting kitchen, past the growling, obviously hostile Fluffy.

"Might we come in and talk?"

"No. Say what you gotta say and get out." I adjusted my black spandex skirt and looked him dead in the eye. "I'm expecting company—po-lice company."

Riggs jumped a little, but Izzy wouldn't let him off. Izzy nudged him to continue.

"Okay," Riggs said, "okay. Here's how it is. It's a known fact that you are the best the Panhandle has to offer. The reason the Tiffany did as well as it did was because of you and the Bomber."

I was going to dispute the Marla title but thought better of it, nodding like I agreed, thinking I should listen so they'd get done and leave. I was tired of fisticuffs and wasting my brain power on ignorants. It was better to listen and get them gone the easy way.

"Your point?"

"Well, Mr. Rodriguez and I are talking about a merger. We'd combine and be the largest venue on the beach." He was waiting for me to act impressed, but that was a pipe dream, so he went on. "We're here to offer you a chance to be the headliner. We'd pay you large, give you your own dressing room, star billing, the works."

The charter-boat captain looked like he was believing his own sell. I was waiting for him to offer a 401(k) and health insurance, whatever shit he could make up to lure me into taking the bait.

"It's an opportunity for you and the girls to work again."

There, he'd said it, what he'd come to communicate. But just in case I wasn't hearing him good, Izzy stepped up to make it clear.

"You see," he said, "we didn't think you'd come if it was just you. But if you don't, I'm gonna personally blacklist them other girls all over town." He looked at me, his hot beady little eyes boring into mine. "You know I can do it. All's I have to do is say I don't want 'em and the other clubs will think they're worse scum than my usuals." He smiled. "Don't think I don't know what the Beaver's reputation is," he added. "And I can make it work for me. There's a clientele that loves the slut; that loves to know they can be bought cheap and thrown out. And now, Sierra, I'm gonna own the other side of the coin."

Riggs gave him a sharp glance, to which Izzy responded by slipping his hand up on the captain's shoulder and patting him like a dog.

"Me and my partner here are going to whisk them other clubs off the map. We'll expand. We'll be bigger and better and stronger than anyone else on the beach or off. So if you wanna work P.C.,

Sierra, if you want your friends to work, then you gotta play the game our way. Otherwise, you and your tramps can flat-back it, 'cause that's all you'll be able to do in this town."

I saw Raydean's porch light go out. The lights inside had already gone out, so there were no surprises when I heard the door to her trailer open and the screen door moan softly in the night air.

All of us heard Marlena's opening statement. The shotgun's blast reverberated, causing Mike Riggs and Izzy to drop to the ground in front of me. The men in the sedan flew out of the car, guns in hand, swinging them from side to side, alternating between covering the men on my porch and Raydean.

Raydean's voice rang out. "I think the party's over, boys," she said. "Let's us all take our toys and go on home."

Lights all over the trailer park winked out as the residents prepared for Raydean's assault against the alien intruders. The lucky thing for us all was that Raydean rarely hit anything but the streetlights. What most everyone didn't know was that Raydean could've taken the hairs off a flea's ass at fifty yards had she wanted to.

I looked down the street at Moose's men and felt them weighing their odds, felt them thinking they should shoot the crazy lady just as insurance.

"Thomas," I yelled, "Moose wouldn't like you to cause undue bloodshed. Raydean's my friend. Let us handle this our way."

Raydean never took Marlena's barrel off her quarry. "That's right," she called out. "You ain't got a dog in this fight. I got it covered."

None of them said a word. They remained behind the car doors, weapons drawn, watching.

I looked down at my two visitors. "You may rise," I said. "Go in peace or you will depart in pieces."

Raydean laughed. Izzy and Mike Riggs slowly clambered up onto their feet, and Izzy actually took the time to brush himself off, like maybe my stoop was dirty or something. Then he looked back up at me, the anger making his eyes sparkle in the darkness.

"You should think about what we are saying, Sierra. If you and your friends want to work around here again, you'd be wise to hook up with us. Otherwise I couldn't guarantee your collective safety."

I looked down at the little shrimp and resisted the urge to pick him up by the lapels of his slick polyester jacket and shake him until his teeth chattered and his eyes rolled back in his head.

"You don't frighten me, Rodriguez," I said. "I don't even have to import talent to take care of you. You are a pimple, an oozing, festering blemish of a person, and I don't do infection." I looked at Riggs. "I don't know what this worm has on you," I said, "but it ain't a quarter of the trouble you'll find if you lie down with this dog. He'll swallow you alive. Don't join up with him. Let Vincent pay you off when he gets out. Let the Tiffany go back to good management and walk away with a little profit. I'm sure Vincent will be generous."

Riggs looked at me, his eyes meeting mine for the briefest second. He was afraid, and I saw it.

"It won't be so bad, Sierra," he said.

"Then you don't understand the concept of eternal damnation like I do."

Raydean's voice rang out again. "Get thee behind me, you agents of Satan. Get thee offa that porch before I commence to blowing your bodies to tiny pieces a bit at a time!"

I looked down the street and saw our landlady, Pat, emerge from her trailer, her silvery white hair glowing in the light of the remaining streetlights. She was heading for Raydean like a gunfighter at high noon, right out in the middle of the street.

Mike Riggs and Izzy Rodriguez apparently decided to take the high road. They moved back down the stairs, making their way to Izzy's car like there was no particular hurry, but Riggs kept looking over at Raydean while Rodriguez took stock of the black sedan that waited in the darkness.

Pat just kept coming her pace slow and deliberate, her intent clear. Order was going to reign in her little kingdom and she didn't much care what she had to do to restore it. She had little tolerance for Raydean's paranoia and didn't particularly like it that I was always dragging Raydean into my schemes. It was just as well that our little vignette was ending before she could walk into the middle of it.

"Raydean," she said, "what in tarnation is it this time?" She looked over at me, checking me out to see if this was my fault, deciding that it was, and not liking the outcome.

Raydean slid the shotgun behind her housedress and smiled. "The Eagle has landed," she said, "and they are ours."

"The party's over," I sang softly.

"Who're they?" Pat asked, nodding toward the Moose mobile.

"They're some out-of-towners looking for excitement," I said. "I'll let 'em know to look elsewhere," I said. "Don't worry about it. They're not hurting anything."

Pat looked skeptical, her eyebrows drawing together in a frown. "Sierra, have you not noticed that they have guns and are crouching down behind their car like they're expecting a fight?"

"Yeah," I said, "but they're from New Jersey. It's like that there. It's sort of the way you say hello or do business."

Pat wasn't having any of it. "If you don't have a resident's sticker," she called to them, "you're trespassing. Now move it along or I'm calling the police."

I would've expected the Men from Moose to laugh at this or, at best, ignore it, but they did neither. Instead they quietly lowered their guns, got back into the car, and started the engine, this time turning on the headlights.

I looked at Pat in surprise, then noticed what they'd all seen and I had overlooked. Two of Panama City's finest squad cars were rolling down the street. Someone had called the cops already.

"Well," Raydean said, her voice slowing to a lazy drawl, "I can see my work here is finished." She looked at Pat. "Reckon we oughta duck into my parlor and have us a cup of Constant Comment?"

Pat looked at the squad cars and started negotiating Raydean's booby-trapped front yard.

"Wouldn't hurt, I reckon," she said. "It's a mite chilly out here. Besides, Sierra can handle this. It ain't no big thing, is it, honey?"

She was smirking at me like I was finally getting a dose of my own medicine, like a grandma saying, "Make a mess, clean it up." I didn't mind.

Raydean and Pat disappeared into the darkened interior of Raydean's trailer, and as I watched, the lights came on one at a time. The two squad cars were sitting in front of my trailer now. No one had moved to leave the vehicles. They were scouting the area, I figured, or worse, waiting on Nailor.

I breathed a sigh of relief when one door opened, but just as quickly sucked in more air when I realized it was Nailor.

"You all right?" he said, his voice echoing in the darkness, as warm and sexy as always.

"Fine," I answered. "Why the escort?"

Nailor was approaching the bottom of my steps. The coat was gone. He stood there in his dark suit, the white of his shirt a bright contrast to the tan that never seemed to fade.

"Well, I was on another call when I heard there were shots fired here." He glanced over toward Raydean's trailer. "I figured it might be the usual, but in light of you seeming to be a trouble-magnet lately, I wasn't altogether certain."

He was looking at me with those dark eyes, communicating on another level, checking in personally. When Nailor checks like that, I melt. I could stand to be checked like that on a regular basis, a dark-of-night, naked, regular basis. But I digress.

"She didn't show," I said. "And neither did you."

"Who didn't show?" he asked, genuinely puzzled. "What do you mean?"

I looked down at him standing there and felt a little twinge of fear ignite inside my gut. He really didn't know what I was talking about.

"I left you a message this afternoon at your office. Yolanda, 'Angel,' the girl from the poker game, she wants to talk to you and only you. She said she has information to give you in return for you hooking her up to leave town. I told her to come back here at eight and talk."

Nailor frowned. "So where is she? She get tired of waiting?"

I looked out into the darkness surrounding the trailer. Even with two squad cars sitting in front of my house, I felt exposed, not safe. The entire world was turning more sinister by the moment and I couldn't figure it all out.

"Didn't you get my message?"

Nailor shook his head. "I haven't been in all afternoon. Haven't even checked my messages. Why didn't you page me?"

I didn't have an answer. Why sound stupid and tell the truth? Hey, I would've paged you but I was feeling insecure? Nah, it was better to look like it hadn't occurred to me.

"I just figured you'd get the message."

Nailor started up the stairs, looking past me and nodding, like we should continue the conversation inside.

"It's no big deal," he said. "She didn't show. Happens all the time."

I didn't think so. I had a bad feeling about Yolanda, but nothing to connect it up with.

"So why are you here then?"

Nailor grinned. "So I need a reason? Okay, I thought I might bring your car when I come back later. You wanna get the keys for me?"

He followed me up the steps and into the kitchen, flipping the light switch off as he came through the door, plunging us into darkness and reaching for me with one sure, familiar motion. He backed me up against the refrigerator, his hands gripping my upper arms with a certainty, his mouth seeking, then finding mine.

"I miss you," he said softly, his lips brushing my ear as he whispered. "Wait up for me, will you?"

He reached up and took the spare keys off the hook by the door, leaned back and kissed me again, then started to leave.

"How long will you be?"

He shrugged, a movement I could see even in the darkness. "It shouldn't take long."

"A homicide?"

His shoulders dropped a little. "Yeah. Probably cut-and-dried, but it'll take a little time."

"What happened?" I was stepping closer to him now, not wanting him to leave, wanting to hear his voice go on and on in the darkness.

"Somebody shot one of the bouncers at the Busted Beaver."

The image of the two men flashed instantly into my head and I wondered which one of them took it.

"Dead?"

"Yep. D.R.T. Dead Right There." He shrugged again. "There's a shooting there once a month," he said. "It's a wonder nobody's died before now. Dope dealing. Bar fights. If it ain't one thing, it's another."

But I was interested now. "Who did it?"

"Don't know yet," he said. "Probably just another punk looking to rob the doorman. A drunk. Somebody with a record. We'll get him."

"Witnesses?"

Nailor laughed. "What, Sierra? You want a job? Nope. No witnesses. The bouncer went out to check the parking lot and didn't come back."

Nailor was leaving now, focused as I was on the shooting. I had the image of the black sedan driving off, leaving me to deal with Izzy's bouncers. Surely Moose wouldn't have sent his men back to take care of them?

I was thinking about Moose and the way he'd been so cold about taking out Dimitri the biker. But that was different, I thought. That was an immediate threat to my safety. This would've been a payback. I didn't think Moose would trifle with a simple payback, not on something as petty as that. He wouldn't risk getting tagged for murder for something that simple. Would he?

I watched Nailor leave, still not able to shake my doubts about Moose Lavotini. Then I remembered Yolanda and started wondering about her, too. Why hadn't she come back? A girl as greedy and street-smart as Yolanda wouldn't stay away from a possible paycheck. Where was she?

I stepped outside and looked up and down the street. There was no sign of anyone. The wind had started blowing and as I gazed overhead, clouds skittered across the sky. A front was moving through. Tomorrow it would be colder, probably gray and rainy. It wasn't my kind of weather, not by a long shot. Still, winter in Panama City beat the gray slushy winter of Philadelphia any day of the week.

I moved inside, my arms wrapped around my sides, contemplating the relative merits of pulling on a jacket and walking across the street for tea with Raydean and Pat. Fluffy was looking unconcerned. She'd pulled up into a tight ball and was snuggled deep into the futon cushions. She was in for the evening.

"Girl," I said, "don't this stuff ever worry you? Don't you ever stop and think, Hey, maybe we can't handle this one?"

Apparently not. Fluffy sighed in her sleep, smiling at some doggy dream that chased across her subconscious.

"It's a dog's life, girl," I said. "No doubt about it."

Thirty

I was thinking that Yolanda was dead. I sat there on the couch next to Fluffy, tossing around the options and realizing that sometimes those irrational thoughts we all have are really instincts that shouldn't be ignored. My instincts told me the only good whore was now a dead one.

When the phone rang, Fluffy and I both jumped. I grabbed up the receiver. "Hello?"

"I have to talk to you, right now."

I rolled my eyes at Fluffy. I was getting a little tired of the husky-male-voice routine telling me we had to talk.

"Listen, who is this and why do you keep calling me? Now either we talk or we don't, but I can't hardly talk if I don't know who it is, can I?" I was a little confused on account of I'd thought it was Moose Lavotini who'd done all the calling, but maybe I was wrong about that, too.

"I don't know what you're talking about. I'm telling you I want you to come down here and get some shit squared away."

I recognized the whiny, impatient voice then: Izzy Rodriguez.

"And why should I?"

Izzy sighed. "Because I know something you don't know and because if we get some shit worked out, your asshole of a boss might go free."

That had me. "Where and when?" I asked.

221

"My club, right now. Use the back entrance so don't nobody see you."

I gripped the phone tighter. "All right, I'll be there in twenty." I hung up and stared at the dead phone. What was with Izzy looking to work a deal? What had him so desperate?

I glanced over at Fluff. She didn't look like this was a mission she wanted to tackle. She looked like she was in for the night, and who could blame her? I was dog-tired myself. I leaned back against the futon cushions. Fluffy stood up, stretched, and moved closer to me before curling up and resting her head in my lap. I stared at her and stroked the soft skin behind her ears. I couldn't help thinking that this could've been me and Nailor.

"Okay, girl," I said, struggling to hop up off the futon. "I'll go. Don't trouble yourself. I got it covered." Fluffy sighed and snuggled down into the cushion. After all, it wasn't her boss we were worried about.

By the time I reached the Busted Beaver, I had a head of steam up and was working on a good lecture for my friend, Rodriguez. If he thought he could scam me into working for him, or calling any of the other dancers back, then he was dead wrong.

I pulled Raydean's car into the space farthest away from the bright lights of the parking lot. I didn't figure it would do me any good to be seen talking to a sleaze-ball like Izzy. All I needed was the word to get back that Sierra was talking to the owner of the Beaver, and the rumors would fly. The others might think I was actually looking to score a job first and cut them out.

I took my time wedging my way through pickup trucks and souped-up street cars, working along the edge of the paved lot, stepping in sand and briars in my attempt to slink past the doormen and the drunken customers. I could hear the music thumping rhythmically inside, pulsing out a don't-you-want-to-fuck-me beat. The clink of glass, the smell of urine and testosterone, all worked to brand the Beaver as a slum club.

I crept up to the back entrance and was surprised to find the door standing wide open. That sort of security risk never happened around the Tiffany, but then, the Beaver probably worked prostitutes out the back. The people around Izzy Rodriguez weren't exactly looking to enter through the front door.

Still, when no one came to meet me and there was no sign of anyone at all in the darkened hallway, I felt uneasy. Maybe Rodriguez was setting me up. Maybe I shouldn't have come alone.

I felt the back pocket of my jeans, my hand running over my Spyderco, then reaching inside to bring it out and open it up. Something was making my skin crawl and I couldn't quite put my finger on what it was. The music was much louder now the closer I got to the stage, making it impossible to hear anything but the throbbing Latin beat. I just kept on moving, right down the hallway, looking for Izzy's office like I belonged there, hoping I didn't run into one of his gun-toting bodyguards.

The gold lettering on the thick wooden door was a dead giveaway. The empty bottles of cheap champagne lining the wall beside the door told me Rodriguez felt he had something to celebrate, or someone to celebrate with.

I knocked and waited. "This is stupid," I whispered to myself. "Obviously the man is busy. Just go now and come back another time." But no, I couldn't do that. I was too curious, too eager to get it over with and go back home.

I nudged the door with my foot, pushed it open, and stepped inside Izzy's office.

"Anybody home?" I called softly, like I was really expecting an answer. I gripped the handle of my knife tighter and stepped farther inside the office. No one was there and the place was a mess. Empty dishes and glasses were piled high on top of his huge desk. Papers were stacked with no apparent care in piles that spilled over onto the floor beside the desk. Izzy's office was just like him, sleazy.

His desk chair was built for a giant, which was funny in light of Rodriguez's tiny stature. I walked closer, thinking maybe to take advantage of the situation. But somebody else had already taken advantage of Izzy Rodriguez. He lay in a thick pool of blood on the floor behind his desk, his chest a bloody mess and his face a contorted death mask.

I didn't have to scream, or if I did, my voice was drowned out by the music and the screaming of a naked woman who stood in the doorway just behind me. She stood there in a little G-string, her arms crossed across her scrawny tits, screaming her little bleached-blond heart out, and pointing at the knife I held in my hand, obviously terrified.

"Oh shit!" I said, and did what any other woman in my situation would've done. I ran—right past the little stripper, right out the exit door and into the darkness. I kept right on going, edging the parking lot, hoofing it for the Plymouth and the relative freedom of the open road, hoping like hell that nobody saw me.

"Okay," I said, once I'd hit the Hathaway Bridge, "no one's back there. No one saw you. That girl will be so freaked out and hysterical it'll be hours before anyone ever knows you were there. So calm down and make a plan. We need a plan." But there wasn't any plan to be made when I was shaking so hard I could barely keep the car on the road.

I focused on breathing, forcing all the thoughts of Izzy lying dead out of my brain. "Just drive," I instructed myself. And I did just that, obeying the speed-limit signs, making sure I stopped without running any red lights, doing whatever it took to get home safely, without a cop getting curious. And I wasn't followed, either. I kept looking into my rearview mirror, just in case they somehow saw me and were chasing me. But the road was virtually empty and the trailer park never as welcoming as it was this particular evening.

I ran up the steps, closed and locked the door behind me, and reached for Pa's Chianti and a thick tumbler.

"Okay," I said, after I'd downed a half a glass. "A plan. I need a plan and here it is." I reached for the phone and started dialing Nailor. I walked across the darkened living room, the phone in hand, and peeked through the curtains. It was as if I'd sensed them.

The black sedan was back in place, this time a little farther away from the streetlight and Raydean's mobile home. How long had they been there? And why did Lavotini feel he needed to do me a favor? What had I done to inherit a mafioso bodyguard?

As I watched, the rear door of the sedan opened and someone stepped out of the car, walking briskly in my direction. It was Thomas the Sleepy Bodyguard. He moved purposefully, his jacket flapping open as he walked, as if he were making sure he could reach his holster without trouble, as if he were maybe expecting a hard time. Given his history with me and Raydean, I could appreciate his apprehension. On the other hand, maybe he just needed to take a leak. Whatever it was, I didn't need him here now.

I hung up the phone. When Thomas hit the bottom step, I pulled open the door and put on a big Girl Scout smile.

"Third door on the left," I said, "just down the hall."

That stopped him. He looked at me with his dumb-bodyguard-on-steroids expression.

"You're here to use the facilities?" No response. "The restroom," I said, "the potty?"

"Mr. Lavotini wants to see you," he said.

"Take a picture."

Thomas didn't flinch. "He says now."

"I'd come, but I'm expecting company and I need to wash my hair."

Thomas had no sense of humor. He moved toward me, taking the first step and stopping, like I should get the message and submit.

"He said now."

I saw him slip his hand behind his back like a cop, like he had handcuffs or something. He was going to take me forcibly if he had to. He was the extended arm of his employer. He'd bring me to his master, one way or the other. I looked at him, sizing him up, aware that the sleeping pills we'd pumped into him were no longer having a visible effect. It was pointless not to go. After all, you had to choose your battles. Maybe laying low with Moose for a little while was a good idea.

I looked over at Raydean's house. There was no sense in drawing her into it either. It was one thing when she had the upper hand and could surprise them, but they were ready for her now. She'd get hurt, maybe even killed. I was not going to risk that, not for a simple meeting with my newfound godfather.

"All right," I said. "Don't get your panties in a wad. I'm gonna go slip into something more comfortable and I'll be right with you."

Thomas shook his head like a dog worrying a bone, or the neck of a small animal. "Nope, we don't got no time. The boss says now."

"Okay, fine. I'll get my coat."

"I'll come with you," Thomas said.

I glared at him. "Obviously we have a trust issue," I said. "That hurts me no end."

Thomas walked the rest of the way up the stairs, following me into the kitchen. Fluffy, choosing her battles wisely, ignored the newcomer. Thomas looked at my coat lying across the back of one of the kitchen chairs and nodded in its direction.

"Okay, I see it, but I have to tinkle first." I glared at him and spun around, walking away from him and down the hall. To my consternation, the man followed me.

"Now one thing I don't do," I said, pausing at the doorway to my bathroom, "is allow company in my bathroom. I need my privacy."

I slammed the door and stood staring at my reflection in the mirror. What now? I couldn't just head off into the night without letting Nailor know.

I looked around, saw a tube of lipstick and figured it was better than nothing.

"Gone to see my uncle," I wrote. "Be back soon. I hope. Wait for me, I need to talk to you."

Thomas knocked on the door.

"Just a cotton-picking minute!" I yelled. "Can't a girl adjust her makeup without you getting all jammed up?"

"Mr. Lavotini said now," he said.

I flung open the door and marched out, slamming it shut behind me and walking quickly down the hallway.

"Does anybody ever tell you that you have a limited vocabulary?" I said.

Thomas didn't answer. It was all work and no play with this boy. What a stick-in-the-mud.

Moose had ensconced himself in the penthouse of the Baywater Condominium complex. I didn't waste time trying to figure how he'd come into such luck. I figured with the mob you just push a button, make a phone call, and you got connections anywhere in the world. This was obviously one of those times, just like having a local entourage that appeared out of nowhere at the Oyster Bar to take out Dimitri and his bikers. The Lavotini Syndicate had connections.

He stood there by the fireplace, the gas logs burning cheerfully behind the glass doors, the air-conditioning set to compensate for the heat. He was holding a champagne flute in one hand and a bottle of Tattinger in the other. It was my lucky day . . . maybe.

He smiled, all white teeth and South Beach tan. He looked rested and hungry, like maybe I was dinner.

"Hello, beautiful," he said. "Have I told you how lovely you look today?"

Being as I hadn't seen him since the fiasco in the parking lot of the Beaver and he had been implying I was stupid yet again, I figured we could manage to omit this part of his daily ritual.

"Nope. I believe you were focused on my ability to handle a situation involving two minor thugs, if I remember correctly."

"Now, baby," he crooned, his voice sliding into a deep Barry White imitation, "you know I didn't mean anything by that. Come on, it's over. Let's drink some champagne and enjoy ourselves."

In the background I saw Thomas stifle a yawn.

Lavotini noticed and smiled. "Thomas, go take another nap or something. Put Carlos on the door, the *outside* door." He stressed the word "outside" like we shouldn't be disturbed.

Thomas nodded and vanished. A moment later a slim, dark-haired man crossed the marble foyer, opened the front door, and closed it silently behind him. Carlos.

Moose seemed not to notice. He was pouring champagne and motioning me to a small table by the plate-glass window. The table was dressed in a starched white linen tablecloth with pale pink roses in a tiny bud vase and candles. Hors d'oeuvres sat on little white plates, scallops wrapped in bacon, bruschetta with roasted red peppers and freshly grated Parmesan cheese, green and black olives. It was all thought out, all taken care of because the Moose had been certain I would come. In the Moose's world there was no argument. It happened the way he planned it every time, without hesitation or exception.

"I don't get this," I said. "I don't understand."

Moose sipped his champagne and smiled. "I think you do, Sierra."

I was waiting for Frank Sinatra to burst into song and come strolling out of a back bedroom. The lights were dimmed, making it easy to see the foam of the incoming surf splashing on the beach twenty-two stories below us. It was a movie set right out of the sixties.

"You think I don't do my research?" He was leaning back in his chair, smiling at me. "At first I thought it was kind of cute, you using my name like we were related, using my reputation to protect yourself. I was flattered." He put down his glass and leaned in toward me. "Then I saw your picture. That's when I knew I needed to watch out for you."

"What? Is there something in my picture that says I'm incapable of taking care of myself? Because I can assure you, I can take care of myself. I was just using your name a couple of times to keep the riffraff off my back. You know how that is. I wasn't really in trouble or nothing."

Moose reached over, plucked an olive from its bowl, and popped it into his mouth. The way he chewed communicated a different message, like he was savoring me, not the taste of some salty Greek olive.

"You never know," he said. "That's why I was watching. That's how come I knew when you did get into something large. That's why I'm here, to help you out of this jam."

I took two huge swigs of my champagne, forgetting completely that this was the good stuff and not the Tiffany's house brand. I could feel the reaction my body was having to the champagne and I didn't want him to know. I was lost, losing control to a Mafia kingpin. I'd been here before. I sure as hell wasn't going back again.

"Listen," I said, "Vincent didn't hit Denny. It's gonna come out in the wash. He doesn't deal drugs and he was only running the game to get himself out of hock to the IRS. I can handle this."

Moose chuckled. I seemed to amuse him. I was "cute" to him.

"Sierra," he said, "don't be scared of me. I don't want anything but to help you." He pushed the plate of scallops toward me. "Come on, baby. Let's have a truce. This is the one place where it's safe. It's not like the movies. You don't owe me a thing for this. Taking care of you is my pleasure."

I looked at him, lulled by the deep tone of his voice and the champagne that was slowly making its way to my head, bypassing my empty stomach, soothing away the vision of Izzy Rodriguez lying dead on his office floor. The alarm bells were ringing in my head, but I was ignoring them.

Moose didn't miss the look, but for some reason he didn't move. Instead he leaned back in his chair again and smiled.

"It ain't that easy, Sierra," he said. "It's not that luscious body I'm after. I'm after you."

That did it. My stomach rolled over and I couldn't look at him. My heart was jumping up and down, choking me and making me squirm in my seat. The Sierra Lavotini fountain of cool was running dry and Moose knew all about it.

"Relax," he said. He poured more champagne in my glass and stuck the bottle back in the ice bucket. "Let's take a little break from you and me and talk about your situation."

"Situation?" I heard my voice squeak and regretted it. How had he found out so quickly? Oh, why didn't I just wear a sign that said "potentially out of my league"?

He was enjoying my anxiety. He enjoyed it like Sister Ignatius used to enjoy it when she'd call on me to read the answers to the math homework I hadn't done. It was Catholicism at its very best.

"I think you're looking at a bargain-basement corporate takeover gone wrong," he said. "I think Izzy Rodriguez was looking to buy out the Tiffany and corner the market on the trade in this town."

"What makes you say that?" I asked.

Moose smiled. "Easy. I asked him what the plan was."

"You talked to Izzy?"

"You could say that."

"When?"

"Earlier."

We were circling again. I was flashing back on the sedan arriving at the Busted Beaver. I had assumed they were following me, but what if they weren't? What if the Moose had been there to see Rodriguez? What if Moose wasn't happy with Izzy's answers?

Moose stretched his legs out in front of him and smiled. He could read me. "Sierra, this ain't Hollywood. I don't drop in to talk to people and take them out if I don't like their answers. But I do find ways to get results. Now Mr. Rodriguez assured me he didn't kill Watley in a moment of inspiration, that he didn't intend to put Gambuzzo out of action any way but legally." Moose shrugged. "But be that as it may," he said, "I do know this: He intended to buy your club from Riggs. And I think I convinced him that there's a better plan."

My heart was pounding. All I could see was the look of agony on Izzy's dead face. Moose had a plan, all right. He was waiting, like I should fall down at his feet worshiping the great idea maker, but I wasn't going there.

He smiled. "All right, since you're too shy to ask, I'll tell you," he said. "Here's what I got to offer. I suggest I buy the Tiffany from Riggs. I'm sure he'll be glad to let it go at a reasonable price. Then we buy out the Beaver and whatever other competition there is in this pissant little town that wants to sell while the getting's good. Then you'll run the action locally, and I'll make sure there's no trouble. It makes money for me, and it makes money for you."

I stopped chewing on olives and stared at him. Was he out of his mind? Did he really think I'd do a Mafia-financed operation? And that "reasonable price" shit, what was that?

Moose continued. "We'll give Vinny a job, don't worry, but a convicted felon can't own a nightclub. He'll be all right. I'll take care of him. When he's done doing his time for the IRS gig and the drug stuff, we'll put him into something comfortable."

I was pushing back from the table, preparing to stand up and give Moose the business about what he could do with his enterprise, when there was an explosion of noise outside the penthouse. Someone was in the hallway, maybe as many as three or four someones, and none of them was happy.

Moose looked up and frowned. "Wait a minute," he said, like I was Fluffy and would stay on command. He stood up and started for the door, not tracking that I was following him. His hand slipped behind his jacket, to the waistband of his pants, pulling out a black gun, dropping it into his right-hand jacket pocket like he expected to reach for it. For one instant I found myself wondering how many suit coats Moose owned that had bullet holes in the right-hand pockets.

He opened the door, took in Carlos standing there with his back to us, his legs spread and arms crossed like there wasn't going to be any way in but through his body. On the other side stood John Nailor and Carla Terrance standing like they were joined at the hip and looking as mad as hell.

"What seems to be the problem, Officers?" Moose asked. He sounded like smooth water, soothing and ready to help in any way he could. What a load of crap, I thought.

Terrance wasn't going to do it easy. She bellied up to Carlos, talking through him to get to Moose.

"We want to talk to you," she said. She saw me, frowned, and then smiled, like "Bingo! I won the lucky number!" She looked back at Nailor, nodding in my direction, as if maybe he hadn't seen me all along. "Look what we found curled up in the snake's den," she said. "You done questioning my judgment?"

Nailor's face tightened, the color flooding it as he took in the champagne flute, the low-cut top I wore, and Lavotini's superior air of ownership.

"It's not a social call," I said, looking at him.

"Neither is this," Carla said. Unless I missed my read, she was in ecstasy.

I looked at Nailor, who wasn't saying a word, and lost my head. "Where's your coat?"

Carla didn't miss a beat. "He doesn't need a coat when I'm around," she said.

Moose, new to the game I thought, laughed. "Aw, I see how it's gonna be now!" He looked at Nailor and shook his head. "I'm glad it's not my problem," he said. "I don't try and keep up two at a time. I find it unnecessary."

I think Nailor wanted to kill him then, but suddenly I was enjoying myself, enjoying the fact that someone was defending me for a change.

Moose's voice hardened. "Let them in, Carlos. Perhaps this will get more interesting if we all sit down and have a more civilized discussion."

Moose smiled at Carla and she looked momentarily disconcerted. Moose didn't wait to gauge his effect, instead he turned his back on the two officers and walked across the marble foyer with all the seeming confidence in the world that they would follow.

He pulled the bottle of Tattinger from its bucket and frowned, then turned and met Carla's gaze.

"Well, looks as if there's one glass left. You a fan of champagne?" he asked. He was smiling again, as if he knew secrets about her, and to my total surprise, she was almost going for it.

"Uh, no," she stammered. "I'm on duty." Then she straightened and reverted to the Carla we all knew and loved. "I want to talk to you."

Moose raised his eyebrows. "Well, I thought that's what you were doing?"

Carla frowned and Nailor looked out the plate-glass window. I figured he was going to let her hang herself.

"There was a homicide tonight at the Busted Beaver, that's a local club in town." She threw that last part in like she was giving him the benefit of the doubt, like he might not know. "You were there earlier today. You and the owner had words. I want to know what that was about."

Moose shrugged. "It was business," he said. "Nothing more, nothing less."

"What kind of business?"

"Private business. It's unimportant."

Carla looked at Nailor, who was still staring at the moon or whatever it was that was so fascinating outside the window.

"Maybe I didn't make myself clear," she said. "This is a homicide investigation. Everything the victim did that day is important. Every discussion. Every argument. Every move he made. It's all part of our investigation."

I set my glass down, aiming for the table and missing. It crashed to the floor and shattered.

"Wait a minute," I said, ignoring the glass. "Why are you picking on him? I had words with that guy earlier today, too."

Carla ignored me. It was John who turned around and stared at me, looking through me as if I had become the enemy or worse, a total stranger.

Carla's cell phone rang. She stepped away from us, flipping it open and listening to the voice on the other end. In the background, Carlos arrived, cleaning up the glass behind me, moving with the slick efficiency of Moose's men.

I couldn't figure it. Why was I getting the fish eye from Nailor? It should've been the other way around. Here he is, ponied up to his ex, not having the decency to put her in her place when she intimates that they're thick as thieves again, and he's giving me the Sister Francis eye? Forgive me, but I don't think so. Of course, there was that little piece about me finding Rodriguez dead and a half-zonked stripper seeing me there. Maybe that was what had Nailor in a funk. In that case, I could understand his confusion.

Carla walked back toward Nailor, gave him the nod, and then stepped back, passing the lead to him.

"Mr. Lavotini, we have a search warrant issued for this property and your vehicles. It's in transit from the courthouse. Would you like us to wait until it arrives or may we start now?" Nailor's face and tone were neutral. It was in Moose's court.

He wasn't playing ball. His face changed into a hard, stone mask of disapproval.

"We'll wait," he said. "I like to see the paperwork all signed and neat." He snapped his fingers once at Carlos and the man handed him a cell phone from his pocket.

"Before I consult my attorney," Moose said, "I'd like to know what your basis is for searching my property."

Carla snapped. "Because, scumbag, you're selling drugs."

Lavotini laughed, but it was an angry sound, a harsh cough of disbelief. "I don't know who you're talking to, lady, but I don't go there."

Carla drew herself up like she was the law and scowled at him. "I never knew a perp yet wasn't innocent. We got drugs, we got a witness, and we got you at the scene of a deal gone bad, arguing over payment. I think we got you, sport."

Lavotini appeared to be unconcerned. He walked away from her and dialed a number, waited a moment, then started talking in low, clipped tones that brooked no argument. He was issuing orders and taking charge. If the police wanted a fight, it was about to get larger than little Panama City had ever seen.

Nailor was watching me. When Carla walked away from us, mobilizing whatever was about to take place, I took my opportunity.

"What in the hell is going on and why are you looking at me like I had two heads?" I asked.

He frowned. "You know, I don't know what the game is here with your 'uncle' or whatever he is to you, but you've gone over the line now."

"What in the hell are you talking about?" A shiver of anxiety spread through my gut, working its way through my body. His tone was so cold, as if he totally bought I was hooked up with Moose Lavotini.

"Sierra," Nailor said, "I'm telling you this and I shouldn't, because somehow I want to believe you're not involved, but it doesn't look good. Nolowicki can put your 'uncle' here at the scene of a murder. Do you know what he's up to?"

Before I could answer, Nailor went on. "He's looking to shake down the owners of all the local clubs. He wants to take control so he can run drugs and prostitution out of them. Sierra, do you not know what kind of animal this is?" Nailor wasn't waiting for answers to anything. "This is the big time, honey. You think because he's smooth and attractive he couldn't be a bad guy? What dream world are you in? Do you not see what's going on? The man's trying to take over here. He's bringing organized crime to Panama City and do you know why?" Nailor was on a roll. "I'll tell you why. Because of you, Sierra. He's here because of you, or don't you get that? You did this."

I couldn't speak. I didn't get a moment to defend myself or to explain. Uniformed officers arrived at the door. Carla presented the search warrant, and the show was on the road.

My "uncle," the alleged kingpin of New Jersey, was deep in conversation with his legal team. His underlings were all lined up in the living room, looking like the cast of The Sopranos on holiday.

Nailor and Carla were deep in conversation as well, directing the search, intent on doing their jobs and righting the wrongs of civilization.

No one noticed when I left. After all, what did it matter? They were all too busy fighting crime to worry about me. I was just the carrier for a deadly virus that had now infected Panama City. I mean, how many people walked past Typhoid Mary when she stood at the bus stop, never imagining that that one woman brought the plague down on their heads?

To my way of thinking, I had managed to wreck everything. Vincent Gambuzzo was no closer to freedom than when I'd started. The girls at the Tiffany were out of work. And Panama City was on the brink of being owned by a mobster who wanted to show his affection and appreciation for my earthly talents.

Thirty-one

I think what we got here, sugar, is a failure to communicate." Raydean was sitting at her kitchen table, plying me with strong, sweet tea, and listening to me cry it all out.

"First off," she said, "the Typhoid Mary metaphor don't work. You are not the cause of the ruination of this town. The Flemish is what done that, and done a good job of it too. I point to them new county buildings and the dog pound as an example." She leaned back in her seat, her head covered in pink foam rollers and her face still sporting a little of the green goop she used as a beauty mask.

"No, baby, what we got here is King Kong and Fay Wray. You're in the palm of that monster's hand and, therefore, you'd be in the catbird seat. Why, honey, with your natural talents, you can wrap him around your little finger. And that other one, that police, he's just temporarily insane, that's all, baby. His little head ain't thinking and his big head's done worked it too much. We can handle all that. What we got to do now, though, is pull Vincent's fat out of the fire and back into the frying pan."

Raydean shook her head again. "You ever think you might have an attention-span problem? You're just all over the place. Give you one thing to work out and you spawn a yard full of problems. Just stick to the basics. Who killed that whiny boy and what will it take to get your boss out of jail and the show back on the road?"

"But, Raydean, it's more complicated than that!"

"Life ain't hard, honey," Raydean said, "you make it hard. Now work a task list. That's what they give us in life skills class down at the nuthouse. They make you do a priority list and then work the list. Isn't your livelihood and the rest of the crew's the most important thing? Don't you think you should put aside your love life for a moment? Do you not think them boys can hold their own dicks long enough to pee?"

"Raydean!"

"I don't call 'em like I see 'em," she said with a wise nod. "I call 'em like they *is*. My brother taught me that. Used to run a baseball club." Raydean sniffed. "Follow the money, Sierra. In a thing such as this, it ain't about revenge or lust, it's money."

I put my head down on the table and sighed. "I'm tired," I said. "It's the middle of the night. I can't do this anymore."

She reached over with one gnarled hand and laid it on my head, as gently as Ma used to do when I was a kid.

"Go on home, baby," she said softly. "Tomorrow's another day. Don't you worry about nothing. It's not like we're alone here. We got each other, always will."

I looked up at her, saw the belief shining in her eyes and had to give her a smile back, like I knew we could do it, a stripper and a crazy old woman. I gave her the smile because I wanted her to think I believed in the concept because she needed it more than I did. The way I saw it at that moment, we were sunk, but she didn't need to know that. I didn't need to take that away from her.

In the morning it would be different. I kept telling myself that the whole way home. I told Fluffy that as I stripped off my clothes and reached for the softest, oldest T-shirt I had. In the morning it would be different. I would wake up with a plan.

But the plan came to me. This time it didn't arrive fully formed in my head. It arrived with the sound all night-shift workers come to dread: banging on my front door.

"Sierra! For God's sake, you got nothing better to do than sleep the night away?"

Pa? It couldn't be Pa. I was dreaming, but his voice just got louder and louder. He was working his way down the side of the trailer, banging on the aluminum siding, making the inside of my house sound like a hollow can. Pa was in Panama City.

I sprang out of bed, grabbing my bathrobe and running for the door. Had the old fool lost his mind? Who was gonna take care of Ma? What did I have to do to make him get the clue that Ma needed him?

I threw open the door, ready to give him the Lavotini business, but then saw Ma, propped up on pillows, lying in the backseat of the blue Lincoln Town Car. She looked to be either sleeping or dead, and for an awful moment I figured she was dead and Pa hadn't figured anything else to do but bring me the body.

"Pa!" I cried, seeing him underneath my bedroom window, banging away. "What's the deal? What are you doing here? What's wrong with Ma?"

Pa, red-eyed with fatigue, his cheeks covered with gray stubble, turned around and looked at me like I was the stupid one.

"Sierra, they don't just bounce back from a major surgery like that," he said. "She's sleeping. She took some of them pain pills and told me to drive or she'd do it herself! She's a nutcase, Sierra. She thinks the only good thing for recovery is Florida sunshine. She says we need a vacation. Now what is that?"

Pa was wearing his faded white long undershirt and a pair of jeans, notched at the waist with a thick leather belt, the same belt he wore with his uniform pants when he was working at the firehouse. He looked tired and wired on caffeine and ready for relief.

"Okay, okay, I gotcha." And I did indeed have the number. Ma wasn't looking for a vacation, she was looking to take care of me, the very last thing she needed to be worrying about.

"Are you gonna stand there," a voice said, "or can we get this young'un inside and into bed?" Raydean had materialized by the Lincoln, peering in the back window, her face softened with concern.

"Big man," Raydean said, looking at Pa, "can you carry her or do you need me to take the feet?"

Pa hid a smile. "If her head rolls off, you catch it," he said. "Otherwise, I think I can handle it."

Ma's eyes fluttered open as Raydean opened the back door and she looked at all of us and smiled. "I thought I was dreaming," she murmured.

"You should've been," I said. "Ma, you shouldn't be making a trip like this so soon after surgery. It's only been a week."

Ma frowned at me. "Good, so the doc won't be none the wiser on account of my post-op check ain't till next week. So long as nobody feels the need to rat me out . . ."

They all turned and looked at me, like I was the one making all the trouble. Great. Just what I needed, more guilt.

Pa reached in for Ma, who slapped his hands away and insisted on walking under her own steam up the steps and into the trailer. Once there, Raydean bustled ahead of her, straight into the guest room, where she turned back the covers and smoothed the sheets for her new patient.

"Just what you need," she said, turning to Ma. "A good lie-down and a cup of my tea when you wake up. How about it?"

Ma was so pale it scared me. She nodded, all the strength worn out of her by the trip. Pa stood in the doorway looking equally worn.

"Big man," Raydean said, "you're due for a nap, too. Sierra here'll get the bags in and see to what needs unpacking. You two rest up." She looked at Ma. "I'll keep an eye on your girl for you." She knew why Ma had come. Raydean had instincts like millipedes got legs; she was just covered over with them.

Ma and Pa, like I'd never seen them do before, shut down. There was no argument, no talk of what needed to be done. They merely crawled into bed and went to sleep, leaving me and Raydean to sort out the details.

Raydean was tickled pink by the turn of events and wasted no time in letting me know.

"It's perfect," she crowed. "I got me a crop of patients and you got you a purpose beyond sorting out the little details of Gambuzzo's life." She rummaged through my freezer, tossing a frozen chicken out onto the counter and sighing.

"You ain't got the fixin's for the dumplings," she muttered. "Reckon I'll go across the street and fetch what I need." She straightened and looked up at me. "While I'm doing that, you might ought to get yourself dressed and prettified. You got to use what God gave you if'n you're gonna catch the bastard."

She didn't wait around to hear what I had to say in the matter, either. She was off, leaving me to do as she said. I wandered down the hall and caught Fluffy sneaking into the guest room. Fluffy knew her priority: Keep watch over the parents.

I stood in the shower, wishing I hadn't forgotten to make coffee and trying to gather my wandering thoughts. Ma and Pa would sleep for hours, I hoped, long enough for me to make serious inroads into taking care of Vincent's murder charge. The sooner I got that sorted out, the sooner Ma would quit worrying.

I reached for the shampoo and tried to figure out how to "follow the money," as Raydean had put it. The killer wanted Vincent out of the way, but why? Pair that up with Izzy Rodriguez being dead and it looked like the killer was after club owners, or control or something. Who at the table wanted control? Who was left still standing?

Yolanda was missing and probably dead. She didn't seem to stand to gain from killing anybody. She was just a hooker, hired to keep people busy, to keep them from noticing what was going on. She'd run screaming from the room the instant the first shots were fired.

Vincent, Eugene, and Bruno were all out of the picture, too. They only stood to lose more with the Tiffany lost to Riggs and their butts in a sling. Izzy Rodriguez had been my prime suspect, but he'd come out on the short end of the deal too.

That left Mike Riggs and Denny's friend Turk Akins as suspects. Riggs had threatened to kill Dennis Watley. He'd won the club from Vincent. Why would he kill Izzy Rodriguez? And Turk Akins had no motive as far as I could see. He could've killed his buddy for screwing his ex-wife and to clear the way to Becky Watley, but the widow had convinced me they weren't looking to kill Watley. No, that didn't make sense.

A third thought occurred to me, a thought that I just wasn't ready to look at until all options were exhausted: Maybe the two murders were completely unrelated.

I shaved my legs. I tried to figure it all out and finally tossed it up in the air. I needed more to go on. I needed to talk to Mike Riggs. I needed to find some other key to this entire situation.

"It's not hard," I muttered to myself, "once you have a plan. I have a plan. One of the people in the room killed Watley and pinned it on Vincent. I'll just find out who, spring Vincent, and call it a day. Bingo!"

I was feeling pretty confident, except that now I was gonna be stuck driving my parents' Lincoln, because my Camaro was still at the Oyster Bar. I walked into the guest room and proceeded to lift Pa's keys silently off the dresser. I had turned around, tiptoeing for the door, when Pa caught me, just like in the old days of my adolescence.

"This time put gas in it," he muttered. "And try to park where you won't get no seagull shit on it."

"Thanks, Pa," I whispered, but he was sleeping again.

I walked back down the hallway, resigned to the fact that I'd be driving Pa's huge sedan. At least it was in better shape than Raydean's Plymouth. But as I stepped onto the porch, I did a double take. The Camaro was on the street. Frankie the biker stood leaning against the right rear fender, a shit-eating grin on his face at what must have been the shocked look on mine.

"Don't you need this?" he asked.

"How did you? You don't even have the . . ."

Frankie pushed off the fender and opened the driver's side door for me, gesturing to the inside of the car. "There's a switch there, temporarily, to start the car. Only takes a minute when you know what you're doing. Once you got a little bit of time, I'll slip that ignition system back in. But this should do for right now."

He leaned inside and gestured toward a toggle switch. "Go ahead, flip it."

I slid into the driver's seat and hit the switch. The car roared to life and Frankie smiled.

"Ain't that cool?" he said. He walked around to the passenger side, opened the door, and got in. "I just never get used to the beauty of your perfect hot wire. It's an art form, really." He looked at me and smiled. "So where are we going?"

I just glared at him. "You could've just asked me for the keys, you know."

He grinned all the more. "I know, but I was getting a little rusty. Besides, I get bored just hanging around."

"Frankie, what are you doing here?"

His smile faded a little. "Well, I got nothing better to do, so I thought I'd bring you your car and tag along if you decided to go anywhere."

"Moose sent you, didn't he?"

"What makes you think that?" he asked, but he wasn't looking into my eyes anymore.

"Enough said. You don't lie good to me, Frankie. It's your eyes. You can't look at me and lie at the same time."

Frankie sighed. "All right, but I'm kind of into the guy, you know? He saved my ass. I gotta help him out a little. He said you had a thing about him helping you and he's a little jammed up right now anyway."

I slipped the Camaro into gear, rolled into the driveway, then backed out into the street and headed out of the subdivision.

"What's going on since last night?" I asked, figuring he knew. Frankie always knew.

"Oh, it was a big time at the penthouse last night," Frankie said. "They must've had an informant because they searched and searched and found nothing until the vice people turned up and started looking in a couple of places no one thought to look, one of them being Lavotini's stash spot. They got fifty thousand in cash and an ounce of rock."

I braked the car, sitting at the stop sign leading out of the trailer park, and just stared at Frankie.

"They popped Moose Lavotini for cocaine?"

Frankie shrugged. "I didn't know either," he said. "But it was in the wheel well of the sedan he and his men ride around in. He was treated and released by morning."

"Moose? Don't you mean arrested and released?"

"Yeah, whatever, but you know how them cops down here are with strangers. I'd say 'treated' is your better word."

"Anybody could've put that there," I said. "If he was dealing dope, it wouldn't be small like that. It's a plant."

Frankie nodded. "Yeah, or else one of his men is trying to make a little side action off of their trip here. You know, some of them guys are local. The man didn't just bring all of his own talent with him. The Syndicate's got enough going up there without bringing the show down here just to help you out."

I looked over at him and he shrugged. "No offense intended, Sierra, but what you got going on is nothing compared to what they got going on in Jersey. Anybody can tell you that. Jersey is like, well, like Dante's Inferno or something. It's evil. This is a vacation for your boy, Lavotini."

I turned out of the trailer park and headed for town on my way out to the beach, still thinking to talk to Mike Riggs, but completely jammed up by this latest development with Moose. My Catholic guilt was kicking into overdrive now. What had I done? Not only had I contaminated Panama City with the Mafia, but I'd gotten my self-appointed savior into hot water, too? And should I feel guilty about my kidnapper getting his ass popped for dealing dope? I mean, even if it was his staff looking to work a side deal, Moose Lavotini was a criminal. Who was I to root for a criminal who routinely killed people?

Frankie reached over and turned on the radio, hitting the buttons until he heard something he liked, Cream blasting "White Room." The man was terminally stuck in his past.

"Where are we headed?" he asked.

"The Tiffany."

"Don't you mean Big Mike's House of Booty?" he said, needling me.

"Hell no, I do not."

Frankie laughed and turned up the radio. Clapton made his guitar scream out the solo lick. Somehow it all seemed appropriate. I was headed to my old club to talk to a man who knows nothing about the business, accompanied by a biker doing a favor to a mobster and currently hiding out from every other biker in the world by coughing up an identity in the witness-protection program. I looked out the windshield at the overcast sky and thought, What's next? What crazy shit could possibly jump into my life now?

Thirty-two

*M*ike Riggs knew what the world had planned for me next, he just wasn't going to come up off it and tell me. He sat in Vincent's Gambuzzo's office, in Vincent's old chair, and hunched back into the leather like a frightened sea turtle.

"I'm not talking to you," he said. "The window of opportunity has closed and I'm not hiring."

"Well, lucky for you," I said, "I'm not looking."

Frankie leaned in the doorway behind us, trying to look imposing. He frowned. He crossed his arms. And every now and then, he'd mutter something that sounded like "bullshit." But it didn't look like it was having an effect on Riggs.

"Listen," I said, "what I got are questions about that night when Watley got capped and you won this place . . . temporarily."

"Nope," Riggs said, "no deal. I'm not talking."

"The fuck you ain't," a deep voice said. "Motherfucker's gonna talk or I'll rip your fucking head off. Good enough deal?"

Eugene "Fully Automatic" stood just inside the doorway, towering over Frankie and holding an Uzi in his hand, pointing it at Riggs, his white teeth shining against his dark skin as he smiled.

"Lady wants to talk," he said, enunciating each word carefully. "I think if she wants you to tell her something, you'll be talking too." He punctuated this statement with a short burst of gunfire that destroyed the paneling above the sea captain's head.

"You got my back?" he asked Frankie.

Frankie nodded, looking a little wide-eyed himself.

"Good," Eugene said, "then we got us a party." He looked over at me. "Go ahead, Sierra, ask the boy what you want. He'll talk to you now."

Riggs was looking from Eugene to me, his face drained of color and his body visibly shrinking into his chair.

"Okay," I said, "let's get started. How about we start with an easy one, like how come you told Dennis Watley you'd kill him the week before he died?"

"Because he was taking my customers."

"What do you mean?"

Riggs shifted in his chair, embarrassed and uncomfortable. "He'd see them coming and offer them a better rate. He'd take them away. It wasn't like I was going to really kill him. A worm like that don't need the actual stomping to get the message."

"All right," I said, "good. Now, what was the deal with you and Izzy?"

Riggs wouldn't answer. He looked down at the desk in front of him, studying the hard wooden surface as if it held all the answers.

Eugene took a step toward the desk and looked to me. "I can pop his fucking knee caps," he said eagerly, sounding as if I would be doing him a favor if I granted permission.

"No," I said, straightening. "That won't be necessary, will it, Mike?"

The captain looked up at me, the fear in his eyes unmistakable.

"You thought you and Izzy had it all sewn up. You two were going to be a big deal around town, but suddenly Izzy's dead and you're afraid you're next, right?"

Riggs nodded, still saying nothing.

"Someone trying to shake you down, make you pay up?"

Riggs looked like I was reading his mind, not knowing it was commonplace, an easy guess.

"Izzy said he'd take care of it, but . . ." The sea captain's voice faded.

"Yeah," I said, "and look what happened. So now you think if you talk, you're next, right?"

Mike Riggs shook his head. "No, that's not it. I don't know nothing. I never saw the guy. I never did nothing but get a phone call telling me to pay up."

There wasn't a sound in the room. Even Eugene seemed to be holding his breath. "So did you?" I asked.

"No. Izzy was here when the guy called. He told him if he was looking to shake me down he'd have to go through him first 'cause we was partners. I didn't get no more calls after that, so I thought it was okay."

I shook my head and looked at Frankie. What a mess. I was crossing names off the suspect list, one right after the other. There weren't but three people left and two of them were missing, allegedly holding the bag on information that could lead me to the killer.

But I was also thinking about Vincent, remembering him saying he'd been set up, even inviting his own arresting officer to the game. Then I thought about Yolanda, paid to keep people busy and distracted.

I closed my eyes and reviewed the events of last night, of Nailor saying they had evidence that Moose Lavotini was selling drugs, that Nolowicki could put him at the murder scene, that when vice arrived they'd suddenly found Moose's stash and money.

I thought about Tinky, dead in Watley's garage. Then I started playing it all back in my head, how whenever somebody died or disappeared, Nolowicki had been in contact with them or at the scene. When Vincent and Moose got popped, who had found the drugs? I thought about Yolanda again, how she only wanted to talk to Nailor when her work would've brought her in contact with Nolowicki on a more regular basis. Why not talk to him? Why tell me to tell Nailor it had to be just between the two of them?

Everybody was out of the way. If Nolowicki wanted to run

protection or silent partner himself up to every stripclub in town, the way was open and easy. He could go to Riggs or any other club owner in town and say, Look what happens to those who don't play my game. And Riggs couldn't call the police because Nolowicki *was* the police. Nolowicki could always tell him that other cops were involved, and maybe they were. By getting Vincent locked up and out of the way, he could terrorize all the other club owners, take over if he wanted, and still look like a paragon of "coply" virtue.

I looked at Eugene and Frankie. They were the only posse I had right now, and somehow between the three of us, it was going to have to be enough. Nailor and police backup were out of the question. After all, Nailor saw me as just trying to protect a mobster and save a junior gangster from a murder rap. He saw me as the cause of all of his problems. He wouldn't help. Nope. We had to prove it was Nolowicki in a way that guaranteed success. I figured that to be almost impossible without Yolanda or Turk Akins—or one of their bodies.

Thirty-three

$\mathcal{E}$ugene and Frankie thought I was nuts. I could tell this by the way they didn't say a word as I laid it out for them, by the way their eyebrows furrowed and they darted glances at each other when they thought I wasn't looking. But at some point, the tide turned, probably the point where I explained about the drug connection being almost impossible in Vincent's case, about how he wouldn't have needed a stupid card game that had no guaranteed pay-off if he had really been running a drug operation. Dope dealers don't need money to pay off the IRS.

Frankie was the first one to offer a suggestion on the Yolanda front. He smiled, stroking his upper lip as if he still had a mustache.

"I got some friends that'll tell us if she's still alive," he said. "Let's go." He was headed for the Camaro's passenger side door without waiting to see what I thought of the idea. Eugene looked like the last kid left on the bench, clutching his Uzi down at his side and staring at the ground like maybe I'd forgotten about him.

"You wanna play?" I asked.

That was all it took. I hopped in the car, flipped my new automatic toggle switch, and roared off out of the parking lot and into the almost deserted street. It was lunchtime and there was almost no traffic. The sky was gray and overcast and the air was still and cold. Up north I could've told you it meant snow, but on the beach-front of northwest Florida it probably meant a long, cold rain.

"Where am I going?" I asked Frankie.

"Across the bridge, back into town. Go to the Pink Pony. That's where my friend works."

Eugene snorted. "That dump? I ain't been there in years."

Frankie snickered. "Then you don't gotta pay for pussy," he said. "And you ain't a biker."

Eugene and Frankie were still sniffing each other out, looking to see who was gonna turn alpha dog. I didn't have time to hand-hold or lead them through a trust walk, so I ignored them and turned on the radio.

"Remember," the announcer said, "if you're going to drink to-night, designate a driver. The local clubs all have free taxi services ready and waiting, so don't hesitate to use them."

"There it is," Frankie said. "Pull up into the parking lot. I'll go get her."

"You can't do that," I said. "The people who are looking for you will be in there. Just tell me what she looks like. I'll go get her."

Frankie laughed. "A, she won't come with you and, B, you won't make it back out."

Eugene leaned forward from the backseat. "Mr. Uzi would be glad to accompany the lady."

We rolled into a potholed lot and parked in the farthest corner. Even in the middle of the day, the Pink Pony was crowded, Harleys ringing the door, beat-to-shit cars taking up the rest of the lot.

"Nope," Frankie said, "I can handle it. I don't see nobody I know here. There ain't no bikes I recognize either."

Eugene and I looked at each other. What's to recognize on a bike?

"I'll come with you," Eugene said. "Just in case."

"No," Frankie said automatically, then hesitated and said, "Lis-ten, these guys are kind of militant, you know? Like Aryan-nation militant."

Eugene laughed. "Then me and Mr. Uzi are gonna have a big time desegregating the place."

Frankie smiled. "We should do that, Eugene, but now is not the time. We gotta pull that girl out of there without attracting a crowd, you get me? You wait here. Be ready because if anything goes wrong, it'll go big wrong."

It was a bad situation about to be made worse by Frankie risking being discovered by the very people he'd helped put in jail a few months back. I couldn't see a way around it, but then, fortunately, we didn't need an alternative plan after all.

A reed-thin girl wearing a dingy white rabbit fur jacket stepped out the front door, a burly man right behind her, reaching out to slip his arm possessively around her waist.

"Well, shit," Frankie said. "Here we go."

He was out of the car and across the lot before I could say anything, walking quickly, hunching into his leather jacket, with his hands jammed into the pockets of his jeans.

There were words—her soothing her disappointed customer, him wanting to dispute the point, Frankie stepping up into his face and arranging the guy's future, pro and con, for him—but I could only guess at what was being said. Finally Frankie walked back with her, talking with his arm around her shoulders, smiling but not giving her a reason to smile back. She looked sullen. He stopped, spun her around, looked down at her, and said something that made her smile, then continued on toward the car.

Eugene moved over as Frankie opened the door and held the seat back for her so she could scamper in.

"Louise," Frankie said, "these are my associates."

He didn't introduce us by name. He was smiling like we were at a cocktail party and he was the host.

"Louise, we are looking for one of your colleagues, girl by the name of Yolanda. You know her?"

Louise was sizing me up, then she shot a sideways glance at Eugene. He gave her a big smile and winked, like we were all about to have a really good time.

"Yeah, what about her?" she said.

"Where is she?" Frankie asked.

"How would I know?" Louise whined. "I'm not her mother."

"Ah . . ." Frankie said. "You are under the impression that this is negotiable information. I'm sorry, did I not make myself clear?" Frankie's tone had changed. It was deep and strong and I wouldn't have argued with him given the opportunity.

"All right," Louise said. "I haven't seen her in a couple of days."

Frankie nodded, satisfied that we were moving along. "Who's she working for?" he asked.

"Nope," Louise said, her mouth trapping shut, looking out the window, making movements like she was leaving.

Frankie wasn't having any of it. "Louise, tell me."

She looked at him, gave him this hard stare like she didn't care who he was or what he had, and said nothing. We sat there for what felt like a full minute before I decided to intervene.

"Louise," I said. "Yolanda's in trouble. She may not be the only one in trouble. I think someone's looking to hurt her and anyone else who gets in his way."

Louise looked at me, a tiny spark of fear crossing her face, then dying out. She was not going to talk.

"Okay," I said, "then how about this: The guy she works for, the guy you guys have to pay off in order to do business, is it a cop?" I rushed on. "You don't gotta say nothing, just nod if it is."

We all waited, watching her head. Finally it came, an imperceptible nod, and then she was out, pushing her way past Frankie, half running in her strappy little sandals into the club, not looking back and glad to be rid of us.

"So," I said into the silence of the car. "Bingo."

I drove out onto the road and almost immediately pulled into a tiny convenience store parking lot.

"Hey," Eugene said, "I don't eat hot dogs. If you're buying lunch, let's go somewhere with real food."

"I'm looking up something in the phone book," I said. "If you two are hungry, go on in and knock yourselves out, but get back out here as soon as you can."

Frankie and Eugene couldn't get out of the car fast enough. Apparently interrogating prostitutes made them hungry. Maybe they weren't thinking like I was, maybe they assumed Yolanda was already dead and time was no longer of the essence. Maybe I was just an optimist. No, change that—I knew I was an optimist, I just didn't want to give up and then find out later something could've been done to save Yolanda.

I stood outside in the cold and looked up Nolowicki's name in the phone book. Nothing. Cops don't list their numbers in the phone book; I should've remembered that. So then I did the only other thing I could do. I called Raydean and she took care of it as only she could.

"Darlin'," she said when she called me back. "It weren't easy. Juanita's only there part-time and this weren't her time, and she had to call one of her friends and, well, anyway, he lives out in the county. You want the number and the address?"

I wrote it down, hung up, and immediately dialed the police department. I asked for Nolowicki and waited, my heart pounding in my chest.

"Ma'am," the secretary said, "he's around here somewhere. Just hang on while I find him."

That was all I needed. "Wait," I said, "how about giving me over to Detective Nailor."

"Now, he's definitely not here. I think he's off until the day after tomorrow. You want his voice mail?"

I said yes, but I didn't really think it would do any good. "John, it's Sierra," I said after the beep. "I really need to talk to you. I think I know something that might help you figure out what's going on. I'm going to check on one other thing and I'll get back to you."

I hung up, my heart pounding, thinking about him and Carla and the locket that I kept in my pocket because I couldn't bring myself to wear it, but I couldn't bear to let go of it either, not just yet anyway, not when I wasn't absolutely sure there was no hope for us. Just the optimist in me coming out, I supposed.

I drove off, heading out toward the county, thinking about Nailor, thinking about me and Nailor, seeing scenes from our relationship like a slide show. I'd been gone fifteen minutes before I even realized I'd left Frankie and Eugene inside the convenience store pigging out on chemicals and preservatives.

"Well," I muttered, "it's only for a little while. Maybe they'll still be there when I get back." Because I wasn't going back until I had looked for Yolanda. Two grown men stranded in a warm convenience store with all the comforts of home didn't need my help, not like a bimbo prostitute looking to work an angle and getting herself trapped by a killer.

I headed out Route 231, moving toward Chipley, looking for the side road that led to Nolowicki's house. I was working out my plan: First scout out his place, make sure Yolanda wasn't tied up and sitting on a hard wooden chair where I could easily see her, and then leave, coming back later with Frankie and Eugene to search the place more thoroughly with a lookout and bodyguard. This was just the preliminary, make-sure drive-by.

I told myself this all the way down his isolated road, which was rimmed with pine trees and spotted with a few mobile homes and tiny stick-built houses. I would've missed Nolowicki's place entirely if I hadn't seen the mailbox almost camouflaged by the green plastic. The house was set back from the road, hidden from sight by the pine trees, but it was easily visible once you made the turn into the driveway.

It was a plain modular home, set on a large rectangle of grass. The backyard was cluttered with pine trees and left natural, but the front was a green square. There were no frills in Nolowicki's life. The house was simple, no curtains, only miniblinds. No flags or flowers to indicate a woman's touch. It was a house without personality. It was also impossible to approach it without being seen, a fact that made me nervous, even though the carport behind the house stood empty and I knew Nolowicki was sitting in his office ten miles away.

My stomach was flipping over and over with monster-sized butterflies. My hands shook as I pulled the car slowly past the house and around to the back where it wouldn't be seen.

"No one is home," I whispered to myself. "We're just checking. If he drives up, I'll tell him I have a drug tip or an informant for him." I stopped the car and got out, standing beside it and listening for any sound that might indicate life. Nothing.

"Okay," I said, my voice shaking a little even though I knew no one was there. "Let's check the back windows first." I stepped toward the house, looking over my shoulder at the carport and the large metal outbuilding that lay beyond it. "Fear is pointless," I told myself. "Your body is having a physiological reaction to a stimulus that is all in your mind. I know this. Freud would back me on it, I'm sure. Pa would tell me I was being a baby and to just do what I need to do."

But, see, I knew Pa wouldn't say any such thing. Pa would say, "You have no business being there. Get out!"

I stood on tiptoe and tried to look in the back window, but like every other window in the house, it had closed miniblinds blocking my view. I couldn't even see through a chink in the side. Nolowicki liked the dark, or privacy.

"Yolanda? Turk?" I called finally. "Are you in there?" I banged on the back door, then stood very still, listening. I heard nothing.

"Okay, then, well, fine," I said. "Just look in the storage building and be gone. Didn't figure anybody'd be home anyway."

I turned and walked down the steps, crossing the backyard, almost whistling with relief. We'd come back later, when it was dark, and raid the place. We'd wait for a night when Nolowicki was gone, like maybe tonight. Maybe he would have a hot date with a prostitute. Maybe he'd fly to Vegas and gamble. After all, he had to do something with the money. He sure wasn't spending it on the house.

I walked up to the Quonset hut and checked out the padlock on the double doors. Whatever Nolowicki had inside, he didn't want to share it with your common criminal. The door handles were wrapped in thick chain, with a padlock attached to it. It looked like quality construction.

"Yolanda?" I called. "Turk?"

No sound. I looked back over my shoulder and thought about returning to the car, grabbing Eugene's Uzi, and blasting away at the lock.

"No, there's nothing like breaking and entering into a cop's house to get your ass locked up."

It was Sister Mary Frances, her voice stuck inside my Catholic mind, reading me the riot act about fair play.

"Wait," I said, "the guy's a murderer. You don't play fair with murderers."

Sister Mary Frances sat back in my head, frowning her disapproval. With us Catholics, fair is fair all the time and right is right and wrong is wrong no matter who the enemy is.

"Fine," I said. It made me feel better to talk to myself, like I actually had company. On the streets in Philly, you had to talk to yourself as a mode of defense. It made people think you were nuts, and nuts is a good thing. Muggers like quiet, mousy sane people, predictable victims. Nuts tend not to realize that the danger of a mugger is real. They tend to attack their attackers, at least that was the prevailing logic on the street.

I was shaking inside and out as I rounded the corner of the metal hut and looked into the only window in the building. Inside I found Nolowicki's stash, sitting up on a trailer, gleaming in the dimly lit room. It was a huge red cigarette boat, the kind Bahamian dope dealers routinely use to outrun the law.

"Holy shit!" I said, ignoring Sister Mary Frances. "The freaking mother lode!" I looked past the boat, trying to take in the rest of the space, hoping to see poor little pink-haired Yolanda all tied up and breathing, but it wasn't to be.

"I should take a picture," I said, walking around to the back of the hut, thinking maybe there was another way in. "I should learn to carry a camera because I'm starting to think I have a gift for this sort of stuff." I was feeling like I was the total shit of homicide investigation. I was picturing myself giving Nailor and Terrance the business, leaning back in a wooden office chair and smiling while they watched me wide-eyed and grateful. I started humming "Who's Sorry Now?"

That's how come I tripped over the well instead of looking down and seeing it coming up on me.

I sprawled spread-eagled on top of the thick wooden lid, not knowing for an instant what had happened or what I had landed on. At first I thought it was like Philadelphia, where we keep our trash in containers buried in the ground beside the row houses. The trash guys would come by, or at least they did in the old days before those robot trucks came along, hop off the truck, lift your trash out of the canister, and batta-bing, they're gone. I figured it was the same with this house. Keeps the animals out of the trash. Out in the county, they probably had trouble with raccoons.

But as I sat on the edge of the big wooden and concrete circle, rubbing my shin where I'd barked it tripping, I realized this wasn't a trash receptacle. For one thing, the lid was wooden and it wasn't hinged like they are in Philly. Being a city girl, it took me a moment to realize I was sitting on a well lid. But it took no time at all to realize where Yolanda and Turk might be now.

I jumped up, turning around and reaching for the lid, trying to shove it off so I could look down inside, shaking and not wanting to see what I figured was waiting.

"Shit," I said, shoving and clawing at the lid. "Don't be in here."

"Why not?" a low voice said behind me. "Two's company. You'll have something to talk about."

I hadn't heard him sneaking up on me. Nolowicki stood in front of me, Eugene's Uzi in his hand, wearing the goofy red satin jacket with his name above the pocket, an unlit cigar hanging from his fat lips.

All the smart-assed comments I usually had waiting at my fingertips vanished, along with the image of Sister Mary Frances and her disapproving frown. Instead I was a blank — a blank focused on the tip of an Uzi submachine gun. This was really not my day.

"I was just . . ." I said.

"I know, you were just going to check and see if I'd stuffed Yolanda down my well." He smiled, but his dark eyes never left mine. "I did. There. I saved you the trouble. The well's very useful for things like that, you'll see."

He looked like we were having a normal conversation, like he'd shoot me with that same expression on his face, like nothing would faze him about killing me and anyone else who got in his way.

"So why didn't you stuff Rodriguez down the well, too?"

I wanted him to talk, to postpone whatever he had planned long enough for me to come up with a plan. But there were no plans. I was stuck. I couldn't run and I couldn't hide. I couldn't overpower a cop with an Uzi.

"He was an afterthought," he said. "No one was supposed to see me. I went in the back to meet with Izzy. He let me in. No one saw us because he didn't want them to. He thought we were transacting business."

"What about Tinky?" I asked.

Nolowicki laughed. "Stupid biker. Didn't know he was shaking down a cop!" He looked at me and for a second there was a twinge of regret in his features. "Too bad you had to find them both. Must've been traumatic. But," he added with a shrug, "it could've been worse. You could've seen me, too. That would've been a shame. This way we prolonged your life a little while, made your boyfriend happy a few more times, eh?"

He was looking at me like I was meat. That was good. If his little head was starting to think, I could deal with it. I can work a little head; it only holds one thought at a time.

"So, that's that," I said, wetting my lips and widening my eyes a little. "I'm toast; you're going to kill me and have a clean shot at taking a cut of all the drug and protection money in Panama City. There's no looking back."

"That's about right," he said. His eyes roved over my body, hesitating at my breasts, then moving south to take in the total Lavotini package. He motioned to me with Eugene's gun. "I'm thinking to maybe make one stop before the train pulls out of the station and you become a pleasant memory in most men's minds."

I tried to look as if I didn't know what we were talking about. Stupid is a hard act for me, but when it's my life, I figure I can do bimbo as good as anybody.

"And what is that?" I asked innocently. I crossed my arms like I was cold, then let my fingers drift slowly down my arms in a long caress that issued an invitation to linger.

He smiled, shifting the cigar from one side of his mouth to the other. "Let's go inside and have a little talk about your last will and testament," he said.

I walked slowly across the grassy yard with the muzzle of the Uzi pressed hard against my back. Sister Mary Frances returned to my head, full of "I told you so's" and rosaries. The fact that Nolowicki was prodding me with the tip of the cold metal gun pissed me off and didn't put me in the mood to work a seduction-based plan.

I took the steps slowly, looking around, hoping to see a means of escape or destruction, but there was nothing. When he finally had me inside, standing in the kitchen, I turned around very slowly and faced him.

"How about a drink?" I asked.

Nolowicki was staring at my breasts, his breathing coming a little quicker. When I spoke his attention shifted back to my face. "Sierra, a drink isn't going to change the bottom line. I'm going to fuck you and then you're going in the well."

I looked right back at him, feeling the color drain out of my face and my fingertips go numb.

"You do know how to put a girl in the mood," I said. "Now, I want a drink." Because, I was thinking, if I'm going to get raped and killed, I at least want some form of anesthesia.

I was looking around the sterile little kitchen, all white, clean, and empty. I was envisioning blood and Nolowicki's mustache sliding down a cabinet door. I thought of Nolowicki himself a tangled mass of Uzi damage and guts. If only I could get Eugene's gun.

I looked at the barren counter, saw a bottle of Southern Comfort, and winced, the worst possible choice for a Wild Turkey girl.

"Give me a couple of shots of that," I said. "I'm no good without a jumpstart on a cold morning."

Nolowicki pointed the muzzle toward a cabinet. "Get the shot glass yourself," he said. "Go ahead."

He was starting to sound irritated, rushed. He wanted to take care of business, then take care of me.

I threw back two quick shots, felt the fire hit my gut, and then turned around to face him again, wishing I'd eaten a hot dog with Eugene and Frankie, realizing I wouldn't be in my current mess if I'd taken time to indulge in a little processed meat.

He was looking at me now, a bulge in the crotch of his pants, his pupils dilated with desire or drugs, I wasn't sure.

"Walk down the hallway," he said. "The bedroom's at the end."

Some foreplay, I thought, trying and failing to kid myself into a problem-solving mode instead of an I'm-going-to-die mode. I looked everywhere for weapons and alternatives, but an Uzi beat everything hand's down. It was too quick, too sure.

"Okay," he said, as we entered his room. "Take off your clothes."

I looked at the bed. It was a double, with a thin blue coverlet made up military-style, so tight you could probably bounce a quarter off it. One armchair sat across the room from me. A TV and stand were wedged next to a highboy dresser. I considered jumping behind the highboy, pulling it down on him, and racing out of the room, but I knew I wasn't that kind of strong.

"I have to pee," I said, trying the last alternative. He wasn't that stupid. He was a cop.

"Fine," he said. "Go ahead. Bathroom's right there."

I walked the few short steps to the tiny master bath and turned to pull the door shut behind me, envisioning myself crawling out the small window across from the commode.

He stopped me with one hand, holding the door open. "Go ahead," he said. "Don't mind me."

I glared at him, hesitating and hating him. Although he was about fifty, he looked to be in good shape, outweighing me and probably much stronger than I was. He put the Uzi down on the bedside table behind us, and I started to think about how I could get to it, all the while unsnapping my pants and pulling them down.

Nolowicki stood in the doorway, reaching for his lighter and preparing to relight his cigar. He was smiling.

"Do you have to smoke?" I asked, wrinkling my nose as he tried repeatedly to get the ugly stump going.

"Do you have to breathe?" he answered.

I shuddered, looking away, focusing on anything but him as I sank down onto the cold commode.

He stepped closer to the toilet, fumbling with his fly with one hand and still trying to light his cigar with the other. He was stepping right up to my eye level, his crotch in my face, the repeated click of his lighter the only sound in the tiny room. He smelled bad—unwashed and sweaty. His breath stank of cigar and garlic.

"I got something for you to do while you're sitting there," he whispered. He reached inside his fly, fumbling with one thick hand, reaching for his penis. He moved closer, the hard stump of wrinkled gray skin and hair looming closer . . . And they say men don't resemble their pets.

I looked up at him, widening my eyes and smiling like this was exactly what I wanted. I slowly licked my lips and stretched both hands.

"I got something for you, too," I said. I reached out to touch him with my left hand, my eyes never leaving his. But with my right hand, I reached over and picked up the spray can of deodorant that sat by the sink. With a swift, sure move, I pushed the button as hard as I could, aiming up into his eyes.

There was a whoosh as the aerosol spray met the lit tip of his cigar, a flash of orange that exploded into a fireball, catching Joe Nolowicki full in the face.

He screamed an agonizing howl of pain and rage, staggering backward, unable to escape the flames that now engulfed his head. I jumped up, pulling at my pants and grabbing a towel. I threw the towel at him, not waiting to see if he used it to put out the fire, then grabbed the Uzi from the bedside table and started running as fast as I could for the back door.

The screams went on and on, echoing in my head as I bolted out of the house and into the backyard, racing for the Camaro. I hopped in, tossed the gun on the seat beside me, and hit the toggle switch. The engine roared to life and I threw it into reverse. Joe Nolowicki appeared at the back door, barely recognizable, his face a black-and-red blob of pain and third-degree burns. He was screaming, running blindly, insane with pain and rage.

I tried not to hit him, swerving as I floored the accelerator, screaming as he bounced off the hood of my car and landed a few feet behind me. I couldn't stop. I couldn't help him or look backward or indeed do anything that would keep me there.

I grabbed my purse, fumbling through it for the cell phone, driving like a maniac down the driveway and out onto the road.

I punched in 911, screamed for an ambulance, and then pulled over when the reality sank in that he couldn't follow me.

"Put me through to John Nailor," I said. "Police emergency."

The communicator's voice was a stable monotone. "Are you an officer?" she asked.

"No. I'm his . . ." But my voice faded. I'm his what? "Associate," I said finally.

I think she thought to give me a hard time but, considering

what I'd told her about the ambulance and the victim in need of assistance, decided to go ahead.

One ring. Then: "Nailor," he answered.

"I need you," I said, and started to cry. "Your vice squad just tried to kill me."

Thirty-four

$\mathcal{Y}$ou can't keep a secret in little Panama City, but we tried. The night the big game went down, everybody close to the Tiffany Gentleman's Club arrived hours ahead of schedule, sitting out in the house like they were attending a wake, drinking and talking to the girls like they were sisters. Of course, Tonya and the rest of us weren't working the club that night. We were still out on strike, still waiting for a miracle to happen, still hungry and apprehensive.

Everybody knew what was about to jump off in the back room. They all knew the stakes and they all knew their future now rested in the hands of one woman, a woman as crazy as bat shit and as brazen as brass-monkey balls.

She sat at the table in Vincent's old back room, her hair in pink foam curlers, her knee-high stockings sagging around her wrinkled white ankles, and with the pockets of her faded blue housedress stuffed to overflowing with money and wrinkled tissues. Raydean was loaded for bear and possibly more.

Mike Riggs sat across from her, his dirty white sea captain's hat shoved back on his head, his face looking more and more like a Saint Bernard's.

The peanut gallery, the warm-up crew, flanked them on either side. Everybody had pink bubblegum cigars sticking out of their shirt pockets or tucked into pockets, a token of Turk Akins's gratitude at being able to come out of hiding in time to witness his daughter's birth.

Pa sat on Raydean's right side, frowning and looking at his cards, a mug of steaming coffee by his right hand. Behind them, Ma reclined on Vincent's leather sofa, covered up in Raydean's handmade quilts, a glass of Pa's homemade Chianti at her fingertips and a comfortable smile on her face.

She was pinking up, looking more like Ma and less like a victim of a holocaust. Whatever Raydean had done to care for her, it had worked. Still, the specter of her disease and her impending chemotherapy and radiation hung over her, preventing the fear from leaving her eyes completely.

Pat sat on Raydean's other side, her white hair gleaming in the light of the overhead lamp that hit the table, illuminating the players but leaving the observers in the dark. Bruno sat next to Pat. Bandaged up, he held his right arm in a navy-blue sling, but this didn't hold him back from playing, because Eugene held his cards for him and ministered to him like a mother.

I figured with the amount of existential and misplaced guilt that Eugene carried for Bruno getting shot, he could turn Catholic without much trouble at all. Hell, the way he looked at Bruno, with his eyes all sad, I figured they might just nominate Eugene for martyrdom.

Bruno's physician, Dr. Thrasher, sat next to Bruno, totally ignoring his patient in favor of a pair of blond-headed twins who sat on either side of him, a little gift from Vincent in appreciation of saving Bruno's life. The doctor was smiling, seeming not to care at all that he'd lost his last chip twice and had to stake his BMW in order to remain in the game.

The only two people missing from the action were Moose Lavotini and John Nailor, both excluded for good reason. The way I saw it, the only thing worse than the Tiffany remaining Big Mike's House of Booty would be for it to fall under mob control. I didn't care if Moose was a nice guy and grateful to me for getting him sprung from the trumped-up drug charges. I didn't care that he was like a magnet, drawing me closer and closer to him. Mob was mob and there was no way to pretty up that picture.

I hadn't invited Nailor for the obvious reason, and because I couldn't deal with him yet, and unless I missed my guess he couldn't deal with me either. If I closed my eyes, I could still see him coming for me: lights and sirens, sliding his car to a halt in front of mine while the others went on to the scene. I could feel the way he took me in his arms, stroking my hair, soothing me, listening to the entire story, then telling me Nolowicki was dead. And worst of all, I could still feel the slight hesitation in his touch, the holdback, the piece of him that wasn't there for me and maybe never had been or, worse, maybe never could be.

So we sat there, playing every conceivable version of poker, from five-card stud, to guts, waiting for the big moment, sneaking up on it. We'd been playing for two hours when Mike Riggs looked up at Raydean and smiled.

"Looks like you're almost out of chips," he said. "Sure you still want to play for the house?"

Raydean took her time looking back at him, eyeing her cards, counting the two measly chips over and over, like somehow they'd multiply if she stared long enough. But then she smiled. It was her psychotic bring-on-the-best-you-got-'cause-I-got-God-on-my-side, crazy-assed smile.

"Let them that's without luck cast the first chip," she said. Fluffy was sitting on her lap, smiling. Fluffy wasn't blinking in the face of danger; she was as nuts as Raydean when it came to cards.

The rest of us pulled our chips back, folded our hands and threw the cards into the center of the table. Suddenly the room was too warm and the air stale and still with tension and expectation.

"Draw to see who deals and call the game," I said.

Riggs leaned forward, picking up a card in his big beefy paw and flipping it over. The Jack of Spades.

Raydean smiled, leaned down toward Fluffy, and said, "The one on the left or that'un on the right?" She appeared to listen, nodded, and then drew slowly from the left. She clutched the card to her chest, then painstakingly pulled it back, a smile slowly crossing her face.

"A big man," she said, looking at Pa and laying the King of Hearts on the table. She looked up at Riggs, cocked her head to the side, and winked. Then she drew the cards in close and began shuffling.

"Raydean," I said, "how's about we rethink this?"

She looked over at me and smiled. It was gentle and filled with love, but it wasn't a smile that would take an argument.

"It's my party and I'll cry if I want to," she said, then began singing softly, "cry if I want to, win if I have to."

It was Raydean's gift and I knew it, but it was also her future. We all knew Raydean had money, but how much? Certainly if she lost, it would take almost everything she had. But then, she had backup. She had me. This was Raydean's way of being in the game, the game where everybody's equal, even the ones who hear voices and see aliens. Raydean wanted to put up her money, all of it, to save the Tiffany. She was a team player and she was one of the family.

When Raydean had shuffled, passed the cards to Mike for the cut, and piled the cards back into a stack, she reached down by her side and pulled up her thick black leather bag. It was stuffed with rubber-banded stacks of one-hundred-dollar bills.

"I believe we counted this earlier and you found it to your satisfaction?" she asked.

Riggs nodded and tossed the keys to the front door of the Tiffany onto the table. Vincent picked this moment to lean over and whisper in my ear.

"Do they let nuts have liquor licenses, 'cause I know they can't carry concealed."

I looked over at him and scowled. "How would you know? They turn your application down?"

Raydean was oblivious to the tension in the room. She dealt the cards, five each, facedown, smiling like this was just another hand.

"Five-card draw," she said. "One-eyed Jacks are wild."

Mike Riggs studied his cards, then looked up at Raydean and said, "I'll take one." He slid a card to the center of the table, smiling as he waited for her to deal.

Vincent's head sunk into his hands. Pat looked away, staring at a spot on the wall above Pa's head. No one was breathing. No one moved except for Ma, who slowly raised her glass to her lips and took a short sip of Chianti.

"It's a sign," Raydean said, sliding four cards out of her hand and across the table, pulling four new cards, facedown, toward her chest. She looked at her hand, then over at Pa. He looked right back at her, smiled and winked.

Raydean leaned toward him, rested her curler-covered head on his shoulder like a child, and slowly revealed her hand to him. He looked, his face a frozen mask, and patted her hand like it was all right, like she'd tried and that was all that could be expected.

"Show," Riggs said, smirking.

"You first," Raydean said.

Riggs laid out his hand, one card at a time. Ace of Spades, Ace of Diamonds, Ace of Clubs, and a one-eyed Jack of Spades.

"Four aces. Does this discourage you?" he asked, chuckling.

Raydean seemed very sad for a moment, looking up at Pa, her eyes questioning.

"Go ahead, honey," Pa said. "Show the man what you got. That's the rules."

Raydean clutched the cards closer. "But they're so pretty all cuddled up like this. I'd hate to expose them to an alien plot or subterfuge."

"Raydean, I'll watch over 'em," Pa said. "You can take them right back up and hold on to them all night as soon as we're done."

Raydean nodded and slowly fanned the cards open. She looked at them, kissed one, and laid her family down on the table . . . a three, four, five, six, and seven of Hearts. A straight flush.

"Oh my God!" Vincent yelled, jumping up from his chair and dislodging a startled Marla.

Mike Riggs was staring at the table as if he couldn't believe it.

Then he shrugged, like in some way it was no big deal. In light of his brush with the entertainment industry, I figured it wasn't.

Raydean let go of Pa and returned to her current reality. She reached out, took her purse in one hand and the keys to the club in the other.

"There you go, baby," she said, handing them to me. "Merry Christmas! I figure that beats a cake any day!" And then she cackled and turned to Ma. "Hey, girl, when we get you up and running, how's about we dress up in camo again and go hunting for men?"

Ma laughed. "I could make us hats," she said. "With feathers and sequins."

Pa shook his head. "You been up in Philly with them Mummers long enough, baby," he said to her. "Sequins'll frighten 'em off. If you wanna catch men, you gotta wear something that don't shock 'em. Try beer cans and fish hooks on those hats and you'll come home with 'em strapped to your bumper."

Raydean was looking a little confused. "Why would you strap a man across your bumper when you could tie him down to the bedpost?"

We were too busy envisioning Raydean strapping a hapless man to her bed to notice the back door giving. When it opened, Eugene was the first on his feet, the Uzi materializing from nowhere, and a ferocious look on his face. Marla, of course, screamed. Bruno reached into his jacket pocket like he'd find anything other than painkillers there, and Pa stepped in front of Ma, pulling Raydean with him.

"Wait, wait!" Frankie cried. "Don't fucking shoot me! I'm the point man."

"They come in peace," Raydean muttered.

Eugene eased the Uzi down an inch or two and stood waiting. Frankie walked into the room, followed by Thomas the Sleeping Bodyguard and Carlos the Slick, who took up positions on either side of the room, watching both doorways and nodding to Frankie, who in turn looked outside and nodded.

Moose Lavotini, appearing very tall and imposing in his Armani suit, stepped into the room and stood smiling at everyone, especially me.

"There was a game and I missed it?" he asked.

"Oh, it was no big deal," I said. "Just a private wager between friends."

Now Moose wasn't looking like there was anyone else in the room but me. His eyes sparkled, boring straight inside me, seeing something, but I had no idea what. He threw back his head and laughed.

"I see how it's going to be now," he said. "You weren't going to be beholden to no one if you could help it."

I smiled. "That's about the size of it," I said.

Moose nodded. "Good," he said. "That's what I like about you."

I was looking at him and thinking too bad. Too bad he's a criminal; otherwise, he might've borne investigating in a closer sort of way.

Everyone else in the room was staring at Moose like maybe he had two heads, not sure if he was okay or the enemy or what. Vincent was the first to pick up on who it was.

"Is this your . . . ?" he stammered. "Oh God, I am so honored," he said, stepping forward and taking Moose's hand.

Moose smiled, then snapped his fingers in the direction of Carlos and said, "Why don't we all have a drink? Carlos?"

After Carlos disappeared into the bar, Moose looked around the room, observing all the unfamiliar faces, smiling warmly, like he really meant it, like he wanted to like them and have them like him back. I stepped to his side, slipped my arm through his, and turned to the others.

"Hey, you guys, I'd like you to meet . . ." I hesitated because I couldn't say "my uncle." So instead I smiled bigger and just said, " 'Big Moose' Lavotini from New Jersey."

Carlos and a bevy of dancers and waitresses arrived at that moment, and trailing behind them was a caravan of regular customers and well-wishers who now knew that the Tiffany Gentleman's Club was back in the right hands and that relief from piss-poor entertainment was on the way. It was all downhill from here, and everybody was gonna end up a winner. Of course, there was one little difference: Raydean had given the club to me, not Vincent.

Champagne flowed. People were everywhere and it was one big party. Even Ma was holding court, propped up on the sofa and greeting my regulars with a smile and a wink. At one point I heard her say to a businessman in a red tie, "So I've been thinking about making her a new costume, something in a transparent plastic. I'm envisioning a shower and the song 'Singing in the Rain.' What do you think?"

I stood there, clutching the keys to the Tiffany Gentleman's Club in one hand and a flute of champagne in the other. I was standing like that when Pa walked up to me, still holding his coffee mug and frowning.

"Sierra, we gotta talk," he said. "In private."

I started to blow him off, to tell him not to worry, Ma was gonna be fine, that I knew running a club was a big responsibility but I had good help. Then I looked over and saw something in his eyes, something that made me take him by the arm and lead him into Vincent's office, shutting the door firmly behind us.

"What is it, Pa?" I asked.

"About 'Big Moose' Lavotini," he said.

I smiled. "Don't worry, Pa. I can handle him. I am not about to get myself linked up to a criminal, not again."

"That's not what I'm worried about, Sierra."

"Then what is it?"

Pa took a swallow of coffee. "That ain't 'Big Moose' Lavotini," he said.

I laughed. "Oh that! I know, the real 'Big Moose' Lavotini is dead. That's his son in there. See, they didn't want to risk no big family struggle, so when 'Big Moose' died, his son took over. Nobody had seen the real Moose in years, so everyone just assumed he was still running the show. Bit by bit, Moose's son has taken over."

Pa stared at me like I had lost my mind. "Sierra, what's the matter with you? 'Big Moose' Lavotini ain't dead. He was all over the papers not two weeks ago. He was indicted on racketeering charges and brought up on arraignment. He appeared in court, old as dirt but still very much in charge of his organization."

I felt a shiver run across my shoulders. "Well, it's his son then, trying to make big."

Pa shook his head. "I've seen his son, Sierra. He's short and fat. That ain't a Lavotini you got in there, honey."

I walked toward the door, opened it, and kept on going until I stood at the edge of the back room, watching the man I had assumed to be Moose Lavotini work the room, charming everyone in it and laughing like he'd known them all his life.

If that wasn't Moose Lavotini of the Cape May, New Jersey, Lavotinis, then who the hell was it and just what was he doing in my life?

I turned back to Pa to ask him what he thought, but he had disappeared. I took a step backward and looked down the hallway toward the front of the house. Detective John Nailor stood there, watching me watch him, waiting for the recognition to click in my eyes, then smiling as it did.

I stood there, locked between two men, one, maybe two of them impostors. From somewhere I heard Raydean's voice drifting out over the crowd: "Well, ain't this just the finest mess of pickles you ever did see? Pour me another one, big man. It's gonna be a long night."

I closed my eyes and exhaled slowly, leaning against the cool concrete-block wall. It was going be a long night, all right. I listened to the sounds of my friends and family celebrating the return of the Tiffany and life itself. I thought about all the assumptions I'd held, all the things I'd known to be true and believed in and then watched blow up in my face. What was going to happen now?

I opened my eyes and pushed off the wall. I crossed the hallway and stepped back into Vincent Gambuzzo's former office, walking to the desk, then stepping around it and over to the huge leather office chair.

"There's no time like the present," I whispered. I turned the chair to face forward, sat down behind the desk, and waited.